THE GOLDEN SCIMITAR

R.E. Robb

Magic Valley Publishers

Published by Magic Valley Publishers

ISBN 0-9716681-1-6

Cover design by Matt Gonzalez
Manufactured in the United States of America

First Edition

DEDICATION

*To all the fighter pilots
who were heroes,
and all the heroes
who were fighter pilots.*

THE GOLDEN SCIMITAR

PROLOGUE

This smooth, silent and deadly German jet fighter was a part of Ackermann and Ackermann a part of the plane. They breathed in unison and felt every sensation of flight equally.

With throttle, stick and foot pedals, Hans Ackermann commanded. With power, speed and maneuverability, the Messerschmitt Model 262 responded. They were unequalled as a fighting team in the air war over the shattered and burning cities of Nazi Germany in 1945.

Always test all of your controls, Hans, he remembered his father saying. *Feel the plane in your fingertips and in your toes and in the bottom of your trousers.*

Hans Ackermann gently depressed each rudder pedal alternately and then caressed the control stick to the left and then to the right, forward and back again, as he had so many times before in so many airplanes. It was a ritual he learned as a boy flying the home-built gliders he and his father had lovingly constructed in a makeshift shed at the side of their barn. He learned to love flying in those fragile wood and cloth airplanes, soaring gracefully over the rolling hills and pastures of central Germany.

You must move the controls smoothly, tenderly, and they will react to your touch correctly, and your flying will be a beautiful thing. Lieutenant Hans Ackermann of Germany's elite Luftwaffe had never forgotten his father's words. Now just that slight force, barely perceptible pressure on the control pedals and a gentle caress of the stick that controls the plane's ailerons and elevators, were sending his jet powered fighter-bomber into subtle gyrations.

The Americans will think I am drunk!

He smiled behind his pulsing oxygen mask feeling the surge of eager happiness he had always felt when flying, even when that act would bring down planes and send brave men to their deaths. But now, as the British and American bombers rained their five-hundred pounders down on his homeland, it had become necessary to put his skills to work to stop them.

Killing had become his profession, no better or worse, nor much different, he reasoned, than that of his mechanical engineer father's. And how he loved to fly! The moral ramifications of what he was doing were of no consequence to him as long as he could fly. His occasional thoughts of the destruction of the American and British aircraft and their crews never kept him from a fulfilling night's sleep

And he was well-suited to this purpose in this one-man fighter plane. He was a lone eagle, better equipped mentally and emotionally to fight - and die, if necessary - solitarily.

He was short and slim and quiet and shy, and at a very young age he had already grown tired of being greeted by his parent's friends and even his relatives with "Hans, when are you going to start to grow?" But for his slight stature, he was physically strong and had quietly developed astonishing stamina, endurance, and perseverance that had won him a shelf-full of collegiate track and field medals.

He was indeed a loner, even while with the raucous cadets of the flight academy, he kept to himself. He silently vowed to transfer to the infantry rather than be assigned to bomber duty where he would be only one of eight or more crew. He disliked teamwork because he knew that he alone could do whatever the task better, without the distractions of less able people. Even in his youth he had only two school friends, Fredrick and Ernst, and both of them were as introverted as he. There were times the three of them would loll on the grass of the school yard for a full thirty minutes while other students ran, laughed and played around them. They watched, but never participated, indeed, they seldom spoke, even to each other. This suited Ackermann just fine then and now, and it was a trait that would ultimately help him survive.

He heard that Fredrick died beneath the rubble of a munitions plant in Stuttgart, leveled by 500-pound bombs from the bellies of American B-17s. And Ernst was never seen again after British Lancaster bombers hit the submarine pens on the west coast of France. They say that he was arming a new U-Boat for duty in the Atlantic when a nighttime attack destroyed two of the pens, his the first.

Ackermann felt that he had two scores to settle; one with the Americans and one with the British. But now, with the defeat of most of Germany's air power, and its infantry and tank battalions on the run in nearly every theater of operation, he knew in his heart that the end was very near and he would, in all likelihood, die in this very airplane, very soon, very alone.

On this day it was the American B-17 Flying Fortress bombers of the Eighth Air Force drawing near. Only a moment before, they were mere specks in the sky. Then, in an instant, they loomed in his gunsight. He squeezed four 30 mm cannon rounds into the fuselage and across the left wing of the nearest Flying Fortress. He stabbed the control to the left and forward just in time to avoid sending his screaming fighter on the same path of destruction on which he had sent his cannon's rounds.

At times like that, the Messerschmitt 262's speed was just as frightening to her pilots as it was to the enemy aircrewmen.

Ackermann had not the time to fire on the second bomber. At nearly 840 km/h, kilometers were measured in half heartbeats. He sped clear of the formation, climbing, rolling and leveling off in a classic Immelmann maneuver. Now he had a moment to take a breath before turning back toward the B-17 squadrons. The increase in altitude would accelerate his speed even more when he started his diving attack. *I am like the eagle*, he thought, smiling still.

He saw the bombers below him and wondered where their fighter escort could be. He scanned the skies, finding them empty except for the American bombers and two German fighter planes darting among them like wasps at a picnic. There were no American fighters. On this day he would not have the opportunity to test this new jet fighter plane and his flying skills against his American or British counterparts. A conflicting perception of relief hovered among his heavy feelings of regret and disappointment.

He pushed the column forward, sending the horizon darting upward. The G forces of the maneuver pressed his head back and against the side of the canopy. His eyesight blurred. A hazy brown image filled his windshield and instinctively, Ackermann fired. His vision cleared and he rocked the control to the right and pulled it back almost to his chest. The responsive jet fighter curved upward in a graceful roll, a mere nine meters from colliding head-on with another B-17 bomber.

He saw the American waist gunners in the square side openings of the bombers as he tore by. He imagined the fearful look on their faces, their terror masked by goggles and oxygen masks. They tried valiantly to lead the incredibly fast plane with their pitiful fifty caliber machine guns, But they succeeded only in spewing a steady stream of lead and empty shell casings from guns made impotent by the Me.262's speed.

He carefully aimed and fired his four 30 mm cannon as he slashed repeatedly through the formations of bombers. Leaving three in flames, he now had to break off and return to his base. With all of its speed and performance, the Me.262 consumed fuel at an incredible rate, and he had used most of his, with only just enough remaining to reach the Jagdverband (Fighter Squadron) 44 air field. And he had not only expended his fuel, but most of his arms as well. The eagle's talons were clipped.

Ackermann throttled back and slid his goggles onto his forehead. He unsnapped his oxygen mask, allowing it to dangle against his left shoulder. The smell of the airplane's hot metal and the dankness of his perspiration replaced the rubbery odor of the mask. His mouth was dry from the flow of oxygen. The taste of the rubber hoses and mask lingered and he longed for the simple luxury of spitting. The thrill of the flight was ebbing, replaced by a mixture of gratitude that none of the enemy's bullets had pierced the fragile skin of him or his ship. But there was as well the recurring frustration of having to return to the earth - an eagle without wings - at least until tomorrow.

Sweat ran down the front of his flightsuit, adding to his discomfort, and he slackened the seat belt and shoulder harness, shifting his weight in the seat. He wiped his eyes, and blinked away the momentary blurring of his vision. Peering over the dappled nose of the camouflaged Messerschmitt, Ackermann could again see the green pastures and the rolling hills beyond Bernberg. Just beyond that would be the Sangerhausen air base lying unobtrusively between groves of multicolored trees. He remembered it all so well. It was the same beautiful countryside he and his father had soared above so long ago. His father would be proud of him this day, he had flown well.

Easing the throttles back and slowing to 400 Km/hr, he could safely lower the landing gear. He adjusted the elevator trim wheel to give the fighter a gradual descent to the airstrip, but he would have to drop below 300 Km/Hr to lower the flaps for landing, and he was still too far from the base leg of his approach for that.

Scanning the instruments and jotting notes onto a pad strapped to his right thigh, Ackermann did not notice the American P-47 Thunderbolt diving on him from above and behind. Not until his attention was snapped from his routine by the rattling sound of fifty caliber rounds tearing through his aircraft's aluminum. He felt the jarring impact as the bullets ripped into wings, fuselage, fuel tanks and control surfaces.

Ackermann caught himself about to ram the throttles forward. He checked that impulse. To do so below 6,000 RPM would have surely stalled the temperamental Junkers Jumo jet engines. He slid the levers forward slowly while rolling the plane to the left and stabbing the control column forward. He had just enough altitude for this maneuver under normal conditions, but as the P-47 emptied its guns into the right wing, the Me.262's starboard engine erupted into flames and lost all power.

As if accepting defeat, the plane suddenly rolled right, nosed up, and shuddered in a deadly stall.

Ackermann felt the leading edge slats bang outward. He knew that there was nothing he could do now that would get the plane out of this low-altitude stall. It would make one last, graceful roll and plummet to the ground. In one smooth motion, he pulled the throttles back, flipped the electrical master switch off, shut off the fuel selector and generator, and released the canopy latch.

The last thing he remembered of the American fighter was seeing it scribe a victory roll in the sky above him. He saw its symbol, the golden scimitar of the 220th Fighter Squadron emblazoned on its bright red engine cowling as the fighter rolled across his gunsight. In frustration and anger Ackermann squeezed the trigger lever on the control stick, sending the last 4 rounds of 30mm cannon shells after his attacker.

His plane was into the ground in an instant. The right wing struck first, shearing off and spreading flames along the fuselage. The canopy was thrown off, exposing Ackermann to a fireball of burning fuel. He flailed wildly at the flames engulfing the cockpit. Writhing in an attempt to release his seat harness to escape the inferno, he kept his eyes tightly closed and tried not to inhale the fire into his lungs. But his breath quickly ran out. He opened his eyes and screamed. He screamed in terror and in agony. He screamed until the fuselage impacted the ground, catapulting him from the flaming cockpit, his body trailing smoke like a discarded cigar. Then the Me.262 exploded.

German soldiers rushed to the scene to find Ackermann face up on the cool, soft grass. They were stunned to discover that he was still alive, but so badly burned that they could not tell where his leather flight helmet stopped and his face began.

He spent seven months in a field hospital before American and British troops marched into the area and the hospital frantically put everyone out. Only partially recovered, Hans Ackermann escaped into the woods, his injuries still seeping blood and ichor.

*   *   *

Captain Harvey Dessault brought the control stick back to the left, smartly ending the snap-roll. He had recorded his second kill of the day, a Messerschmitt 262. The German jet was too low on fuel and ammo to fight back, intercepted at its most vulnerable time.

This old Jug would be no match for that Kraut tiger in a dog fight, he thought. The "Jug," an Americanization of the British designation of "Juggernaut" for the American-built P-47, was a solid, tough and efficient fighter plane, but it was well documented that it was far behind the jet-powered technology and firepower of the enemy's new Me.262 jet.

Dessault knew that kills were most likely to be scored on the Me.262's when they were caught low on fuel and preparing to land, as was the one he had just jumped.

Time to get out of here, old Scout, he decided.

He pulled back on the stick to gain some altitude and was shocked by the sounds of steel shells tearing at his P-47. He pushed the stick forward and rolled left, frantically looking for the source of the bullets that were ripping his fighter apart. There were no other aircraft in sight, only the billowing flame and black smoke marking the trail of the Me.262 he had just sent spinning toward the ground.

The P-47 began to shudder. Dessault rolled-out level and quickly checked the instruments. All normal. He eased back on the stick and the plane suddenly jerked to the right. The stick went limp in his hands and the shudder became a violent vibration that put the plane into an uncontrollable dive. Dessault popped the canopy and bailed out.

He saw plane with its red nose and the golden scimitar emblem hurling towards the earth. Shreds of the tail section were flapping in the slipstream. Some pieces were being torn off and fluttering about in the air like a score of berserk butterflies. *That lucky kraut*, he thought. *Got me with a wild shot!*

He saw the Me.262 smash into the ground, then saw his P-47, the tail section almost entirely gone, plow into a grove of trees and explode in a huge ball of red, yellow and blue flame. A sick feeling knotted Dessault's stomach and he thought he might vomit.

The feeling disappeared as his attention was snapped upward by the unmistakable "Tweeng!" of a passing bullet. It tore through two of the shrouds and punched a hole in the canopy of his parachute. He looked down and saw a lone German soldier leaning back against his sidecar motorcycle, idly taking potshots at him.

Dessault unsnapped the strap on the holster cradled by his ribs, pulled out the Army-issue Colt .45 and fired three shots back at the tiny figure on the ground. The man jerked upright, jammed the rifle into the sidecar, jumped on the motorcycle, and tore off through the trees, zigzagging so as to present a more difficult target.

Dessault heard himself laughing. He wondered if he was going a little crazy. Here he was, hurling towards the earth, on a collision course with a Nazi rifleman, and he felt an odd kinship with him. They were both scared to death.

Dessault hit the ground and before he could regain his footing he was set upon by four German Soldiers. They held him down and stripped him of everything but his flightsuit and underwear. They roughly yanked him to his feet and guided him toward a ragged German Army truck, its radiator belching out spasmodic puffs of steam. Dessault saw the German soldier who had shot at him; a boy of perhaps 14 years, standing next to his motorcycle, Mauser in hand. As they passed, Dessault looked into his eyes and saw a look of fearful triumph. He silently thanked God that he'd not shot the kid.

Then a blinding flash of light and the explosive scream of a thousand sirens pounded through his brain as the German boy clubbed him unconscious with the butt of his Mauser to the back of his head. Dessault crumbled to his knees and was thrown face-first into the truck by his captors.

The German boy did not watch, but turned and mounted the motorcycle, proud to have contributed to the Nazi war effort.

The control wheel jerked in Lee Conroy's hands as flak exploded a mere fifty yards below his B-17 bomber, one of thirty three planes in a formation directly above the smoldering wreckage of Ackermann's Me.262. Shards of jagged steel from the exploding shell casing fell back toward the earth, their designated purpose unfulfilled. The B-17 Flying Fortress shuddered and rocked and was rattled again by the shock wave of another exploding antiaircraft round. Although war-weary from months of Allied bombing, the German antiaircraft gunners had lost little of their accuracy, and none of their tenacity. But their prey, the American B-17 and B-24 bombers, were flying just barely above the range of their 88 mm and 105mm shells.

The B-17 pilot, Lieutenant Lee Conroy, briefly scanned the flight instruments. He was relieved that his airspeed, altitude and attitude were still stable. His concentration on his plane's condition was suddenly shattered by his copilot's booming voice.

"Something's shaking, Lee, I can feel it in the wheel."

Lieutenant Walt 'Wally' Weaver was a thin, ex-radio announcer from Pittsburgh who reveled in the sound of his own deep voice. Weaver was loud and was always sweaty, but he was a steady, smart pilot. "Two-to-one says we've got a shot-up prop."

Conroy nodded, afraid that if he spoke his voice might be even the least bit shaky. He couldn't imagine the affect on his crew if their Skipper sounded edgy or, God forbid, slightly hysterical. He pressed the intercom button on the control wheel.

"Andy," he said, straining to keep his voice calm

and as soft as possible, "how's the fans?"

The Flight Engineer, Staff Sergeant Dan "Andy" Andrews, also served as top turret gunner. From the turret's bubble above and behind the pilot, he looked out over the more than 103' of wing span. He quickly checked Number One engine outboard on the left wing, and Number Two inboard of it. On the right wing, the inboard engine was Number Three and Number Four was outboard. He saw no smoke.

Andrews looked over his left shoulder toward his pilot, "All four turnin' just as sweet as Nelly at the dance, Lieutenant."

It was Sergeant Andrews' and Lieutenant Conroy's third mission over Germany in this plane. A mere five minutes ago they had survived a lone German fighter attack without any evident damage. They felt lucky today. In fact, every one of the crew of eight men considered it lucky that they were assigned to this ship.

Flying as copilot just a month before, Conroy had fought a crippled B-17 in for a belly landing at an allied base near Foggia, Italy. Their pilot was blinded and dazed and had one hand smashed. An anti aircraft round had exploded right in front of the windshield, tearing away most of the nose of the ship. With a hundred and sixty mile per hour blast of wind in his face, Conroy, with Andrews handling the throttles and flaps, slicked the crippled B-17 onto the deck as smoothly as buttering a piece of toast. They had gained a reputation as two "lucky" airmen.

But Conroy didn't believe that any one or two persons brought good fortune to any airplane or its crew. It was all a crap shoot, and he'd already had a good helping of sevens and elevens. He knew that a lot of the luck was in the equipment. This plane, a Boeing B-17E named *Belly Dancer* by the crew, was new, and she was proving to be the best Conroy had ever flown. And his crew was good too. *An experienced crew has a way of making luck work*, he thought.

The box formation of "A" Flight's eighteen B-17's was just ahead. *Belly Dancer* was the Number Five Plane in "B" Flight. "C" Flight's planes were behind and above him, out of his sight. The box formation had been developed by Wing Commander Curtis LeMay and was proving to be a brilliant success. The planes held better defensive positions in the grouping, and his theory of Synchronized Bombing had greatly improved the effectiveness of the daylight raids.

Conroy glanced left and right. The number two and three planes of "B" Flight, Captain Jess Martino and Lieutenant Billy Hansen, were snuggled in close to him and maintaining their positions so well that Conroy smiled.

"Martino and Hansen must be lonely," he said to no one in particular.

Weaver grinned behind his oxygen mask and nodded back at Conroy. Then his eyes widened and he shot a finger toward Conroy's windshield.

A green and brown dappled blur blanked out the view ahead as a German fighter plane, its guns blazing streaks of fire, slashed across the nose of the bomber and out of sight to the right.

Conroy felt the impact of the Nazi's cannon shells and the sudden lurch of the big plane. The B-17 shuddered again as nine of its 50-caliber machine guns threw streams of lead after the fighter.

Andrews shouted, "Number three's hit. Number four is smoking and blowing oil all over the place!"

"Shut down four," said Conroy. A billow of chalky white fire extinguisher C0-2 powder burst from number four's engine cowling and trailed aft, joining the plane's contrail in the cold German atmosphere.

A moment later, "Better shut down three as well, Skipper, its about to tear itself off the wing!" bellowed Weaver. He was already killing number three's ignition and shutting off its fuel supply. He jerked the red and white diagonally striped handle labeled "Fire".

With the two engines on the right wing no longer providing power, the plane was losing precious altitude at an alarming rate. The engines on the left wing were pulling the big ship into a circling dive to the right. Now, banked at more than 45 degrees, the failing bomber sliced downward. Conroy, with Weaver helping, had the control wheel cranked hard to the left, trying to straighten out the crippled bomber's flight path. He silently thanked God that neither of the two engines had caught fire. He smashed the intercom button, "Smitty, salvo the bomb load."

Without answering, Bombardier William Smithers released 10,000 pounds of bombs with the single press of a button. A shudder and a sudden surge of altitude as the weight of the bomb load left the belly of the B-17 was the only answer Conroy needed.

Conroy was bitterly angry having wasted their lethal load of 500 pound bombs on the German farm land below. He had been eager to dump them right down the stacks of the targeted German steel mills.

Then *Belly Dancer* and Conroy's luck ran out. The wounded ship had fallen into the range of the German antiaircraft gunners below. The explosion of a well-placed antiaircraft shell tore *Belly Dancer's* left wing off, sending the Boeing Flying Fortress bomber spiraling crazily toward the earth.

Conroy smashed the intercom button, screaming "Bail out! - Bail out!" His final agonizing realization was that his last verbal command indeed sounded hysterical.

The bombs that hurled earthward from Belly Dancer's underbelly were clustered together in a single mass of destructive power, blindly falling toward the German countryside. The entire load of 500-pounders hit the ground within eight seconds, blasting huge craters into the earth, showering a farm house and barn with dirt and debris.

From deep below the innocence of the scene a massive explosion erupted as the last American bomb exploded. The earth heaved upward and the trees shuddered and swayed with a hellish force. Flames shot upward from a jagged fissure immediately igniting a farm house and its barn and turning them into a roaring inferno. Then the earth settled, collapsing into itself, to leaving only the panicked flight of birds and billowing black smoke from the burning structures as a transient record the event.

CHAPTER ONE

Scott Austingrove had spent six full days driving from one farm to the next, climbing over fences and wandering around people's property searching for just the right arrangement of farm house, woods and pasture. He knew from the start that it would be tough finding a particular farm in a general area of southern Germany almost fifty years after the fact. All he had to go on was what was described to him by an admittedly memory-challenged elderly German who died before he could pinpoint it on a map.

Swell, thought Scott Austingrove. *Now it's starting to rain.* He pulled his collar closed and fumbled with its button. *Well, I'm going to take one quick look around, then get out of here.*

Austingrove's trip to Germany and the week of probing the back woods was a gamble, he knew, but the stakes were enormous; a cache of Nazi airplanes still undiscovered from World War Two would be worth a fortune. But he had not found anyplace that fit the dying German's recollection, he was exhausted and discouraged, and now he was getting wet.

He had come to Germany just as the spring thaw had begun, a time when warm showers give birth to swarms of brash, young and aggressive gnats. Now they spun crazily in the mid-morning gloom, diving at Austingrove in suicidal aerobatics as he walked among the debris of the abandoned farm. Except for an occasional wave or slap across his face, he remained intent, wholly involved in his search for any evidence that this place could be the site of an underground World War Two fighter factory. So intent that he was totally unaware of the still, dark figure crouching behind the crumbled fireplace of the bombed-out farm house.

The rainfall increased. He tugged his coat up tightly to his chin and strode off toward the remnants of the structures, his soggy pant legs kicking up spray from the wet grass like the wakes of speeding boats.

He didn't see the man arise and step back from the protection of the brick fireplace. The dark figure shuffled backward, then ambled with a lopsided gait into a line of trees behind the house. Concealed there, he straightened and loped toward a rotting pile of wood that was once the barn.

Austingrove sensed more than saw the movement. He stopped and scanned the old homestead. He had an uneasy feeling and wished that he had not come to this remote, dismal place alone. He struggled to calm himself, dismissing the motion as perhaps that of a rabbit or deer fleeing his approach.

He stepped into the rubble. The smell of the damp, rotting wood mingled with the aroma of wet grass as he maneuvered among the shattered stones, bricks and shards of glass of the old house. He moved around the crumpled fireplace and almost missed seeing a pair of fresh boot prints in the soft dirt. He squatted beside them. They were only just then filling with water from the now steady downpour. He had seen something moving after all, and now it was obvious that it had been neither rabbit nor deer.

His decision to leave the dilapidated farm house coincided exactly with the splat of a bullet against the decaying brick. The reverberating report of the rifle came a hundredth of a second later, its roar echoing across the still landscape. By that time he was in mid air, diving into the brush, not knowing if he had been hit, praying he had not. He landed hard, rolled, and stumbled to his feet. Without looking back, he sprinted across the sodden field to the rented Mercedes.

Scott Austingrove wheeled the car onto the road and stood hard on the accelerator. As the landscape sped by, his alarm began to turn to elation. He realized that whoever shot at him must be hiding something and it was probably exactly what he was looking for.

As the adrenaline of his flight began to subside, Austingrove felt a stab of pain in his right side and back as the sedan bounced across a rut. He reached back, pressing the painful area. He felt an ominous stickiness. He glanced down, finding the floormat shimmering with an unmistakable dark crimson sheen. *Oh, damn. I'm bleeding, and I'm bleeding bad.* Dizziness began to overtake him and he passed out just as the car reeled into the hospital's parking lot. It smashed through the double glass doors and slammed to a stop as it collided with the admitting desk.

Hans Ackermann slid the aluminum panel across the opening, shutting out the light. He carefully placed the ancient Mauser rifle, its barrel still comfortably warm from firing, into the wooden case by the entrance hatch. He sat in the cool darkness trembling, not from the exertion of ambush and escape, but from age. The shaking had come upon him slowly over a period of years. Now, at over sixty, he had become accustomed to the constant tremor. He was out of breath too, but that would pass - the shaking would not.

He wondered who the man was who had been looking so carefully around the farmhouse. In nearly forty years, he had only seen a handful of people there, mostly curious passersby looking at the remains of the house and the collapsed barn. This place had been his home, but more than simply that, it was a haven for him since the war and there was no need for him to think it would not continue to be, he reasoned. But this man was different than any of the others. He had carefully probed every inch of the property. *He was looking very hard for something,* thought Ackermann. *Perhaps he is looking for my Jagdverband!*

Rested, he climbed down the steps cut into the sloping hill of dirt. In the darkness of the cavern, he took each step perfectly, for he himself had carefully sculpted each into the face of the twenty foot high wall of hard soil. Every step was exactly the same width. Each had precisely the same rise and depth. It had been a time consuming task and he had used it for exactly that purpose; to consume time. He had nothing else, only time. But now, he feared, even that was becoming short.

Ackermann confidently took the bottom step and walked blindly ahead, the cement floor softly echoing under his heavy boots. With the practice of nearly a half a century, he walked forward until he came up against a heavy steel table. He reached for the object in its center, then groped in his jacket for a match, struck it, and lit the blackened wick of a large brown candle.

The candle's radiance spread across the huge underground room, illuminating the table and neatly arranged stacks of magazines and newspapers. An empty glass stood among brown, rust-stained rings on the table's top. To the right, an officer's cot (an officer's, he knew, merely because it was provided with a mattress), a small wooden table he had lovingly built, a hanging locker and a wooden foot locker, all painted a dull, fading brown, was the sum of his furnishings.

He slipped out of his tattered military overcoat. He hung it carefully on a hook that jutted from one of the steel beams supporting the wide ceiling.

Ackermann looked around the cavernous underground plant. It was 60 meters wide and much longer than the meager candle could illuminate. Huge steel beams made up the overhead. They were covered with a mosslike growth and areas of pealing gray paint. The cement ceiling was supported by tapered I beams that leaned inward along drab cement walls. Just beyond Ackermann's area, a rusting, steel door enclosed a generator room and inside it there was another tightly sealed room for batteries.

He admired his meager furnishings. Everything was carefully placed so that it could be found easily in the dark. He could spend weeks if necessary in this cavern and not be inconvenienced in the least by the darkness. He had done that in the past - he could, and most likely would, do it in the future.

Occasionally, especially during the long German winters, he would run out of matches, food or reading material and have to crouch in the darkness, alone with his thoughts and the sounds of the scurrying rats. He would walk about and do exercises the Luftwaffe had trained him to do. Even after two or three weeks of darkness, he still had his sense of familiarity with his confines, his self confidence, his sanity.

There was a time, he couldn't remember for how long or how long ago, that he shared this cavern, and his life, with Elisia. He had discovered her crouching, scared, cold and hungry behind the stone wall of the collapsed farm house. It was soon after the American and British troops swept through the area. She was a nurse at the field hospital where Ackermann was treated and was in hiding, fearing for her life. He took her in and they lived in blissful solitude for almost nineteen years, Then, suddenly, it was over. One afternoon he came back from the village of Wolfshütte and found her body on her cot, covered with ravenous black rats. She had died peacefully in her sleep, he didn't know why or of what. He buried her under the dirt steps, and cried for weeks.

He tore a piece of bread from a small loaf, placing the remainder carefully in its bag and stepping around the row of lockers. As always, he felt his heart jump and his breath stop. There, barely illuminated in the light's perimeter, stood the fearful sharklike profile of a Messerschmitt 262 "Schwalbe" fighter/bomber of World War Two.

Hans Ackermann stood for a moment admiring

the perfectly preserved aircraft. He walked to the Me.262 and slipped his toe into the step on the outboard side of the number one jet engine's nacelle. He swung himself up onto the wing and climbed into the familiar, snug cockpit.

In the semidarkness the instrument panel, and especially the controls on his left and right, were shadowy shapes, but Ackermann knew each square centimeter of the plane's interior. He rested his hand on the throttle knobs and looked through the small front windshield and over the nose of the craft. It was all so familiar, even the musty smell of old aluminum, plastic and leather. With his finger tips, he gently moved the mixture handles back and forth, as if adjusting the powerful jet engine's fuel requirements.

Through the small windshield, the flickering candle sent bursts of light ricocheting over the smooth aluminum nose of the Me.262. In Ackermann's eyes, and in his mind, those flashes were the muzzle blasts of WWII 50-caliber machine guns on a 220th Squadron Golden Scimitar P-47. Each flicker was another round of lead death tearing toward him, ripping at the fragile skin of his Messerschmitt, sending him and his Me.262 into the ground.

And the fire! God, the fire! Ackermann's hands were soaked with sweat and he shook with emotion as well as palsy. The last of the bread was crumbling in his grip. With an animal-like guttural groan he pushed himself up from the plane's seat almost in a panic. Free of the cockpit, he calmed, wondering why he subjected himself to the torture of reliving that horrible day. True, he loved the aircraft, but he hated the memories it evoked. Yet, he was unsure if he wanted to forget the war or continue to relive it. Either way, it seemed to him that the choice was not to be his.

Scott Austingrove slowly awakened to a throbbing ache in his back and right buttocks. The mists of his blurred vision shrouded the room, but he knew he was at the hospital in Munich. He remembered driving there. A ragged spear of pain stabbed into him as he made the first tentative move to get up and out of the bed. Falling back, he closed his eyes, cold sweat pulsing from his forehead, and waited for the throbbing to ease. Slowly, as the discomfort left, bits of memory returned. He recalled brief moments of awareness of the doctors hurriedly examining him, and from the soreness of his backside, he knew that they had done some serious poking around.

Austingrove's eyes snapped open at the sound of a scuff of hard-soled shoes on the well worn linoleum of the wardroom. A tall man, darkly dressed, emerged slowly and ghostlike through the haze of Austingrove's perception. His vague image stood at the foot of the bed, tapping something on his upturned left palm with obvious impatience. The man's form seemed familiar, but Austingrove could not tie him to any particular time or place.

As full consciousness approached, he became more aware of his surroundings and was startled by the discovery of a young doctor at his left arm, fussing with a clear surgical tube. He looked back toward the tall man. His image became clear as he moved forward and injected himself between the doctor and Austingrove.

"Mister Austingrove," the tall man's voice was guttural, snapping Austingrove's attention fully to him. "I am Police Inspector Karl Schwerin. Will you please tell me the circumstances behind your gunshot wound?"

It was spoken not as a question, rather a subtle, yet definite order.

"He has no gunshot wound," said the doctor, a sharp edge of annoyance honed into his voice. He gave the Inspector a frowning glance. "We merely removed foreign particles, primarily chips of stone, imbedded in his back and backside." That said, he assumed an air of disinterest, going to the window, jotting notes on a chart.

Austingrove broke the uneasy silence, "Well, I was out sight-seeing in the country. I don't know exactly where," he lied. "I heard an occasional gunshot. I figured it must be a hunter." His voice was raspy and his throat ached. He stopped and sipped from the plastic cup at his bedside.

Inspector Schwerin looked at him thoughtfully, "You do not know where you were?"

"No, no I don't, but I remember I was by the stone wall of an old farm. I heard the shot and then the projectile hitting the wall. I didn't know that I was hurt. Then I felt the blood running down my leg, so I came here immediately. That's about it."

Austingrove recalled diving into the brush, rolling, and sprinting to his car. He was unaware of the extent of his injuries. Crashing the car into the hospital got him immediate attention and he was examined and quickly rolled into an operating theatre. They found that one of the fragments of stone that penetrated his side was dangerously close to his kidney. The surgery took two hours of careful probing until it, and all of the other jagged shards were removed.

He couldn't tell this German policeman or anyone else where he had been or why he had been there, that would lead to a discussion the peculiar actions of a beautiful German woman, her mysterious companion, and the story told by her dying father that had compelled him to come to Germany. He knew now, however, that his premonition of danger he had held was indeed real, and he suspected that she had lied to him, and that, he reasoned, was why he must go back to the old farm. He knew exactly where it was and he had to find whatever it was that someone didn't want him to find. But the next time he'd use a little more caution, and bring his boss, Major Harvey Dessault.

*   *   *

He and Dessault had performed in the Liberty Bell Aero-rama Air Show in Philadelphia, just sixty days earlier. Austingrove's performance for the crowd of 38,000 went well and was the first of four flights in the Dessault Flying Museum's F-86 fighter at the two day show. Austingrove was wiping droplets of fuel from the glistening wing of the antique jet when he was startled by a tug at his sleeve. He turned and looked into a pair of the brightest blue eyes he'd ever seen.

"I am Hilda Göettz," she said. Her hair was rolled into a large bun on top of her head. It was the kind of hairdo that reminded Austingrove of a big cinnamon roll. She was tall, and he had guessed she was in her late forties. "You are with the Dessault Aircraft Museum?" She touched the logo above the pocket of his flightsuit.

"Yes, Ma'am. What can I do for you?"

"I have been sent to find someone with an interest in German airplanes from the war. My father, Albert Flueger..." She paused, looking at Austingrove as if the name should mean something to him. Seeing no glint of heightened interest, she continued, "My father is in the Hoskins-Borner Hospital, Downtown. He is old. Old and very ill. He is dying. He sent me here to locate a company or a person that would hear his story of an underground jet airplane factory. Your museum might be interested?"

Austingrove saw the beautiful blue eyes become just slightly dampened. *Please don't start crying,* he thought.

"Well, Ma'am, it's not my museum. But I know that I would be interested in talking to your father."

Her face brightened, shedding years from her age. "When can you come see him? Please don't wait too long, he is gravely ill."

"Well, I guess I can be there tonight. About six?"

"Wonderful," she squeezed Austingrove's hand, "He is in room three-fifty on the third floor, his name is Albert Flueger. He will be expecting you. Thank you, thank you." She turned and hurried toward a black Mercedes Benz idling alongside the hangar. A younger woman sat in the back seat and a large man was at the wheel, a newspaper partly obscuring his face.

Austingrove watched her beautiful, long legs swiftly carry her away. He silently wished she were younger - or he a bit older.

The Hoskins-Borner Hospital was a private facility in an area of Philadelphia that had been bypassed by prosperity and embraced by poverty. Austingrove avoided the rickety-looking elevator and took the opportunity for exercise, sprinting up the worn stairway to the third floor.

He found Albert Flueger erect in bed, pillows stacked up under him like a sandbagged dike at flood time. An oxygen tube encircled his head, its two nozzles poked into his nostrils. He stared at the ceiling, unblinking. The man's eye sockets were like two heel marks in a muddy field; black, sunken holes. His skin reminded Austingrove of old, sunbaked airplane tires; cracked, gray, and chalky. The old man's face was expressionless. Austingrove was uneasy. He felt the chill of impending death. Along with that, the room smelled heavily of sweat.

"Mr. Flueger," Austingrove said, "I'm Scott Austingrove. Your daughter, Hilda, asked me to come see you."

Albert Flueger showed no response except that his dark eyelids slowly closed. When they opened several seconds later, a pair of penetrating blue eyes were staring directly into Austingrove's. Hilda indeed had been passed her father's eyes.

"Why did Hilda send you?" His voice was unwavering, much stronger than the body that produced it appeared to be.

She told me that you wished to talk to someone. Someone who has an interest in warplanes of the Third Reich."

"And what is your interest?" Flueger asked.

Austingrove stepped closer to the bed. "Well, I'm a partner in the Dessault Aircraft Museum. At the museum we restore and maintain a number of antique jet aircraft, In some cases we even fly them. We have planes representing many nations." Flueger's eyes never blinked. This unnerved Austingrove. He looked away, then said, "And I also work as a correspondent for *Jet Fighter!* Magazine. There is great interest in planes of your era."

Flueger's eyes were locked on Austingrove's as if trying to look into his soul, penetrate his thoughts and decipher his true motive for being there. "I know not of that magazine," he spit out the word magazine as if irritated him. "Come tomorrow with papers proving who you are, and about this 'museum'."

"OK, Albert." He was eager to leave. "Take care." As Austingrove hurried from the hospital he thought of what a stupid thing that was to say to an obviously dying man; "Take care."

After the next day's performance, he quickly refueled and cleaned up the F-86 and immediately left for Hoskins-Borner. Albert Flueger perused Austingrove's personal papers, a Dessault Aircraft Museum brochure, and a copy of *Jet Fighter!* magazine as if they were the Dead Sea Scrolls. "I must have your pledge that you are who you say you are, and that you have only just met Hilda, exactly as you have told me."

Austingrove was beginning to tire of the old man's suspicious nature. "Well, look, Albert, I'm only interested in helping you and your daughter with whatever it is that you need. And yes, I am who I am, whatever the hell that means."

"Very well, sit. I have something to tell you." He reached out and grasped Austingrove's arm. "You must tell no one what I'm going to tell you. Not even Hilda. No one." He released his grip and relaxed back into the pillows, the exertion telling on his frail body. "You must promise me that."

"Of course, Albert."

Albert Flueger's dark eyelids closed again. There was a moment when Austingrove wondered if the man had gone to sleep. Then his eyes slowly opened, as if recovering from some sort of trance. He began to speak as if reciting lines from a script. His voice, edges frayed with emotion, was no longer as strong as it had been at first. "I hated Hitler and what he was doing to Germany. He was a *Wahnsinniger*, a madman, without morals or conscience. And I was an aircraft worker, building the planes that this fool sent to destruction on a daily basis. I held my tongue. To speak out would have meant a tortuous death at the hands of Hitler's Gestapo."

Austingrove pulled a small note pad from his inside jacket pocket and began to make notes.

"I was just as much a prisoner as those in the stalags. No prisoner of war suffered any more than I. And it was not merely suffering of the body, it was of the mind too. Many of us were forced to work so many hours that we would drop from exhaustion. Only then would we be allowed a few hours of rest." He pulled at the neck of his gown as if it were a yoke. His eyes began to glisten with the first tears of emotion. "I was afraid. Too afraid to speak out against the Nazis. But then, we all were. We worked as told and prayed in silence for our freedom."

Austingrove again felt the itch of impatience. "You worked in an underground airplane factory, is that right, Albert?" he prompted.

"Ja, it was a huge facility. There were many assembly lines that could build a hundred fighter planes at a time. Yet, above ground there was no sign that anything was there. We were only taken out from there and brought back at night, so I saw little." He stiffened with intensity and gripped Austingrove's hand, "I know it is still there. I know it has not been found since the war." He fell back, exhausted.

"How do you know that?"

"I have searched the military records for many years, both American and German. It was in the area that became Western Germany. I went back to find it many years after the war. I found the town, Wolfshütte, but could not find the factory. My memory was not so good, Mister Austingrove, but I know that it was somewhere among the forests southeast of a town named Wolfshütte, and it has to be still."

Austingrove was skeptical, but realized that if a World War II underground Nazi aircraft plant existed, yet undiscovered, it would hold an incredible treasure of aviation artifacts. "What kind of fighter planes were you building there, Albert?"

"The main assembly line was producing Herr Willy Messerschmitt's new jet-propelled design, the 'Schwalbe' model two-sixty-two. 'Schwalbe' is the small, forked-tail bird you Americans call Swallow. The two-sixty-two was a twin engine fighter-bomber..." His voice trailed off and his eyes closed.

Austingrove thought that perhaps Flueger had gone to sleep. He rose to leave. He didn't want to pressure this frail old man too much. He would return in the morning.

"Don't go!" Albert Flueger was alert, straining to rise, his eyes bright again, burning with intensity. "I must tell you the rest - tonight."

Austingrove skidded the chair closer. "All right, Albert. Go ahead."

"There was a farm at the edge of a forest. To the south a hillside covered with small trees. The road nearby led to a grass airfield, then on to Wolfshütte. The planes were towed to the airfield at night for delivery to Luftwaffe squadrons."

Flueger told of the layout of the plant, the equipment and the lives of those who labored like ants in an underground hell. Austingrove asked few questions, but wrote everything down. As tired as he was, he was sure that he would not remember it all the next day.

Finally, Flueger's voice weakened and he turned to Austingrove, "I can still see it so well, but it was not where I thought it to be."

"Remember, Albert," said Austingrove, "things change in so much time. The farm might be gone and the trees would be much larger. Or they could be gone as well." He stood, wanting to leave. He needed some sleep, badly, and he'd return early tomorrow. "I'll come again in the morning. You try to remember all that you can. I'll bring a map for us to look at, OK?"

Flueger pointed a shaking, bony finger at Austingrove, "Remember, tell no one, Mister Austingrove." His hand fell back to the bed. "I hope I will still be able to be here for you tomorrow."

The next morning, Austingrove returned with a map of Germany only to find Flueger's bed empty. He had a grim feeling that he'd seen the last of his link to the underground German aircraft plant.

In the waiting room he found Hilda Göettz, a wad of tissue crumpled in her hand, her eyes red and swollen. She looked very, very tired. The only other occupant of the room was a lone man, slouched in a chair, reading a newspaper.

"Mister Austingrove, he is gone." She stood, swaying, as if about to collapse.

"Sit down, Ma'am," said Austingrove. He held her around her shoulders, feeling them rocking with quiet sobs. Her head pressed into his chest and he smelled the sweetness of her hair, better smelling than cinnamon rolls, he thought.

She straightened, "What did he tell you?"

Austingrove remembered Albert Flueger's admonition not to tell anyone, not even his own daughter, Hilda. He knew that he must not violate his oath to the dying man. "Well, He told me of his work during the war. He said that he'd tried to find an aircraft plant after the war, but he couldn't." He stood to leave. "I'm sorry. I'm not much help, I'm afraid."

"That's all he said?"

"Yep, pretty much." said Austingrove. "He was angry because he couldn't remember more."

"You brought a map," pressed Hilda Göettz.

"Yes, Ma'am."

"Well, what did he show you on the map?"

"Not a thing. I only brought the map today." Austingrove turned. "Sorry for your loss, Ma'am." He felt Hilda's eyes on his back as he left the room.

Austingrove stood at the curb, hoping to snag a taxi. He saw Hilda Göettz and a large, dark man hurry out of the hospital and disappear into the parking garage. A moment later a black Mercedes Benz sedan roared past him, blowing a cloud of dirt and street debris around him. Austingrove recognized the driver as the slouching man in the waiting room. That realization created rippling chills along his spine.

Now, only two months later, he felt that indeed, he was finally very close to finding Herr Flueger's concealed aircraft plant. And someone with a rifle knew it.

"Did you see anyone?" The inspector asked.

"No, Sir, no one." That was true, he thought, he hadn't really seen anyone. "It must have been hunters. They didn't expect anyone to be around there, I reckon," he offered.

The inspector was becoming impatient with Austingrove's slow, vague answers. He asked three more questions, repeated two previous ones, smiled, politely thanked Austingrove, and left.

"Your injuries are quite serious, Mister Austingrove." The young doctor had moved to the bedside. "To prevent an infection, and to be sure we have removed all of the debris, we will keep you as our guest for a few days." He suddenly smiled, "Did you really drive your car into the Emergency Room?"

"I guess," said Austingrove. "But it's OK, it's a rented car."

The doctor laughed and pressed the wall switch. The room darkened except for a small fluorescent bulb above the bed and Austingrove could see a narrow, black strip of the evening sky between the plastic-like window curtains. He watched a pair of shimmering landing lights of an airliner course across the narrow gap and was asleep before the high-pitched whistle of its jet engines reached the darkened room.

CHAPTER TWO

The F-86E slashed across the field in a shimmering blur, rolled on its side and circled a full 270 degrees. When it leveled out, its red-ringed nose was pointed directly down the east-west runway of the Fullerton, California Airport. Dust blew up in curling vortices from the undercarriage as the two main tires "fweeped" in unison on the asphalt strip. The nose gear slowly lowered to the tarmac in time with the decreasing speed of the silver fighter plane.

The Sabre Jet, a veteran of the Korean conflict, turned smartly at the end of the runway and taxied toward the Dessault Aircraft Museum hangar. The canopy slid back. To that point it had been opaque, a bright star of reflected sunlight, but now the pilot was exposed, already pulling off his helmet. He placed a yellow ball cap on his head and a pair of sunglasses on his tanned face. He deftly swung the plane around in front of the Dessault Aircraft Museum hangar, and rocked it to a stop.

The General Electric J-47 turbojet engine was still coasting down. Its whine diminishing as the pilot sat in the cockpit, jotting notes into his flight log. But unseen, his hands shook and he sweated profusely. He jumped down from the wing, slid a set of wheel chocks in place and strode past the golden scimitar painted on the aircraft's bright red nose.

He walked as a soldier would; determined, long, strong strides, parachute and helmet hanging from one shoulder, the other arm swinging, back straight, head up, eyes straight ahead. And indeed, he still considered himself a military man even though he'd not been on active duty in nearly 5 years.

A patch on the left breast of his tattered 1960s-era flight jacket said, "DESSAULT MAJ. U.S.A.F." and a red shoulder patch sported a golden scimitar, the curved battle sword of the ancient Persians.

Major Harvey Dessault entered the cool interior of the hangar. He wiped the sweat from his brow and scanned the aircraft arranged side by side, nose to tail, wings overlapping. There was one empty spot for the F-86 Sabre about to be refueled outside. The rest of the planes, all jets, were equal to a display of classic military aircraft you might find in Washington D.C.'s Smithsonian Air and Space Museum. The beauty of each of the perfectly restored, historically significant aircraft was enhanced by the reflection of its undersides in the painted and polished hangar floor.

An F-84 Thunderjet sat with its open snout pointed at the back wall. The F-84 was Republic Aviation Corporation's finest jet fighter. Almost 8,000 had been built from 1946 to 1952.

Next to the space for the F-86, crouched an olive drab Bell P-59B Airacomet.

The P-59 was America's first jet-powered fighter plane and this plane was one of only two 1945 models remaining. It was flyable. The other was atop a pedestal at the entrance to Edwards Air Force Base in the California desert. Both still carried Air Force paint, numbers and insignia.

The high tail of a Gloster Meteor Mk III stood out above the low slung P-59. The Meteor was Britain's first jet fighter, a twin engine, single place, low wing beauty. It was the only allied jet fighter to be operational in World War II. This example served out its final active duty years with the Royal Canadian Air Force and still wore their insignia.

A brilliantly polished Vought F7U Cutlass faced the hangar door and stood like a cobra about to strike. With its stubby nose high above the floor on a long forward landing gear, it looked as if it was about to leap to flight. The Cutlass was a 1950s era Navy carrier-based twin engine fighter, America's first tailless fighter. In appearance, it would fare well alongside modern swing wing fighters with its twin wing-mounted vertical fins. In performance it would be a goose against a falcon, as it was woefully underpowered. The F7U was the first American aircraft with afterburners on its twin turbojet engines, but even with that, its speed was disappointing. It saw only limited service. For many aviation enthusiasts, however, it would still rank as one of the most beautiful fighting planes ever built.

The rest of the classic planes included a Russian MiG-15 brought to America during the Korean War. A North Korean pilot defected to the South with it, affording the Americans their first chance to test and evaluate an example of Russian technology. It was said that Chuck Yeager had once flown this very plane. A U.S. Lockheed T-33 jet trainer - One of Dessault's favorite planes - and an F-104J Starfighter dressed in the red, yellow and black of the Belgian Air Force, complete the Museum's inventory. He breathed a huge sigh.

Each of the aircraft displayed a golden scimitar on its bright red nose stripe.

To the right, a flight of steel stairs led to a balcony backed by a row of glistening glass office windows and doors. One door stood open and a young man in a blue jumpsuit leaned out.

"Up here, Major, hurry! Telephone!" Cody Gordon, Dessault Museum's Master Mechanic darted back into the room.

Dessault reluctantly turned away from the jets,

flopped his ex-government-issue parachute and helmet on the equipment rack next to the stairs and took them two at a time.

Entering the office, he pulled off his tattered flight jacket. His flightsuit beneath also bore a faded emblem of the Golden Scimitar, symbol of the 220th Fighter Squadron, positioned on the right breast. He slid down into his huge, black leather executive chair, filling it completely, and swiveled around to the phone.

"Dessault," he announced.

Dessault's office, although 1950s stylish, was as immaculate as the hangar and the aircraft below. The carpet was a rich textured crimson and the walls were tastefully paneled with individual planks of dark wood. A single high-backed chair faced the desk. A pleated leather sofa and a small, square table faced a bookcase that covered the north wall from floor to ceiling. Each of the bookcase's eight shelves were arranged with rows of fine leather volumes interspersed with photos of family, friends and aircraft in gold, silver and wooden frames. There was no clutter, no mess, not even on the vast expanse of the man's desktop. The only thing truly out of place in the room was his ragged Vietnam era Air Force flight jacket.

Dessault was retired from the Air force. He had almost immediately placed most of his savings in peril by joining Scott Austingrove in starting an aviation magazine. They called it *Jet Fighter!* and it emerged at a time when young executives and wealthy flying enthusiasts were discovering the thrill of flying a surplus jet fighter or trainer. It had taken only five years for it to catch on. When it did, it rapidly became the leader, establishing a new field in aviation publishing. *Jet Fighter!* was eagerly bought out by a huge broadcasting/publishing company. Dessault took a position on the Board of Directors and Austingrove continued with the company as associate editor, mostly because he simply loved the work.

Dessault started his jet fighter collection about then, more by accident than by design.

A small air museum located in Orange County's John Wayne Airport was going under. The MiG and the F-86 was their main attractions and Dessault's generous efforts over the years at providing publicity for the museum was repaid when he was offered first chance to buy the aircraft. He had added to his new collection over the years as opportunities arose. As the museum grew and began to fly demonstrations at air shows across the United States, Dessault took on Austingrove as an equal partner.

Major Dessault had admired but a few men. Scott Austingrove, however, was one man who had earned every bit of respect and admiration the Major could ever have for anyone, this even included his own family.

He recalled however, that this had not always been the case. In fact, he remembered that once in a muddy field in Vietnam he called him ignorant, a jackass, and the stupidest bastard he'd ever known, even though Lieutenant Austingrove was risking his life to save him. The young lieutenant had just grinned at him and continued to drag him on through the marsh.

"You were heading the wrong way, Sir."

"Let go of me Lieutenant," Dessault growled. The pain shot up through his legs with every lurch and against every bump. "I'll court martial you, damn it, Lieutenant."

Austingrove paused just enough to get a better grip on the Major's flightsuit and then he dragged the 205 pound airman into a flooded rice paddy. The buoyancy afforded by the water made Austingrove's load somewhat lighter. This hastened their retreat toward a stand of tall reeds and brush that bordered the northeast corner of the rice paddy.

The humid air made Austingrove's chest pound and the slimy bottom of the flooded field made him slip and fall face first into the muddy water three times before they reached the cover of the reeds and collapsed.

"You damn fool," Dessault was still raging. "You lost your aircraft, Mister."

"With all due respect, Sir, so did you." Out of breath, Austingrove's words came in short bursts, just like the ones from the MiG-23's cannons that had taken out Dessault.

"You were crawling right toward a column of

about fifty Reds, Sir. I had to get you turned around." Dessault didn't hear, he had passed-out again.

Austingrove had chased the MiG off with the last 5 rounds from his F-100 Super Sabre's 20mm cannon before his Flight Leader's parachute had settled Dessault into the soft muck below. Then he flew low over the Major twice, indicating which way he should go, but the dazed pilot continued to drag himself toward the enemy troops. Austingrove could see them spreading out to search for the downed pilot. Any more overflights would just serve to steer them to him, he reasoned.

Gun magazines empty and his entire store of rockets spent, he pulled the F-100 up and over and headed back toward the pilot on the ground. He dumped the speed brakes out, throttled back slightly so as to steady up the plane's flight and pointed the jet's nose directly at the column of troops. He slammed his helmet visor down and raised the left ejection seat handle. He felt the blast of hot air as explosive charges blew the canopy off. He adjusted the plane's heading slightly, raised the right handle and squeezed the grip. The ejection seat fired him free of the falling jet at a mere 600 feet of altitude.

The aged and war-weary F-100 slammed into the ground just ahead of the advancing communists and exploded into a fiery hell that engulfed the stunned troops and their heavily loaded supply trucks.

That old, tired F-100, affectionately referred to as "Hun" - G.I. lingo for "Hundred" - had gone out taking out more troops in five seconds on the ground than it could ever be expected to get in future air combat.

Austingrove landed on his feet, a mere 20 yards from Dessault. He dragged the unconscious pilot to the cover of the reeds. He bandaged the man's left leg and splinted the right.

Dessault came to. "That was a damn fool move, Lieutenant," were his only words before the pain made his world black again.

When the daylight's haze slid into darkness, Austingrove carried, dragged and at one point, rolled, his Commanding Officer to the shoreline of the South China Sea, nearly two miles away. A patrolling evac helicopter homed-in on their emergency beacon, snatched them off the beach and airlifted them straight to the hospital at Dong Hoi.

That was six years ago, thought Dessault, and I haven't sworn at him since.

Dessault straightened and hung up the phone. For the first time, Cody Gordon saw the big, gruff Major shaken, stunned. "Sir?" he said.

"Scott's been shot," rasped Dessault.

Austingrove was awaken by a nurse changing the intravenous solution tapped into his arm. It was only that morning, he remembered, that he had found the old farm, and it was definitely in an area similar to what Albert Flueger had described. On that basis, he began poking around, looking for anything that might indicate a hidden underground installation.

He knew that Hitler's Germany, in the later part of the war, was still able to continue to build hundreds of fighters and bombers, even though their factories, industrial areas and railways had been bombed to smoldering shambles by Allied air raids, day and night.

This amazing feat was accomplished by an incredible network of cottage industry. Parts were being manufactured in barns, shops and even in the kitchens of the homes. They were then transported by cars, vans, wagons and horses to assembly plants hidden in unlikely locations in Germany, Holland and Poland. Some of these assembly plants were huge underground caverns with assembly lines that could accommodate the construction of up to 100 planes at a time. Completed aircraft were usually moved at night, along country roads to outlying air bases where final flight readiness was accomplished.

An underground aircraft plant west of the city of Munich, at Augsburg, was found after the war, totally destroyed by bombers of the 9th Air Force. Another near the town of Ulm farther west was also razed. These factories were all in the southeast, an area of Germany to which Albert Flueger had led Austingrove.

Albert Flueger said that German records showed that there were too many parts supplied by too many suppliers for the number of planes produced. No large cache of new or destroyed parts had been found. He felt that at least one of the underground plants was still pretty much intact at war's end. He insisted that somewhere there had to be a huge stock of airplane parts - or airplanes - in an assembly plant yet unaccounted for.

Austingrove had been searching yet another farm field that stretched nearly a kilometer from east to west. Covered with rich, new grass, it was an obstacle course of hundreds of ancient indentations, remnants of bomb craters created by American and British World War II bombers more than 40 years previously. Each depression, the sharpness of its edges eroded smooth, was filled with water from melting snows. Atop the icy water, bits of man's trash floated among nature's castoff branches, twigs and leaves.

To the south, a tree covered ridge ran 800 meters east and an equal distance to the west. Patches of snow still clung to its shaded areas. The long ridge looked as if it were a parapet, there to protect the field from an assault from the north.

A bombed-out farm occupied the northeastern corner of the site, its house and barn leveled except for the remnants of the home's fireplace and one stubborn corner of a stone wall. A constant, light rain dampened the stones, reviving for a time the original luster and beauty for which they had been selected decades before.

Austingrove continued his walk among the craters, a gnarled stick in his hand dripping water. A gray overcoat open down the front, hung loosely over his wide shoulders. It swung back and forth as he walked, hurling rain from its hem. His shoes and pant legs were wet to his knees. Stopping at the next crater, he saw his reflection on the surface of the pool. His face, tan from years in various aircraft cockpits, held wide set, dark and intense eyes. At almost 40, he was neither handsome nor ugly, but his unique features often held a person's gaze until they decided if they were impressed or appalled.

He wasn't a large man, but he carried himself as if he were. He had a swaying stride reminiscent of a cocky sailor, but he was ex-Air Force, an aviation historian and a correspondent for *Jet Fighter!* magazine and had never been to sea. Those who knew him knew that he sported no cockiness, and Austingrove knew that his boss and co-worker, Major Harvey Dessault, an ex-Air Force fighter pilot and co-owner of the Dessault Flying Museum in Fullerton, California, would condone neither arrogance nor cockiness in his staff.

His image wavering on the icy water reminded him of the night flights when he could see nothing outside of the plane, only his face, encased in his red, white and blue helmet and illuminated by the soft red instrument lights, reflected back at him from the plexiglass canopy. He slammed the stick into the water, shattering his reflection and spattering his coat and pants with dirty rainwater.

Even after five years, remembrances of his Air Force career brought sudden anger. He had been grounded for intentionally sending his perfectly good Super Sabre, F-100 fighter crashing into the ground. The Board of Inquiry ruled that he had acted irresponsibly, causing the unnecessary loss of a million dollar fighting plane without considering that his action took out an undetermined number of enemy soldiers and resulted in the rescue of a downed American pilot.

There was no court martial, but he was grounded for the duration of his squadron's involvement in Vietnam. When he returned home, he felt that his father and brother, both ex-Air Force fighter aces of WWII and Korea, were ashamed of him, never including him in the long, pool-side bull sessions spent recounting their flying experiences.

After all, he reasoned, they knew that he had destroyed only a single plane during his career as a fighter pilot, and it was his own.

CHAPTER THREE

ice landing. Dessault uncoupled his seat belt as the Luftansa MD-11 rocked gently along the taxiway. Always the professional flyer even when a passenger, he had admired the pilot's finesse during the eight-hour flight. He too had once experienced the same enjoyment of flying he knew this pilot felt. It was in the way the Luftansa Skipper made sweeping, graceful turns and in the gentle handling of the huge airliner. He felt that he could tell when a pilot enjoyed flying - it was evident in the aircraft's every movement. No jerky or hesitant motion. Like dancing with a princess, it was smooth and rhythmic.

He used to have that feeling in the F-105 and in the F-86. Yes, even in the little "T-bird," the T-33 trainer. He had the joy of flying in the Air Force too, but now all that remained was a paralyzing fear. A fear that crept into him at some undefined moment, and he suddenly became afraid, and was still terribly afraid of dying in the flaming wreckage of one of the planes to which he had dedicated his life.

His thoughts turned back to Austingrove, the only real friend he'd ever had. A man that would lay down his fortune and indeed even his life for him. They first met in Nam. He had become Dessault's wing man by virtue of his flying ability, certainly not his kill record. He had not a single MiG to his credit.

Dessault lost track of Austingrove until three years after being discharged from the Air Force. Looking for work, Dessault's progress in finding a flying job was zero. The outlook for any employment was dim. There were just too many pilots, just too many ex-military people looking for work.

He had left his resume' at a charter airline in San Diego and then strolled out through the hangar, onto the flightline.

"Major!"

Dessault unconsciously ignored the call as he stood admiring a line of brightly colored private aircraft on the ramp next to the charter airline. The PacSeaAir hangar faced the N-S runway, shielding the aircraft and those attending to them from the sea breezes that swept across San Diego Harbor. It had a huge skyscape mural in bright oranges, whites and blues that held his attention.

"Major!" The call came again.

The skyscape depicted two ultralight aircraft, one looping, the other banking around a towering cloud. It made him want to strap on one of the little ships and soar off into the afternoon wind.

"Major Dessault!"

The sudden realization that the call was to him startled him. He turned, shielding his eyes from the bright Southern California sun, but he was unable to see into the dark interior of the hangar. His eyes adjusted slowly. A figure was coming toward him. Thin, tall, not close enough yet to make out who it was.

"You have any need for an old, experienced wing man?"

The man that stepped into the sunlight had a wide grin and an easy casualness that made Dessault feel immediately at ease.

"I'll be damned, Scotty, my man!" Dessault grabbed Austingrove's hand and began pumping. "Damn good to see you Scott! What are you doing these days?"

The two men reestablished their friendship that day and when the opportunity came to go to work together, they didn't even have to discuss it.

Dessault and Austingrove started *Jet Fighter!* magazine and later, Dessault's Flying Museum.

*   *   *

The gentle rocking motion of the plane as it rolled to a stop and the brightening of the cabin lights gently brought Dessault back to the present. He looked out the window. The rhythmic flash of the strobe light on the belly of the MD-11 reflected on the wet ramp like the pulsing of a pumping heart. He again thought of Scott Austingrove lying in the Munich hospital, he silently prayed that his friend was going to be OK.

"I'm OK," said Austingrove. "Get me out of here, will you.   All of the nurses have hair all over their legs and armpits, and the food's terrible. Let's go."

"You're not going anywhere until I talk with your doctor, Ace, so just relax."

Austingrove's attending physician spoke excellent English and filled Dessault in on the injuries and surgery. "He must stay here for another forty-eight hours, then remain in bed for at least another seven days," he said.

"Look, Doctor, we have a flight out of here tomorrow, back to The States. Can you release him to me if I promise to keep him down?"

The doctor reluctantly agreed after Dessault explained that they may not be able to pay for a longer stay. They checked-out of the hospital the next day, checked into a hotel, and checked-out a map for their drive to the razed farm house near Wolfshütte.

It had stopped raining but a gray overcast accentuated the gloom of boredom felt by Dessault and Austingrove. They lay propped on their elbows with only a coarse canvas tarpaulin separating them from the damp grass. For the past six hours they had been watching the bombed-out farm from the ridge that ran along the south side of the property. Cold and tired, they never looked away from the site. They took turns, constantly scanning the area through a new pair of Leitz binoculars.

This was their third day of observing the place where Austingrove had been fired upon. They arrived early each morning and stayed until the sun slipped behind the tall trees to the west. They would like to watch during the evening as well, but the moonless nights would hide any activity below. Besides, the uncomfortable, damp and dull pastime would be unbearable without the promise of a hot shower, dinner and drinks, and the soft beds that awaited them each evening at their hotel.

Austingrove had turned onto his back, trying to relieve the throbbing of his wounds. "Kind of keep an eye on the old barn area, Major," he said. "I think that's where the shot came from."

Dessault grunted and swept the glasses across the short distance between the house and barn. A black bird flashed across his field of vision. Startled, he glanced over the top of the binoculars, and watched as the bird cut a graceful arc toward the trees to his left. He looked at the trees for a moment, then scanned the ones to his right. He put the glasses to his eyes again. He gazed at the trees adjoining the pasture below. Something had been bothering him about this place. He had not been able to pinpoint it, but now he knew what it was.

"Damn, Scott, look at those trees!"

Austingrove glanced at Dessault, shrugged, rolled over onto his elbows and began to study the trees covering the ridge. "Well, I don't know what kind they are, but they're pretty," he said. "So what?"

Dessault rolled over onto one elbow. "Look, all of the trees on this hill are the same type - Aspens, I think." There was rising excitement in his voice. "They are all about the same size. That means they are all probably about the same age."

Austingrove picked-up the binoculars and leveled them back on the farm site. "Thanks for the lesson in horticulture, Pal, but I repeat, so what?"

"Look at all the rest of the trees everywhere else," Dessault swept his arm in an arc. "They are all different kinds - some small, some huge, young ones and old ones." He said.

Austingrove lowered the glasses and looked around. His backside ached and he was in no mood for puzzle games. His release from the hospital was contingent on him staying down for at least seven days. He had no intention of doing that, but the pain made him irritable.

"See what I mean?" said Dessault, "Trees on this ridge look to have all been planted about the same time, a long time ago. They are all the same type, like out of a nursery or something."

"Well, Yeah, I see what you mean - so, what do you think that means?"

"It means that this entire hill along here was made by somebody. This is a giant pile of dirt and all these trees were planted to camouflage it," Dessault said. "And that means, Old Scout, that all this dirt had to come from somewhere."

"Damn!" Austingrove dropped the pair of Leitz'. "Tons of dirt from building an underground plant! That means we must have found that puppy! There is an underground assembly plant or parts depot or something down there, right?"

"Wouldn't surprise me," said Dessault. "But remember that there is also somebody down there with a gun."

As nightfall moved upon them, the men gathered up their belongings and worked their way down the backside of the hill to their rental car parked just off the road to Munich.

"I think the only way we are going to find out what is down there is to flush out whoever might be there," said Austingrove.

"Sure, you're probably right about that. He must come and go early in the morning and after dark," said Dessault. "Tomorrow let's get there even earlier and I'll go down and poke around. If you see someone, whistle and I'll take cover."

"Well, great. And what if you get shot?"

"If there is someone there, I don't think he would kill anyone. He probably just wants to keep people away," said Dessault. "Besides, we don't know if there actually is anyone there or not. And if it turns out that there isn't, we could lay around on that hill forever, looking and waiting."

Five minutes later Austingrove wheeled the rental car out of the thicket and onto the road to Munich. Neither he nor Dessault saw the Police cruiser fall in behind them.

Austingrove rolled out of the comfort of the hotel bed, reached for the lamp on the table separating the beds and snapped on the light. He stood, aching from the surgery and the days on the cold ground and threw a pillow at Dessault's partly covered head. A direct hit, the pillow startled Dessault into wakefulness. "Dammit, Scott, that was a rotten way to wake a guy up."

"It's just as rotten to have to get up at this miserable hour," said Austingrove.

The men ate huge breakfasts in the hotel restaurant. Then, with Dessault driving and Austingrove napping, they drove the dark German highway to the farm site.

Tired and with muscles aching, they struggled to the top of the ridge and began the routine of setting-up their observation position. "I'm heading on down there," said Dessault. "There's enough light now for you to keep an eye on me, OK?"

Austingrove nodded.

Dessault uncapped the binocular's lenses and

swept the area below. Then, he thought he noticed movement. He focused back on the barn area. "We've got something, Scott, take a look at the right corner of the barn."

He knew Austingrove's eyesight was sharper than his. He handed him the glasses.

In his excitement, it was difficult for Austingrove to hold the glasses steady.

"What did you see?" he said. "Is that shadow moving?"

"I don't see anything moving." Austingrove took a deep breath, exhaled, and looked again through steadier lenses. "Yeah, yeah," he said. "The grass, no, it's not a shadow. The grass is moving!"

The men watched as the dark figure of a man emerged from what appeared to be a grass covered trap door near one corner of the barn. He looked cautiously about and slowly stood. Confident that no one was watching him, he walked with a slightly lopsided gait to the tree line. He paused, looked back, then moved off through the trees in the direction of the village of Wolfshütte.

"Unless that's one damn big rabbit, there's your big hole, Pal," Dessault said. "Let's wait a few minutes and then go down there and take a look."

"Let's go now!" Austingrove was on his knees. He groaned in pain from the sutures in his backside and crammed the glasses into his overcoat pocket.

Dessault figured that it would take them five minutes or more to make it down the steep, grassy slope and across to the spot where they saw the man. "OK, let's go, but take it easy and keep an eye on that tree line in case that guy decides to come back."

The men slid and stumbled down through the trees. Like two kids heading for a sandy beach, they hurried toward the abandoned home site.

They went immediately to the spot where the man emerged. Dessault was on his knees, feeling around in the grass, looking for some sort of seam or opening edge. Austingrove was working along the side of some old stonework and what appeared to be the remnants of a blacksmith's forge.

It was Dessault who hit pay dirt.

"Here!"

He pulled up a section of sod that had been carefully stitched to a square patch of canvas. This exposed a metal panel with a hand grip cut into it. He pulled at it. It slid smoothly back, opening a three foot square access hole to whatever lay beneath.

Austingrove was trembling with the greatest excitement he could remember feeling. He looked around, then said, "Damn, Man, this is it! We've found something big!" And he slid down into the entrance.

Light from the square opening illuminated a row of dirt steps that led down to a cement floor. Austingrove took each step carefully, squinting into the darkness. Dessault slid through the hatch, momentarily blocking out the daylight. Austingrove stopped and listened. He wondered if anyone else was down there. If there were, he and Dessault would be perfectly silhouetted targets.

As Dessault moved down the steps, Austingrove was again able to see. His eyes were beginning to adjust to the darkness and images beyond the column of daylight were beginning to emerge. They were at one end of a huge room.

Standing in the center was Ackermann's steel table, with his matches and candle. Austingrove went to the table and scratched one of the old kitchen matches across its top. He lit the candle and picked it up.

To his right he saw someone's living quarters. A wall with a steel door was straight ahead, and to his left . . . He raised the candle high and walked slowly toward the form that began to grow in the flickering light of the candle.

"My God, Major. Oh, my God, look at this." His voice was unexpectedly loud, echoing throughout the chamber.

As if it were a huge pagan idol, the profile emerged of what many believe to be the world's most beautiful fighter plane of any era: a perfectly preserved and maintained 1945 Messerschmitt Me.262, "Schwalbe."

In the half-light, the dappled camouflage paint of this twin jet German fighter/bomber emphasized the sharklike sleekness of its fuselage. More than thirty four-feet long, it tapered back to the raked tail standing more than twelve-feet above the hangar floor.

The sides of the fuselage sloped down and outward, curving into a triangular cross-section, providing room for the landing gear when retracted.

Every line, every curve, was a masterpiece of aircraft design.

The cockpit was boldly positioned half way back and high on the fuselage. Its bubble canopy accentuated the smooth lines of the aircraft. Nacelles hung one from each of the thin, slightly swept wings, each housing a single jet engine.

Its tricycle landing gear served to give it a slightly nose-high stance, imparting a look as if somehow it was proud of its lineage and fearlessly competent in its purpose.

After nearly fifty years, the black swastika on the tail, edged in white, could still be seen. The Roman numeral 3 of Nazi General Adolf Galland's elite *Jagdverband* (fighter squadron) 44, and the German cross on the fuselage was as if it were painted yesterday.

The Messerschmitt 262 was called "Schwalbe" the Swallow, but unlike that gentle bird, it was armed like a tiger, it fought like a berserk bear and flew like every pilot's best dream.

Behind this bird stood another. Hands shaking, Austingrove raised the flickering light and could just make out a third in the row.

Dessault recognized the first two as model Me.262A-1A's, single-seat fighters. The third appeared to be a rare two-place B-1A model, a radar-equipped night fighter. Twin streamlined sixty six-gallon external fuel tanks hung beneath its fuselage. The drop tanks became necessary when the fuel tank behind the pilot was removed to make room for the radar operator. The planes were brand new, and had been waiting nearly fifty years at this secret assembly line to be flight tested.

They couldn't know that these three Me.262's represented Able Flight of Hans Ackermann's Jagdverband, and that he considered them to be his very own Nazi underground fighter squadron.

Just beyond the third plane, the overhead of the huge hangar was collapsed. There were, Austingrove was sure, more fighters in various stages of construction buried back there. They would have to stay there. Somehow though, Austingrove and Dessault would take these three back to America.

Dessault had not spoken a word. He stood at the side of the first plane, tenderly caressing the smooth aluminum skin. Finally, he whispered, "Scott, the hell of this is, we can't tell anybody about these planes."

Austingrove knew that he was right. The present German government was an ultra-right regime of the highest order. It emerged after the unification of Germany, when a Neo-Nazi political arm had begun to take great strides in the cities of the renewed country. This instilled fear in some, and so inflamed the right, that their political clout grew. Running on an antiradical platform, they were elected into power and made their first order of business the total annihilation of the entire Neo-Nazi movement. Additionally, one of their primary goals was the complete eradication of all history of, reference to, and remembrance of, Nazi Germany. In this they were making great strides as well. The book burning of the 1930s had returned. This time it was the opposite faction, Nazism, that was targeted.

If the present German regime were to discover and seize these aircraft, three pristine examples of aviation history would surely be totally destroyed. Austingrove could not allow that.

Austingrove walked around the wing and stood next to Dessault at the nose of the first plane.

"How do you suppose they stayed in such good condition all these years?"

"The only thing I can figure," said Dessault, "is that the man we saw leaving here - probably the guy who shot at you - has been maintaining these planes for a very long time. And without harsh weather, sun and wind to deteriorate them, I guess they could last almost indefinitely down here."

"I don't believe that to be possible, Gentlemen." Dessault jerked around to the sound of the voice, the rapid movement nearly blowing out the candle. Austingrove appeared to snap to attention as if a ranking officer had just entered.

In the column of light at the bottom of the steps, Inspector Schwerin stood holding a nasty looking black pistol aimed at their chests.

CHAPTER FOUR

ang! The kitchen door no sooner slammed shut than Hans Ackermann was tearing at the white butcher paper on top of the trash bin. Once every two weeks he ventured into the village of Wolfshütte to find food and hopefully, some discarded clothing. Today had been very good. He had a pair of pants that, although quite large, could be made to fit. The food he had gathered from the few houses and the single cafe in the tiny village would carry him through until the next week.

The villagers knew Ackermann. He had been foraging in their trash and garbage for longer than most of them could remember. The few times they had tried to talk to him, he had run off, a panicked look about him. Everyone considered him an ancient casualty of a long ago war, harmless and pitiful. Much of the food and clothing was left intentionally for him, most of it by people who could ill afford the contributions. Yet Ackermann considered them, each one and all, a threat to all he held dear; his Jagdverband, his freedom, his pride. They would take all of that from him. And they would mock and ridicule his appearance as well.

He loped through a back yard and into the forest. A few moments more and he was on the road that would lead him back to within a few hundred meters of the underground assembly plant.

He rigged a strap over his right shoulder for his precious bundle and pushed his ragged hat from his forehead exposing his face to the sun.

Hans Ackermann's nose was a small lump in the middle of a face full of scar tissue. His right eye sagged grotesquely down onto his wrinkled cheek. His mouth was a lip-less slit, in a permanent snarl. He had not a single hair on his face. No eyelashes, eyebrows or trace of a beard. He had been so terribly burned that the only few scraggly hairs that showed grew randomly from his seared ears.

The skin had been burned away on his right leg so that there was not enough left to allow him the comfort of straightening it. He walked awkwardly and painfully.

But the damage was not restricted to his body.

He was horribly injured inside as well. He had once been a proud and daring Luftwaffe Lieutenant. In his mind, he now felt that he had sunk to humiliating depths.

Ah, the glorious days of the Third Reich! He had been General Adolph Galland's most promising fighter pilot. With seven kills in the very short span of two weeks, he would surely become one of JV-44 Squadron's top aces by the end of 1945.

Then he bitterly recalled his fourteenth sortie, when he was almost out of fuel in a brand new jet-powered Me.262, an America P-47 Thunderbolt flamed Ackermann as he neared his landing approach. He was into the ground in an instant and into the hospital for seven months.

Ackermann turned off of the road and weaved his way through the trees until he came to the farm. As he always did, he stopped and scanned the area. The familiar crumpled ruins of the farm and the solitude of this place gave Ackermann a warm, almost happy feeling. Perhaps he was the luckiest of all the old Luftwaffe pilots. He had his own quiet world and his own Jagdverband as well. But he missed Elisia. She was the only person who had not recoiled at their first look upon his face. They were so in love and so happy. But now, happiness faded with the memory of her. He knew in his heart that there would never be another to share his life, his home, his Jagdverband.

He walked slowly toward the broken barn. As

he reached the side of the house, he stopped. *The entrance is open!*

Oh, no, have I become so old and forgetful? He had forgotten many things before, but never anything so important.

He cautiously approached the sliding panel. He heard voices.

He knelt at the edge of the opening and looked down into the hangar. He saw Inspector Schwerin standing at the base of the steps, his pistol casually hanging in his right hand. Ackermann bent forward, reaching into the open arms locker at the top of the steps and felt the cool steel of his Mauser. He slowly brought it up out of the hole and carefully positioned himself for a shot at the intruder.

He levered a round into the chamber. The clatter spun Schwerin around and the pistol came up like a cobra, spitting fiery venom from its stubby nose.

Ackermann fired once. The 7.65 mm slug tore into the door of one of the lockers. It missed Schwerin by nearly a meter.

Austingrove dove for Schwerin. He was just a tenth of a second too late.

Ackermann took a .38 round just below his collarbone. The slug mushed into his fleshy shoulder, gouging a curving path as it went. The second bullet tore a prune-sized piece out of his right forearm. A third would have taken him in the forehead had not Austingrove's collision with Schwerin sent that shot wide.

Austingrove had Schwerin down, but the German was a tough street fighter. He tucked his legs under Austingrove and with one mighty shove, catapulted the younger, lighter man backward, smashing the small wooden table to pieces as he fell. The tough policeman dove at Austingrove, driving him hard against the lockers with his shoulder. Austingrove's head smashed hard against its steel. He drove his arms up between Schwerin's, forcing the release of the German Policeman's grip, and desperately swung at the man's jaw. He missed and fell back, his vision beginning to tunnel. He had an odd metallic taste in his mouth as he thought, *Oh, shit, I'm going to pass out*. He did so, not realizing that Schwerin had hit him once again.

Dessault was busy scrambling for the .38. He snatched it up but had not had time to raise it level when Schwerin rammed into his chest, using his bald head as a battering ram. Dessault flew backward, landing in a heap at the foot of the dirt stairway. He still held the pistol, but as he gasped for air, Schwerin reached down and took it from his hand. Schwerin slowly raised the weapon, aiming it at the top of Dessault's head. "You are becoming troublesome. I think it is time to rid myself of the aggravation of having to contend with you."

Dessault looked up into the nasty end of the black pistol. His eyes showed no fear with the prospect of a sudden, violent death. Then Schwerin's head jerked sideways, the gun fired, and he fell face down on the floor. Austingrove stood looking down at Dessault, a table leg hanging loosely in his hand. He kicked the pistol to him. "Want to shoot him? He was going to shoot you."

Dessault looked distastefully at the pistol in his hand, "Hell, no." He got up, jammed the pistol into his belt, and went to work tying Schwerin's hands behind him with scraps of electrical wire.

Austingrove noticed that the underground hangar was deathly quiet, even through the gun's blasts were still ringing in his ears. He leaned back against the row of lockers. He wasn't sure if the man outside had been hit, or if he was still there and able to fire that rifle. If so, they may yet be in danger.

His jaw ached and it hurt to speak. "We had better get under cover in case that guy up there wants to try another shot," he said.

Dessault grabbed Austingrove's arm and turned him around. Bright red stains were forming across Austingrove's shirt. "You've ripped out some stitches, Scott," said Dessault. He pulled up Austingrove's shirt tail and guided him to the bunk. "Sit down and I'll see if I can get the bleeding stopped."

Dessault retrieved the candle and began to rifle through the steel lockers. He found an ancient first aid kit in the third, that even though it was World War II vintage, the gauze and tape appeared to be usable. He pulled off a section of blood-soaked bandage and pressed an gauze pad on the opened wound. He tightly taped it. The blood stopped flowing.

Dessault walked over to the steps and held the candle high. "There's blood all over up there. I think he must have been hit."

He pulled the .38 from his waistband and shifted it to his right hand. He carefully climbed the steps and peered over the edge of the opening. The man was unconscious, face down. The Mauser was some three feet away where he had involuntarily thrown it. He rolled the man over.

"Christ! Scott, hey, Scott. Come look at this."

Austingrove painfully rolled off the bunk, pulled down his shirt and climbed out into the dull sunlight. He quickly drew up as he saw the man's face. "Oh, my God," he felt bile begin too churn its way into his throat. Still shaken from Schwerin's punches and the loss of blood, the sight of Ackermann's grotesque face brought on a wave of nausea.

"Man, he sure had one hell of an accident of some kind," he said. He looked away and the sickness passed.

Dessault pulled away Ackermann's old coat and unbuttoned his shirt. He tore the front from the shirt and wrapped it tightly around the forearm wound. "Looks like he's just one more victim of Hitler's madness," he said.

The two men carried Ackermann to the cot and stripped him to the waist. Using the old first aid kit, Austingrove began to bandage his wounds.

Dessault sat at the steel table, the big, black gun

in front of him. He still shook from the assault and his ears were still ringing from the echoing reports from the pistol and the old rifle.

"Scott," he said. "I think we're getting in 'way over our heads here. We've got a wounded man. We've got an unconscious policeman. We've got three unflyable old airplanes with only two pilots. And we're stuck in a big hole in the ground in a foreign country."

Austingrove was stunned. He had never heard a negative word from Dessault. The bandaging finished, he walked to the table.

"We can't let this get away from us, Major. We have a chance here to really do something great. Saving these planes and getting them home will be one hell of a contribution to aviation history - not to mention what it'll do for the two of us."

Dessault looked dejected, whipped. "Well, How are we going to get three, big, damn airplanes out of this hole in the ground? It's three thousand miles to the States. How we going to do that without anyone seeing us?"

"Come on, Major, you know that anything really worthwhile has its risks."

When you were in the hospital in 'Nam you told me that our lives are just like flying; if you're at the controls it's an exhilarating, enjoyable experience. If you're merely a passenger, it's really pretty dull." Austingrove watched Dessault's expression, hoping for a brightening of his spirit.

"On the other hand," he continued, "if you're on the ground, looking up at a plane flying over, you probably just envy both the pilot *and* the passengers. We're at the controls here, Man. If you let this go, you'll regret it for the rest of your life."

Dessault gave him a condescending look and shook his head. "Bull sweat," he said, "you forgot that sometimes the weather is so bad that it's crazy to fly. And well, right now the weather around here stinks."

This angered Austingrove. "Look, I'm not going to let anything or anyone stop this project." He slammed his fist onto the table. "We're going to get these planes out of here even if I have to *fly* the bastards out!"

Austingrove and Dessault were silent for a moment while that statement sank-in. A grin started to spread across Austingrove's face like the first light of dawn on a distant horizon.

"You've lost it. You've slipped your moorings, Pal," said Dessault.

"Look, why can't we fly these old birds out of here?" His eyes flared with enthusiasm. "You and I have flown all kinds of jets, and there's no reason we can't get these babies airworthy and fly them as well."

"C'mon, Scott," said Dessault, "you don't have any idea what kind of shape these planes are in. How do you suppose we'd get them out of here? This place is a bombed-out mess. It might take months to make them ready. We'll surely be discovered by then."

"Well, we can sure as hell give it a try," said Austingrove.

"And we'll end up spending our old age in some dingy damn German jailhouse too."

Austingrove glared at his friend and began to rant. "Every damn time I have a chance to do something big, something worthwhile, some damn thing screws it up." He paced to Ackermann's cot and back. "Not this time, Major. This time we're going to make it. This could be the biggest thing you or I will ever accomplish in our lifetimes, and I'm not going to let *anything* screw it up."

Dessault kept quiet. He had never seen his friend like this. Although he knew that Austingrove would never turn on him, he felt that he should stay silent, allowing him to gather himself together.

"I was screwed in 'Nam. The only thing I wanted was to do was get was my five kills. My dad flew in World War Two, in the Pacific, and he was an Ace inside of three weeks. My big brother took out seven MiG's in Korea and came home a big-ass hero." He paced, his anger reddening his face. "I get stuck on crappy ground attack missions in 'Nam for three years and came home like a dork with no kills. While my dad and brother patted each other on the back, I was treated like a high school dropout."

Austingrove knelt beside Schwerin, going through his pockets. He pulled out a key case.

"I'm going to go find his car," He was calmer now. "I need some air and a little time to think. You can stay with these guys, or if you want to pull out and head back home, that's up to you." He headed for the stairs. "I hope you'll stick with me on this, Major. But if you don't, I guess I'll understand."

"I think its crazy, that's all," said Dessault. "I'm not too hot for the idea of spending the next twenty years in a German prison."

Austingrove just grunted and went up the steps, closing the entrance hatch as he went out. *Jesus, he was worried sick when I was shot,* he thought, *Now I leave him alone in a dark hole with two unconscious strangers who would both like to kill him when they wake up.*

CHAPTER FIVE

Light from bulbs discolored with age struggled through eight dirty windows. Yellow, trapezoidal patterns spread side by side on the ramp outside the steel hangar's doors. As Cody Gordon paced, each of the eight forms flashed in turn up his legs, then rolled across his shoulders, allowing his grim expression just the slightest splash, and then sped down his back. Finally, each pattern of light fell back to the cement to await his next passing.

The rest of the airfield was dark.

Gordon felt naked in this lonely place. He wore light gray slacks, a white shirt, a loosely knotted tie and a blue sports jacket. A black raincoat dangled over his arm, at the ready for the unpredictable

Germany weather. He looked to be just another American in Germany on business, and he was.

He had been pacing the ramp for nearly half an hour since the German taxi driver had dropped him outside the airfield's rotted wood fence. Without so much as a raised eyebrow, the cigarette-puffing cabby had driven off into the night, leaving him alone in this remote place. He had stood for a moment at the sagging wooden gate. It had been left wide open, inviting him to walk right into the old airdrome. So he did.

Of the three buildings on the field, this hangar was the only one lighted. There was another steel hangar, and what appeared to be a wooden shop building. A boarded-up control tower protruded up from the side of the shop and in the dim moonlight the single runway looked to be of unkempt grass.

Gordon felt vulnerable, exposed as he was in this deserted place in a totally foreign country. He jumped at every sound in the night and every movement of shadow. Even those borne of his imagination.

He had first stayed pretty much out of sight as Austingrove had suggested, until he determined that there was probably no one within 10 kilometers of this deserted rural airstrip.

"Damn, I wish they'd get here," he said aloud. Then even louder, and throwing up his arms for emphasis, "It would be nice to know what the hell is going on, Guys!"

He glanced around the darkened airfield, knowing that no one, certainly not Austingrove and Dessault, had heard him, yet he checked anyway.

He stopped at the corner of the hanger and turned his head toward the road. He sensed the noise before actually hearing it. Then it became audible, a faint pop-pop-pop of a small, two cycle engine. It began to reverberate off the side of the steel building. He stepped back into the shadow of the hangar, peering down the narrow road that had brought him there.

A vague form appeared, traveling fast. It looked to be a man hunched over a small motorcycle running flat-out, without lights.

The machine slowed, turned and wobbled through the open gate. Its rider straightened, and even with the backward baseball cap and trench coat, Gordon recognized Scott Austingrove. He stepped out of the shadow of the hangar. Austingrove swerved the motorbike in surprise.

"Ah-ha! There you are," he said, grinning. "How about a ride, soldier?"

"Scott, what the hell is going on?" Gordon was more tired than angry, but he scowled at Austingrove anyway, just to get some answers. "You bring me six thousand miles, have me shuttled out to a 1940s airport to stand in the dark for two hours. I'm hungry, dammit, and my feet hurt!" His tirade was beginning to actually make him angry. He softened. "And where in the hell's The Major?"

"Hop on my Noble Steed here, Cody, and I'll bring

you up to speed on the way to the plant. Dessault's there."

Gordon slipped into the raincoat, picked up his flight bag and flopped it in Austingrove's lap and threw his leg over the rear seat of the rusting motorcycle. "Plant? What damn plant?"

Gordon didn't hear Austingrove's answer as the motorcycle lurched forward, exhaust popping, and reeled out onto the road.

"I didn't want to tell you on the phone, but we have found a Nazi aircraft assembly plant just a short distance from a little town called Wolfshütte." Austingrove was talking over his right shoulder as the motorcycle sped down the country lane.

"And Cody, its damn amazing. There are three brand new Messerschmitt two-six-two's sitting there like they've been waiting for us for forty five years. One of them is a rare, two place model. With a little hard work, I think we can get them airworthy and fly those suckers out of here."

The wind in his ears and the noise of the old motorcycle was making it difficult for Gordon to understand what Austingrove was saying.

"Slow this damn thing down, Scott," he said. Austingrove immediately backed off of the throttle a bit.

"Hey!" said Gordon. "It sounded as if you said we're going to fly a couple of Messerschmitt two-sixty-two's from here."

"Three," said Austingrove. "They're a little stiff,

but I really think we can make them flyable with a few week's work. Who's going to fly them and where they'll fly them to is what is going to take some doing."

"Well," said Gordon, "You're crazy, but I'll take a look, and if they are as you say, then we'll do our damnedest to get them out of here, one way or the other." Austingrove smiled. He knew that would be Gordon's reply; a simple "Let's go for it."

Austingrove filled him in on his hospital stay, their confrontation with the German police lieutenant and the old German who still lay unconscious in the underground hangar.

Gordon was stiff and cold when Austingrove finally wheeled the machine off into a forested area some minutes later. They walked quickly through the trees while Austingrove continued to fill him in. He told him how he had driven Inspector Schwerin's car to the far side of Munich. He explained how he had parked it on a dark side street, leaving the keys in it, and walked the six miles back across town. Incredibly hungry, he had gone into a haufbrau for something to eat and a German beer. In less that 20 minutes, he had bought the old motorcycle and a bottle of schnapps from the owner of the tavern.

"The Major has some reservations about who these planes belong to," Austingrove explained. "He's not too hot about being a part of smuggling them out of Germany."

"Crap, doesn't he know about the government here? If they had found them first, they would have blow them all to hell and no one would ever see them again," Gordon said.

"This *Deutschland immer zuerst* (Germany always first) regime is anti-everything, especially anything that reminds them of Nazi Germany or World War Two. Dessault must realize that."

"Well, he's coming around, but I think a lot depends on what the wounded German guy says. I believe that whatever this guy thinks will swing him one way or the other. He'll know the true condition of the planes, and may know for sure what the German government would do if they got their hands on them."

They stopped at the edge of the field and carefully scanned the opposite line of trees before continuing on to the entrance of the plant. Austingrove slid the panel back and Gordon groaned as he bent into the opening.

Dessault had rigged some battery powered lanterns and the interior of the assembly plant was lighted far better than it had been since their arrival.

Gordon's first words were "Good God Gertie!" He dropped his bag at the bottom of the stairs and walked as if in a trance to the first Me.262.

"My God, its beautiful," he said softly. "and absolutely cherry in every way."

He never used the term "cherry" from his old hot rod days for anything that wasn't an absolute perfect original or beautifully restored. He walked down the port side, slowly rubbing his hands along the cool aluminum skin as if hoping to absorb some of its form and substance.

"There is no damn question about it," he almost shouted. "We've *got* to get these babies back to the States!"

Austingrove was glad that Dessault hadn't left. There was, however, a tenseness in the air between them now. They no longer joked or engaged in making fun of each other with the relaxed, good humor that they had enjoyed before. Even when Austingrove tried, Dessault's silence told of his feelings. Their long friendship wasn't ending, but it was traversing some bumps.

Gordon too noticed the change in Dessault. He approached him that evening. "You know, Major," he said. "It's like Scott once told me; life is a lot like flying. If you are at the controls it can be exciting and..."

"Gordon, I'm the one who gave that worn-out pep talk to Scott," said Dessault. "Look, I'm not a hundred percent hot for this whole damn idea, but I'm not running out on you guys either. Yet."

"OK, Major, no sweat," he turned away and went into the generator room.

To Gordon's back, Dessault said, "So you believe that old 'Life-is-a-lot-like-flying' crap, huh? Well, I'll be damned."

*   *   *

Inspector Schwerin had come around. "The crimes of attempted murder and kidnapping will get you a considerably long stay in our prison. Let me go now, before the charges become more serious." he said.

"Easy there, Pard," said Dessault. He had put on his worn Air Force flight jacket. It seemed to give him a air of confidence and reaffirm his leadership position.

"As I understand it, your fellow countryman here took a shot at you, and if you want to put that old Nazi into your jail, why, I reckon you'd be doing him a huge favor. And as for kidnapping, you came here of your own free will. You alone accosted these two men. We haven't taken you anyplace, and I doubt if the boys here have asked for any ransom. Hell, you wouldn't be worth much anyway."

Dessault grinned at the Lieutenant. "Sure, maybe we are committing unlawful detention, maybe assault, but attempted murder and kidnapping?" Dessault put his face close to Schwerin's, "Nope, I don't think so, Pard."

Schwerin spat at Dessault, but the American turned aside and the spittle sprayed past him.

"You may find out differently," the German snarled.

Dessault walked past Austingrove. "Nasty old bastard, isn't he," he said.

The entrance hatch slowly slid open sending a wedge of sunlight onto the dirt stairs. Austingrove and Dessault ducked behind the lockers. "I thought you said this is a secret place," whispered Dessault.

I thought it was."

The hatch slid closed. Austingrove peered around the edge of the locker. A dark form moved down the steps and cautiously edged toward Schwerin. It was a woman.

Austingrove saw the Inspector's gun on the table and considered making a dive for it. He glanced back to the figure. She was approaching slowly, swinging a black object back and forth in front of her. Austingrove knew that it could only be a gun.

"Hurry," said Schwerin. "Get my gun from the table and untie me!" The woman dropped his pistol in his lap and went to work untangling his bonds.

Released, Schwerin stood, his pistol jammed into his waistband. "You will please come out now, Gentlemen," he said in English. "Now you will call your friend, Mister Gordon, please."

Austingrove called out to Gordon as the woman stepped out into the light. "Hilda, Hilda Göettz!" he said.

The gun still in her hand, she said, "I am sorry Mister Austingrove, but he has my daughter and will kill us both if..."

Austingrove realized that he had been taken-in by this beautiful German woman with the fascinating blue eyes. And now he remembered where he had seen the man before; leaving the hospital with Hilda

Göettz. "You set me up to find this place for you, didn't you."

"That is in the past," said Schwerin. "You should be more concerned with your future." He waved Gordon to join Austingrove and Dessault.

"OK, Schwerin," said Dessault, "now what?"

"For you, Major, *this* is what is *now*." Schwerin stepped up to Dessault and threw a right cross that smashed into Dessault's cheek bone. Dessault slammed back into the lockers, toppling one and falling unconscious on top of it. A pall of dust billowed up around the men.

"Now, you two," Schwerin pointed a blunt forefinger at Austingrove and Gordon. "You two will do as you're told, unlike your Great Leader there," he pointed a stubby thumb at the unconscious Dessault, "or your fate will be worse than you can imagine. Keep in mind, Gentlemen, that I could dispose of all of you, bury you in this filthy hole and no one would ever connect me to your rotting corpses." He sat on the edge of the table, shifting the gun in his belt to a more comfortable position.

"I am not a barbarian, however, and I've promised lovely Hilda that there will be no violence as long as there is cooperation. *Your* cooperation, and *her* cooperation."

"Your government will destroy these planes, Schwerin," said Austingrove. "Doesn't that bother you? These are priceless aviation artifacts that can never again be duplicated. Why the hell would you allow them to be destroyed?"

"You take a lot for granted," said Schwerin. "I don't recall saying that these aircraft will be turned over to anyone in the German government. Did I?" Schwerin began to pace in front of the men. "My father was a Luftwaffe pilot. He taught me the value of aircraft such as these, and when Hilda told me of her father's knowledge of the secret aircraft plants in Germany, I attempted to get him to tell me." Schwerin stopped pacing.

"But he was a stubborn, un-trusting man. He wouldn't tell even Hilda. So, when the opportunity came to arrange his deathbed revelation to you, we took advantage of it. We have been following you ever since the air show in Philadelphia."

"Are they valuable enough for you to murder three or four people?" Said Gordon.

"Again, you people are taking things unsaid and saying I've said them." Schwerin frowned at Gordon.

"I have no intention of murdering anyone. Unless, of course, it becomes necessary to my own defense." He smiled. "But then it wouldn't be murder, would it? I have no idea how you expected to get these planes out of here and out of Germany, but whatever you had in mind will not work without cooperation from many government officials. I have that advantage, Gentlemen, and I assure you that I will be unchallenged at any border. My position has advantages. My crew will be free to disassemble, load, and take their trucks with the airplanes inside any place I wish. Even to America!" He made a guttural, choking laugh that turned his face red with the exertion.

"And in case you might be wondering, Mister Austingrove," said Schwerin, "Hilda's father was a mean, selfish man who would not trust even his own daughter. I am not sad at his passing."

"I wasn't wondering about that at all," said Austingrove. He pointed at Schwerin. "I was wondering how a scum-bag like you was ever hired as a policeman."

Schwerin pushed Austingrove in the face, sending him stumbling backward. "Shut your mouth or there certainly will be a murder to contend with."

He told Austingrove and Gordon to carry Dessault into the generator room. He motioned Hilda inside and carefully checked for any possibility of escape. Satisfied with the security of the room, he took Hilda by the arm and left, slamming the steel door as they went.

Austingrove heard the steel bolt clatter closed, imagining its echoing ring as the sound of the falling blade of a guillotine.

From his cot, Hans Ackermann watched and listened as the two strangers, Inspector Schwerin and Hilda Göettz, planned their next move. He had awakened when the man hit Major Dessault and the locker crashed over. He watched as they herded the Americans into the generator room. Unsure of who they are and what their motive might be, Ackermann lie silently, unmoving, hoping to find out.

"I must arrange for the trucks and mechanics, and I will be gone for perhaps two days," said Schwerin.

Hilda looked up from her purse where she had just concealed the small Baretta pistol.

"You are not leaving me here alone." Her statement was of fact, not questioning.

"You will stay," said Schwerin, "to make sure that those in the other room stay in the other room." He tossed a stubby thumb over his shoulder.

Ackermann shut his eyes as the woman turned, looking toward him. "They cannot get out, and I'm sure that old man will not help them," she said.

"We cannot take that chance, and you will do as I say, Hilda, or you may find yourself in there with the Americans."

Ackermann eased one eye open and saw the woman take up her purse, saying, "Don't threaten me, Karl. You would have none of this if not for me. And I am not staying here alone. It is important that those who will be working here know that I have the same authority as you."

Her voice was rising with anger, and she started for the stairs. "When you are not here, I must be able to direct and manage the workmen. We started this together, and now we will go together to arrange for the trucks."

Ackermann saw Schwerin ease the pistol from his belt. He almost called out to the woman to look out, but held back, fearful. She saw it too and fumbled in her purse for the Baretta. Schwerin's shot echoed with a thunderous boom in the cavern. Vermin scurried at the noise and Ackermann involuntarily jumped. Hilda Göettz was blown backward as the slug smashed into her chest. She made a loud grunting noise and was dead long before her mind realized what happened.

Schwerin calmly put the pistol back in his waistband, slipped on his jacket and unceremoniously drug Hilda Göettz up the dirt stairway and out through the entrance hatch.

Ackermann was confused. His world, a world that had been so secure, was suddenly alive with strangers, guns and terror. He lay shaking, unable to grasp how any man could kill in such a cold-blooded manner. He realized that his life would be less than nothing to this *Wahnsinniger* (Madman), as would the lives of the three Americans closed up in the generator room. He should escape, run and find a new place to live, perhaps at the old airdrome on the road to Wolfshütte. There were abandoned buildings there.

Ackermann's arm ached as he tried to rise from the cot. He remembered the man that killed the woman had first tried to kill him. He had only wanted to scare those out of his home, he would not have killed anyone. Even when he had a perfectly simple shot at the man who was looking for his Jagdverband, he intentionally missed. He only wanted to be left alone. *Perhaps the Americans will protect me from the man with the gun,* he thought. *But then again, perhaps not.* He decided that he must leave his refuge and let the strangers do as they wish to each other.

He swung his legs over the edge of the cot and instantly became dizzy. He hung his head, waiting for it to pass. Slowly, he rose from the cot and took the first tentative step toward the exit. At the second step he realized that he was still much too weak to make it outside, let alone to the airdrome. As nausea, pain and weakness overcame him, he decided that he had no other choice but to free the others. He would have to take his chances with them.

Ackermann fell to his knees and crawled toward the generator room door. His vision narrowed as darkness forced itself upon him and he struggled forward, a strange ringing in his ears. He reached out for the latch and cried out a pitiful moan as he fell forward into darkness.

Austingrove leaned back against the cold steel door. It had been perhaps an hour since they heard the loud bang that they agreed must surely have been a shot. Perhaps Schwerin had killed the old German. It would be a cowardly act, shooting a old, sick and wounded man while he slept. But he doubted if

Schwerin had any scruples at all.

He closed his eyes and tried to imagine the room as it was when it was lit. In the darkness he recalled a clutter miscellaneous electrical parts and wiring, sections of steam and water pipe and plumbing fittings. He realized though, that the ceiling was several feet thick and the door was solid steel. None of the puny pieces and hunks of equipment would be stout enough to get them out of there, he reasoned.

The other side of the rear interior wall would be buried in debris. Tons of cement, steel and dirt from the bombing cave-in would present as formidable a barrier as the thickness of the overhead.

He listened to Major Dessault's steady, heavy breathing and wished The Major had left this hell hole when he had the chance. *What a stinking way for us to die,* he thought, *starving to death in a hole in the ground, like a bunch of trapped gophers.*

It would be better, he decided, if Schwerin came back and shot them. At least it would be fast. He didn't relish a slow death. But deep in his heart, he knew that somehow they would get out of this. He shook off the thoughts of death and began to try to think of a way out.

As if on cue, a clatter and a thump startled Austingrove. The steel door moved. A thin sheet of light created a white perpendicular wall through the edge of the door. Austingrove pushed, but the door would open no further. He peeked through the crack and could make out a leg, Ackermann's leg, unmoving on the floor.

"Cody, I think the wounded guy has opened the latch and passed out again. Give me a hand."

Together, the two men shoved the big door and Ackermann's dead weight just far enough for them to squeeze out of the room.

After checking the hangar for Schwerin and Hilda, they lifted Ackermann back into his cot. Austingrove found Hilda's purse next to a puddle of fresh blood. Streaks of crimson made a zig zag course up the stairway.

"Geez, Cody," said Austingrove, "I think Schwerin has killed the woman and dragged her out of here."

Gordon looked sick as he stared at the pool of blood that was already beginning to dry, the bright red becoming a darker crimson at the edges. "That lousy piss ant," he muttered.

"Yeah, where did that scum bag run off to?" Dessault had recovered and was leaning heavily on the steel table. Gray dirt covered his flight jacket, his face was blotchy red and his hair looked like he just came through a hurricane.

Austingrove went through the contents of the purse, handing the gun to Dessault. Dessault removed the clip, checked to see that it was full and snapped it back into the grip of the semiautomatic.

Not knowing when Schwerin would return, the three men each took a two hour watch, one squatting alongside the entrance hatch while the others, one with the pistol, stayed concealed behind the row of lockers. It was the third watch, Gordon by the hatch, when it slid open, sending blinding light into the hangar. Schwerin looked down through the opening, then, seeing Ackermann on the cot and no one else, he stepped onto the top step.

Gordon could not see if Schwerin was holding his pistol, so he took no chances. He kicked hard into Schwerin's legs. The big man collapsed backward, giving out a agonized growl and tumbled down the steps. He landed at the bottom in a heap, Austingrove and Dessault holding him down. The German kicked violently and struggled to reach his gun. With all of his strength and with great pleasure Dessault hit him twice. The second punch broke the policeman's nose, sending blood spattering across the floor to blend with that of Hilda's.

Dessault rolled the man over and manacled his hands behind his back with the Inspector's own handcuffs. They dragged him over to the side of the hangar where he'd be out of the way and propped him up against the wall.

Tired, dirty and aching, the three men celebrated, each with a paper cup of Austingrove's schnapps.

For the next four days, Austingrove was busy cleaning the bugs, rat's nests and dirt from the control surfaces and interior spaces of the three planes. He thoroughly inspected every electrical wire, control cable, hose, line and fitting and was amazed that other than flat tires and an accumulation of dirt, there was little to indicate that these were planes of World War II vintage.

One obstacle became immediately apparent. The Junkers Jumo 004-B-2 jet engines were fitted with a starting engine. It was a small, single cylinder, two cycle, gasoline engine. The starting engine would carry the rotation of the powerplant up to 800 RPM, at which time the pilot would depress the ignition button on the throttle, starting the jet engine. Then the small starting engine would shutdown. Five of the six starters for the jet engines were missing. They had never been installed.

This setback didn't stymie Austingrove. He removed the one available starting engine, bolted it to the battery cart, and using a fabricated extension shaft, made a portable starting cart. Each engine would have to be started in turn. Then the cart would be rolled to the next. It would be time-consuming, but necessary. It would also mean that if any of the jet engines were shut-down en route, it could not be restarted again.

Dessault began an inventory of the contents of a bank of more than forty steel filing cabinets. They extended along the south wall from the tail of the first plane until they were lost under the collapsed ceiling beyond the third aircraft. He laid out three stacks of manuals, one for each of the three intact aircraft. The old books included maintenance manuals, parts books and unused flight logs. But his greatest find was an entire cabinet full of flight manuals. Although they were printed in German, the most important flight information could be deciphered because it mainly involved numbers; airspeed, engine RPM, fuel and oil pressures, takeoff and stall speeds and a full range of flight data that they must know if they were to attempt to fly the Me.262's out of the country.

Dessault sat at the steel table, apparently absorbing the numbers, but his thoughts were filled with concern about his ability to fly the Me.262 jet.

He had long ago lost the self-confidence to climb into any plane's cockpit, mash the throttle to the firewall and fly the heart out of it.

He skidded the chair out, shaking off the dismal thoughts, and walked to the nose of the first ship.

My God, you're beautiful, he thought. *It would kill me to smash you up.* He laughed aloud. *Yes, it might at that!*

Gordon busied himself as though he had every confidence of success in what they were going to do. He gathered three sets of tools, cleaned and arranged them and rolled the ancient boxes one beside each plane.

In a dungeon-like area behind a soundproof steel door he located a huge coal-fired steam engine that powered the plant's generator. The generator was necessary for lights and compressed air. He was busy trying to get it fired as Austingrove came over to him. "The German guy is starting to come around."

Without a word, Gordon turned and hurried over to the old man on the sagging cot. He got to him just as his eyes fluttered and opened.

"Kann ich bitte ein Glas Wasser haben?"

His voice was weak and hoarse. When he spoke, the slit that was his mouth barely opened, just enough to slightly expose black and broken teeth.

"'Wasser' is water," said Dessault. He had come up quietly behind Gordon.

Gordon spun to the sound of his voice. "Can you speak German, Major?"

"Just a little. Remember, I flew Jugs over here in forty-four and forty-five."

Gordon returned with the old coffee mug full of water and raised the German's head, holding the cup to his lips.

The man kept his one good eye on the golden scimitar insignia on Dessault's flight jacket, looking as if he expected the Major to do something injurious. He pulled his head back and Gordon sat the cup next to the cot.

"Amerikaner?"

"Ja," said Dessault. "Sprechen Sie Englisch?" His German was almost unrecognizable after nearly fifty years of non-use, but the old German Lieutenant understood.

"Ja, I speak some English," he said softly.

"Ich fühle mich schwach..." His voice trailed off, his eye closed and lay back to sleep.

"What did he say?" asked Austingrove.

"He said something about feeling weak." Dessault turned and went back to his books. At his back, Hans Ackermann watched him go, his one good eye just barely opened.

"You will all be feeling weak after a few years in our jail," muttered a revived Inspector Schwerin.

Austingrove took another motorcycle trip to Munich and stocked up with as much food and drinks as he could manage on the two wheeler. He bought some disinfecting salve and fresh gauze and tape.

On the way back through Wolfshütte, he stopped at the cafe and purchased three complete orders of Kartoffelpuffer and Brockworst for their first hot meal in almost a week.

Inside the underground hangar, Gordon was sitting with Ackermann. The German was awake and talking earnestly with the American. Dessault was at the table, pouring over the Me.262 flight manuals.

Austingrove slid through the hatchway, juggling his bags down the stairs and just made it to the table before dropping half the load. He slid the pile of the manuals aside and began to unload the bags, separating the hot food into three parts. He carried one to Schwerin. Another to Gordon. Ackermann was aroused at the smell of the food. Austingrove gave him the entire plateful.

"Scott," said Gordon. "This is Hans Ackermann. He flew Messerschmitt two-six-two's during World

War II."

Austingrove was impressed and knelt by the man's side. "Ackermann, how are you feeling?" The German was cutting a sausage into small pieces and carefully placing them through the small lipless slit of his mouth. He chewed slowly and ignoring Austingrove's question finally said, "You must go away and tell no one of this place. You will do that, ja?"

"We will do that, no," said Austingrove.

"We are here to take these aircraft to the United States. To protect them and secure them as museum pieces for future generations to see and learn about. These planes are priceless examples of your countrymen's skill as aerodynamicists, designers and craftsmen. You certainly want that preserved, don't you?"

Ackermann stopped chewing and looked up at Austingrove, a deep sadness in his battered features.

"They will not be preserved," he said. "The Deutschland Ersters will take them from you and they will be destroyed like all of the things that were built during the Third Reich."

"Believe me, Ackermann, we have the means to spirit these ships out of your country without anyone knowing it, ever." Austingrove didn't fully believe that, but he had to get Ackermann on their side. His expertise and knowledge of the Messerschmitt would help them immensely. Besides, he'd like to see the old man have a better life during his remaining years.

"You will have to take them all to pieces. You will have great truckloads to try to clear the border. The D.E. will catch you there. You cannot go around the border crossings."

Austingrove leaned down, putting his face near Ackermann's and in a conspiratorial voice said, "We're not going to go *around* the border checkpoints, my friend. We are going *over* them."

Incredulous, Ackermann stiffened and twisted his face to Austingrove's.

"You want to *fly* the Schwalbes to *America*?"

His one good eye was bigger than Austingrove would have believed it ever could be.

"Du bist wohl verrückt! yelled Ackermann, "You are mad!"

Austingrove laughed. "We're not going to fly them to *America*, Hans. To *England!* And *you* will be with us!"

CHAPTER SIX

Dessault had connections in the United Kingdom by virtue of his purchase of spares over the years for his Gloster Meteor and MiG-15. He had also purchased four de Havilland Tiger Moth trainers a few years before for resale to a flying club in Arizona. They had been packed carefully in cargo containers at Roughscuff Field, a small private airstrip near Ipswitch in the east of England, and shipped on board a British container ship. The containers were unloaded in New York and trucked to California without a mar, scratch or dent on their fragile contents.

Dessault knew they could do the same thing with the Me.262's if only they could get them to Roughscuff. His colleague in England was Tennison Barquelay, a man of some stature in British social circles. Barquelay seemed to have the uncanny ability to shred red tape like a tiger clawing balloons, and was never without a cheerful word or at a loss for an original and clever solution to almost any problem. They had become friends during Dessault's tour of duty in England. Barquelay was head of the photo evaluation section of Royal Air Force intelligence and would debrief the pilots while reviewing their gun camera footage. Dessault routinely shot a lot of film, shot a lot of ammo, and shot a lot of enemy planes, so the two men had spent a lot of time together.

Dessault put the Pilot's Manual down, rose from the table, stretched and called the others over.

Austingrove looked tired and Gordon looked worse.

"We need to get organized here and get this project underway in a serious, professional manner if we expect to succeed." Neither of the men said a word as he paused, so Dessault took full command as he had a tendency to do in all situations.

"Gordon, you're doing a great job on getting the support equipment squared away. Concentrate on the generator so we can power up some batteries and have compressed air and sufficient lighting. Dig around and find some tires. Looks like we'll need all six mains, but only one nose gear tire. Find them."

He paused and in a quiet voice; "Are you with us on this project?"

Gordon glanced at Austingrove, looked back at Dessault, then to Ackermann. Ackermann tilted his head to one side as if listening for Gordon's answer. He swallowed, then muttered, "Yes, Sir."

Dessault carried on, "Scott, check out every system you can on each of the planes until Cody gets you some electricity. Get the tires on these babies and install the batteries as soon as you get them." He begin to pace. "Check all the fluids; hydraulic, engine oil and check out the instruments as best you can. Blow out the pitot systems as soon as you get air, clean up the cockpits and repack four parachutes. It would be nice if we had communications, but the mechanical and electrical is most important. In your spare time, see if you can dig up some sort of truck or tractor for a towing vehicle. That damn motorcycle of yours won't tow these planes out of here."

Austingrove smiled at Dessault, "Are *you* with us on this project?"

"Hell, yes, but I still don't like it." And for the first time in more than a week, he smiled.

Dessault had commanded men pretty much his entire life and it came naturally to him now. "I'm flying to England to see Tennison Barquelay and arrange for transportation of these birds. Hopefully, we'll be able to land them at Roughscuff Field."

"Scott, you'd better study up on the Pilot's Manual, and perhaps you can convince Herr

Ackermann here to answer any questions you might have."

Dessault held up a khaki colored Me.262 Pilot's Manual. "I'll be flying the second plane, so I'm taking one of these manuals with me to study. While I'm in England, I'll see about getting another pilot, someone who might be helpful in getting the planes ready as well."

He began to cram things into his flight bag, his voice dropping. "I don't want to leave you guys here with all the work, but I don't dare contact Barquelay on the telephone, God knows who listens in."

Ackermann awoke to the sounds of metal tools against metal aircraft and the squishing noise of a hydraulic jack raising one of the planes. He peered across the hangar. Austingrove was jacking the main gear of the first airplane off the ground. Gordon was in the generator chamber freeing up the governor on the steam plant. The inspector was asleep and Dessault had not returned.

Ackermann sat erect on the cot. He had watched these men for three days now and had time to evaluate his feelings toward them and their impossible scheme. He understood that if the German government discovered these planes, they would surely destroy them immediately. He could not allow that, nor could he dissuade these Americans. He had no alternative, whether he was ready or not, his Jagdverband 44 would fly again.

Gordon entered the hangar, stifling a yawn, and saw Ackermann trying to rise from the cot. He went to his side. "Hans, are you feeling well enough to be getting up?"

"Ja, I must lay around here no longer. *Wir haben viel Arbeit vor uns!* (We have work to do!)"

From across the hangar, Austingrove saw the grin on Gordon's face and a grimace that might be considered a smile from Ackermann. He wiped his hands as he walked over to the two men.

"You two on your way to town to chase the fräulines?"

Gordon turned and smiled at Austingrove "Lieutenant Ackermann is signing on for the duration."

Austingrove was sincerely pleased. He had been hoping the German would voluntarily help them. He was the only one with hands-on experience in the Me.262.

Ackermann sat back down and sipped at the glass of water that was always at his bedside.

Gordon was suddenly talkative. "Before Hans was shot down in nineteen-forty-five he was assigned to this assembly plant as a sort of quality control inspector. He says that they were bombed only once. It was a lucky hit. The roof of this place has more than fifty-eight inches of reinforced concrete and armor plating. But it caved-in back there. That's where the bombs and ammo were stored. That one, heavy hit set the whole mess off."

Austingrove crouched by the cot. "At this stage

of assembly, how far were these planes from being ready to fly, Lieutenant?"

"When they leave here, they are in need of only fuel. There is ammunition in the cannon's magazines and each gun is bore-sighted and test-fired at the air-drome just before the planes are, I mean, *were*, flown to their assigned squadrons. Here, we completely serviced each aircraft and tested all of its systems. The very last thing to do was to put the batteries in. We did all the tests before that with a mobile battery cart. The aircraft batteries are in a battery room next to the generator room."

"How did you get the aircraft out of here?" asked Gordon.

Ackermann pointed up to the corner of the ceil-ing. "The roof is hinged there. On both sides, and it is lowered by the use of cables to make a ramp up to ground level. The generator drives two big electric motors that lower the ceiling." He pointed to boxlike humps in the steel framework of the overhead.

"It is a ramp, and there was once a yellow line on the floor showing where the ramp comes down to." He took another sip of water. "The *Zugmaschine* (tractor) we used to pull each Schwalbe up the ramp and to the airdrome is buried under the cave-in over there by the stairway."

"The Major asked me to 'dig up' a tow vehicle." said Austingrove. "I don't think he realized how lit-erally he was speaking.

*   *   *

For the next four days, the three men worked practically around the clock. Ackermann paced between Austingrove and Gordon translating the Pilot's Manual aloud and answering their questions. He went over the material again and again, etching it into the two American's subconscious, much as had been done for him as a young cadet by his Luftwaffe classmates.

Austingrove went plane to plane, piece by piece, system by system, testing, repairing and adjusting the myriad of components and systems until he was satisfied that each was functioning absolutely as good as it could be under these peculiar circumstances. But with only three hours of sleep in the past 48, he was slowing. Each step, each time he had to lift, pull or shove anything, it was becoming increasingly difficult.

Cody Gordon had worked miracles. The steam plant was running and the leaking air compressor was pumping just enough pressure for the tires. A bank of 10 aircraft batteries were being charged, two for each plane, with four spares. They were serviced with still usable acid found stored in ancient rubber bladders. But like Austingrove, Gordon was having difficulties staying alert and awake.

Ackermann was charged up and pumping far better than the machinery or the other men. "Since you are unfamiliar with the kilometer markings on the instruments, I have marked each airspeed indicator with colored lines for you to fly by."

He paced between the men like a stern school teacher, gesturing and waving a Pilot's Manual in the air. "All you have to remember is *rot, weiss, blau, braun* (red, white, blue, brown). You will find that the red mark is your stall airspeed, white is takeoff airspeed, blue is the best cruise speed, and brown is your landing airspeed."

Austingrove had heard this so many times that he thought he might expect to see those markings in every plane he ever flew thereafter.

"You must be very careful as you taxi," continued Ackermann. "The nose wheel has a shimmy damper brake that makes steering most difficult." He paused, looking from Austingrove to Gordon to ensure that they were listening.

"You must use the engines as well as the brakes to turn. Next to the throttles there is a spring-loaded switch that controls the stabilizer trim. Set it to plus one degree. The degree indicator is just ahead of the switch. Pressing it forward trims the nose down, pushing it rearward raises the nose."

"At one hundred ninety kilometers per hour, carefully raise the nose wheel from the ground. The Schwalbe will begin to fly off the ground at two hundred."

Ackermann raised his raspy voice for emphasis, "Do not raise the landing gear until you are at two hundred twenty kilometers per hour. Remember that. Level off to gain airspeed. You will need to press both brake pedals to stop wheel rotation, then raise the gear." His voice softened, "The landing gear makes very much loud noise coming up. Do not let that alarm you. It is simply German wartime engineering."

Cody Gordon started digging at the dirt slide that buried the tractor and blocked the lowering of the ramp.

"Flying at such a low altitude," Ackermann continued, "you will have only just enough fuel to make it to Ipswitch. Do not exceed the cruise throttle setting or you may find yourself swimming in the Channel."

Ackermann put down the manual and dragged a canvas piled with dirt from the slide to the other side of the hangar. He sat for a moment, then, when he was sure the other two's attention was wholly into their work, he rose and quietly slipped through the door into the generator room.

Hans Ackermann hurried to the rear of the chamber. The steam generator was running poorly, surging up and down, rattling like a washing machine full of spoons, but it was supplying electrical power nonetheless. He knelt and shoved a wooden packing crate of wire scraps aside. This exposed a small tunnel, the hole he had dug more than forty years before. A rancid stench of mold, rot and decay hung like a barrier, invisibly barring the passageway. Ackermann lay on his side and slithered like a weasel through it, into the adjoining room.

He stood. He scanned the cold and musty cham-

ber. There were no windows, no ventilation. It was
the first time in half a century that the room was
illuminated by more than Ackermann's weak candle-
light. One dirty, naked bulb hung above a long table.
It was a wooden conference table with eight straight-
back chairs and it dominated the area. The table
was strewn with rotted papers and remnants of what
were once leather briefcases and portfolios. Four of
the chairs held other remnants, the decayed carcasses
of once elite Nazi officers. Rotting bones and ragged
Nazi uniforms lay in piles, the bodies decomposed to
unrecognizable litter. Bones, some with black shreds
of rotted flesh, lay everywhere, dragged about by
hungry rats.

There had been pictures on the wall, but all but
one were scattered across the filthy floor. The one
remaining was of Adolf Hitler in a brown uniform
with a red armband. The armband held the swastika of Nazi Germany. His right arm raised in sa-
lute. His face twisted in a self-satisfied smirk.
Ackermann had replaced that one fallen photograph
when he dug into this chamber after the bombing. It
had taken him nearly three weeks to dig through the
six feet of concrete to those souls trapped there. By
that time they were all dead, asphyxiated, and the
rats were busily engaged in their grisly task.

A folding table sat against the western wall of
the room. It held a huge field radio. It was covered
with dust and decay, its brown paint peeling off. It
had been silenced when the south wall collapsed, sev-

ering its power source. A rotted, brown uniform hung loosely over a decayed corpse that dutifully sat at the radio. The radio operator had died at his post, and he was still on duty, one bony hand pressed against an ancient tuning knob.

Against the opposite wall, a sofa held a pair of corpses. One, obviously a man, was in civilian clothes, a floppy hat draped over the white bones of his skull, bits of flesh and hair clinging to it. The other was a woman. The shreds of a flowered dress dangled from her form. Her hat had rotted away, leaving the brim to fall around her neck like a yoke.

The two cadavers held hands.

Had it not been such a tragic scene, the skeletons, the floppy hat and the rotted bonnet could have been a Halloween display.

At the end of the sofa sat four traveling bags, their contents spilling out through decayed seams.

Unaffected by the taste of rotting death, Ackermann straightened and strode to the couch, rats scurrying at his approach. He snapped to attention. He saluted smartly.

"Mein Fuehrer," his voice was young, strong and commanding. It reverberated throughout the concrete chamber.

"The aircraft are being prepared. We will be moving them to the airdrome shortly and depart at first light. I will pilot your aircraft, my Fuehrer, and Major Dachendt will pilot the other. As you have so wonderfully planned, we will take you to The Azores where a Dornier flying boat, at this moment awaits to transport you to South America."

He took the silence of the corpses to be affirmation and approval of his report.

But Ackermann knew that the planes would not be ready "at first light." He also knew how Adolph Hitler could erupt into a rage upon hearing what he had no desire to hear. Merely by saying the wrong thing, Ackermann could be taken outside and shot. By stalling, he may be able to blame others, perhaps the three Americans, for the delay. Better they be at the end of Hitler's riding crop and Luger pistol than he.

He also knew that Major Dachendt was long dead. An American aviator would be flying Adolph Hitler. *An American!* Ackermann would have to justify this change of pilots. He must wait until it became too late for the Fuehrer to demand an explanation or insist on a different pilot.

Things were not going as perfectly as he would like, but at least there was some progress being made. The first progress, he thought, in such a long, long time.

Ackermann clicked his heels smartly, saluted, bowed to the woman. He turned and rigidly marched to the opening in the wall. Only then did he bend, his shoulders sloping, his right leg bent back. He was once again the burned, crippled and deformed, sixty-year-old German, World War II, ex-fighter pilot.

*   *   *

"Captain Dessault, Old Boy!"   In Tennison Barquelay's mind, Dessault still held his 1945 rank. This was neither the result of poor memory nor disrespect, but merely an affirmation of his fond memories of their previous relationship.

"Hello, Tenny, my friend. It's been too damn long. How're you doing?"

"Ah, quite well, Harvey. And I agree, it has been much too long since we've had an opportunity to bang about."

Dessault was eager to get to the business that brought him to Ipswitch. "Are you still in tight with the Air Ministry and using that old field on the coast?" he asked.

"My dear friend, you might say that I am the Air Ministry and yes, we use Roughscuff Field for all of my aviation endeavors. My, you are in such a hurry! What do you need of me, Harvey?"

Dessault explained the situation to Barquelay, who became more and more excited as he learned of the planes and of their attempt to spirit them from Germany.

"Oh, yes! Yes, indeed," said Barquelay. "You get them here, and I assure you, we'll have them disassembled and stowed in ship cargo containers and off to the States in no time."

The two old friends discussed the project over a dinner of lamb and potatoes and more than a sufficient amount of Irish whiskey to wash it down. The details were finalized with a handshake.

The following day, Barquelay took Dessault to Roughscuff Field. The change in the old airdrome stunned Dessault. An industrial complex had replaced the pastures surrounding the field and the strip was now 12,000 feet of shiny cement with new approach, runway and taxi lights and a modern, concrete tower.

"Sure isn't the old grass strip of the forties and fifties, is it?" said Dessault.

Before Barquelay had a chance to answer, a gray streak flashed in from the east, coming low, loud and fast. By the time it had shot down the length of the runway, the plane was just barely recognized by Dessault as a F.Mk 3 Tornado, Britain's top fighter plane. It pulled up, executed two snap rolls, and returned to scream over the field inverted at what must have been close to Mach one.

"Who the hell is that crazy bastard?" Dessault yelled over the noise of the jet fighter.

Tennison Barquelay stood quietly, his chin cradled in his right hand, not answering Dessault's question. He turned and walked slowly toward a large hangar with a Barquelay Aviation sign above the massive doors. Inside, he stopped and turned to Dessault.

"That 'Crazy Bastard' happens to be my Daughter, Bridgett."

"Oops!" said Dessault. "Damn, I'm sorry Tenny, I didn't know."

Barquelay laughed, "That's quite all right, Harvey. I've called her worse on occasion."

The Tornado landed and taxied up to the open hangar doors. Barquelay stood defiantly in the center of the opening as the fighter's engines coasted down with a whine, and the plane's roll slowed. The pilot brought the nose of the plane right up to Barquelay, its pitot tube pointed right at his forehead. He stood his ground and the spear-like protuberance stopped a mere four inches from him.

The cockpit canopy hinged open and a bright pink helmet was pulled from a head of dark hair that fell to the pilot's shoulders. The rear vision mirror, standard on almost all fighters these days, was adjusted, and additional adjustments were made to hair and lipstick. She threw a leg over the side of the plane and stabbed her toes into the hinged steps on the side of the plane's fuselage, helmet in hand, and gracefully lowered herself to the hangar floor. She was thin, too thin, thought Dessault, and walked, no, bounced, in a manner reminiscent of an athletic teenager. He was unsure of his first impression.

The men moved aside as ground crewmembers pulled up to the plane with a small tug dragging a rattling tow bar. They began to attach the tow bar as Bridgett Barquelay leaped on her father. He feigned anger, telling her to "Buzz off, you nasty child." They scuffled for a moment in mock battle and then hugged warmly.

"Harvey, this mad child is my daughter, Bridgett.

Bridgett, here now, try to act your age." There was a light in his eyes Dessault had never seen before, but he knew that it was the glow of his pride and love of his rambunctious daughter.

"Oh, finally I get to meet Captain Harvey Dessault, my Daddy's Number One Hero!" Her voice was totally feminine and with a British accent that sent pleasurable chills up Dessault's spine.

Dessault reddened. He certainly never expected that Barquelay would have ever characterized him as being a hero.

"I think your Daddy exaggerates a little," said Dessault. "But it's very nice to meet you, Bridgett."

She gave him a smile that would have made a younger man pass out face down on the asphalt. Dessault just turned more red.

Dessault checked out of his bed and breakfast lodgings in Ipswitch and spent his final day and night at Barquelay's Felixstowe estate on the North Sea coast. After dining on a light, typically British dinner, they enjoyed gin and tonic, a pipe for Tennison Barquelay, and Dessault sampled a small Honduran cigar, Barquelay's favorite import. The talk was about airplanes and the military, but mostly about their project of bringing the Me.262's out of Germany.

Dessault gained a huge amount of respect for Bridgett during those hours. She was knowledgeable and sensible when it came to aircraft and the job of flying them. She had served in the Royal Air Force, graduated from their test pilot school, had gained two college degrees and now flew for the Air Ministry.

At thirty-one, she wasn't as young as Dessault had first thought. And he hadn't asked her if she'd be interested in joining them in the Me.262 project. Usually open and direct, Dessault wondered himself why he hesitated. It was as if he was a teenager again, nervous about approaching a girl. But this was business, not romance, he reasoned. There was no reason not to ask her. His thoughts dissolved as he became aware she was speaking to him.

"We've only just finished the evaluation of an experimental collision avoidance system for the Royal Air Force." She was sitting on a thick, orange rug in front of the fireplace, the two men in facing chairs.

"The flight today was the final one of almost eighty of the in-flight, near-miss collision tests. I'm really quite glad it's finally over. I guess I did the aerobatics just to let off steam."

"Don't believe her," said Barquelay. "She does that sort of thing all the time, just to infuriate me, Y'know."

He slid a bronze ashtray to the edge of the table at his side and tapped his pipe's ash into it. He stood.

"Don't keep the Captain up all night, Bridgett. A man can only endure so much of your chattering - believe me, I know - 'night all."

Bridgett took Dessault's glass, refilled it and then curled up on the plush rug, now just inches from him. "Tell me more about your German fighter plane project, Captain Dessault."

"Ah, just 'Harvey,' Bridgett. I left my Captain's rank in Vietnam," he said.

"In fact, we need another pilot to get the Messerschmitts out of there. I'm a few hundred hours short of being proficient in any kind of jet, let alone a foreign, antique twin, and I was hoping to roundup someone like yourself, someone who had the time and the talent...and most importantly, the passion to go after this crazy idea."

She looked at him with total amazement. "You think that I would go to Germany, risk everything I've worked for, to go down into a hole and steal an old-time, never flown, German fighter plane and try to keep it in the air all the way to England?" She leaned forward, folding her arms across his right knee, looking up at him.

"Sorry, Bridgett, I just thought it might be of interest to you." He felt as if he'd been slapped across the face for suggesting such a thing.

"I'm just a little apprehensive about my ability. I've only flown our Sabre and tee-thirty-three trainer a couple of times in the past few years and know that you'd be more proficient than I am, in any airplane."

She stood, bent and kissed him tenderly on the forehead. "I'm teasing. I was hoping you'd ask me. You must tell me more about it in the morning. But for now, it sounds as if I may be your pilot."

She went to the stairway, pausing at the first step just long enough to give him a warm smile. "Do you really think I have *passion*?"

The evening was the most pleasant Dessault had experienced in years. He went to bed that night a little drunk and a lot eager to get back to Germany and the Messerschmitts hidden underground.

Rain began its spattering tap dance on the roof and windows of the old manor as an uneasy sleep took his thoughts and turned them into fragmented dreams of flying, and fighter planes, and skinny young girls with daring attitudes.

CHAPTER SEVEN

Scott Austingrove was deep into the first serious sleep he'd had in four days, flaked-out on a pile of dirty packing material. He had sprawled there in total frustration five hours before, his anger grown to the point where he thought, *If I don't get away from these damn airplanes, I'm liable to take a sledge hammer to all three and let the Germans have the miserable wrecks.* And at that point the fact that the stinking packing material was a home for a family of rats didn't matter. All that mattered was sleep, even if for just an hour or two.

He was plagued by rotting fuel lines, leaking inner tubes, cracked tires, frozen bellcranks and control levers, rat-eaten electrical wiring and a million other age and disuse relate problems with the three aircraft. And then there was Inspector Schwerin.

"You are pitiful," said the Inspector, "you waste your time. You keep me prisoner. You have no chance of getting these antique piles of trash out of here. You will be caught and you will spend a long, long time regretting your stupidity - in our jail, of course."

"Go to hell, Schwerin," said Austingrove.

"Oh, no, my American friend, it will be you and your friends who will go to hell."

"Screw you!" He threw a spanner wrench against the far wall of the hangar and stomped off to find a place to be alone and get some restorative sleep. Schwerin laughed at him, but Austingrove didn't hear.

It seemed to be only moments later that Dessault's booming voice snatched him from his dreams. He raised up on one elbow and rubbing his eyes with the back of a grimy hand, saw the still fuzzy image of Dessault and Gordon at the old steel table. Ackermann stood to one side, eyeing Dessault. There was another figure too. This one Austingrove didn't recognize.

He wanted to flop back into his rat's nest and sleep some more, but Dessault's voice brought him fully back to wakefulness.

"Scott, you look like hell. Why don't you get up and clean yourself up. Christ, man, we've got company here."

Austingrove sat up, ran his fingers through his hair. He rose unsteadily and walked over to the group. Then he saw that the forth person was a young, attractive and familiar-looking girl.

"Bridgett?"

She turned, "Hello, Scotty." Her smile was warm, but there was a glint of fearfulness in her eyes.

He felt flushed, blushing like a teenager. "I'm...ah, I'm glad to see you," he lied through tight lips.

She quickly turned away, hoping he wouldn't blast off at her. The last thing she wanted to do was to create a problem simply by being there.

"You two know each other?" said Dessault.

"Yeah," said Austingrove. "We've met."

They certainly had met. They met five years before on the third day Austingrove was at Roughscuff Field. He was overseeing Barquelay's mechanics getting the Tiger Moth biplanes ready for shipment back to the States. Bridgett Barquelay had nearly ran him down as she drove her bright green Jaguar convertible directly into the hangar in which they were working. She ignored him and pulled the roadster alongside the first shipping container.

"What exactly do you think you're doing?" she asked one of the mechanics who was carefully sliding a cushioned wing into the container.

The man stopped his work. "We've been ordered to prepare these 'Moths for shipment, Ma'am."

"By whom, may I ask?"

"Oh, by your father, Miss," he said. "Mister Barquelay."

"And where are they to be shipped?" She was propped up on the back of the driver's seat.

Austingrove stepped to the rear of the Jaguar. "America, Miss Barquelay," he said.

She turned, "America? What in the world for? These are our cadet trainers for the Youth Aviation Program. You can't just take them away." She looked distressed.

Austingrove saw her concern and realized it wasn't about *her* loss, but for the loss to the Cadet Pilot Program. "These Tiger Moths will be completely restored and exhibited in America. They've become classic aircraft, and they should be kept in perfect shape and preserved for future generations to see and appreciate."

"But our Cadets..." she said.

"Before you get too worried, come with me." He took her hand as she swung her legs over the door of the convertible and dropped lightly to the hangar floor.

"Where are we going?" She suddenly realized that they were still holding hands and pulled hers away.

Austingrove grinned, "Next door."

They entered the next hangar. Two Cessna 172's were being readied for flight. They were like new, white with red trim.

"These are your replacements." The Cessnas were more modern and would serve as much better trainers than the old Tiger Moth Biplanes.

"Oh, my," said Bridgett.

"And look back there," said Austingrove.

Bridgett moved alongside the first 172 and peered into the rear of the building. "My God! Is that a Tee-Forty-Five?"

"Yes, Ma'am, and it will bring your cadet program into the twenty-first century." The T-45 is a single jet-engined two-place trainer built by McDonnell Douglas. It is capable of 1,038 Km/Hr and can reach Mach 1.2 in a dive. This example, painted with the same white and red as the 172s, and equipped with a Rolls-Royce turbofan for power, is the ideal jet trainer.

"A fair exchange?"

Bridgett's eyes glistened with excitement, "Oh, yes, God yes!" She grasped Austingrove's hand with both of hers. He could feel her excitement pulsing through the veins of her grip.

That started a week that Austingrove still felt were the best seven days of his life. They spent every free hour together until the evening of the seventh day.

They were dancing at the R.A.F. Station Ramsgate Officer's Club. She had been especially loving, keeping close and speaking softly. Austingrove was leaving the following day, back to Dessault Aviation to setup the shop area for the Tiger Moth's reconstruction. He was aware, and surprised, that he was so fiercely dreading having to say good-bye to her. He felt that she was feeling the same remorse. In his sadness, he began to imagine how it would be if they were together permanently. They both had an avid love of anything "Aeronautic," as she would say, and they were able to agree on most things, and work through the others with humor, rather than rancor. They could enjoy wild all-night parties or quiet times at the seashore with equal enthusiasm.

Her enlistment in the Royal Air Force would end in a little more than a year and he wondered how she'd take to joining him at Dessault Aviation at that time. He decided to put out a feeler.

"It's going to be rough leaving you tomorrow to go back to the States," he said. "I really wish I could take you with me. I'd have a great time showing you every town in every state." *That sounded clumsy,* he thought, *like a snot-nosed, swooning teenager.*

"And all the airdromes too, I'd wager." She was dancing closer than she had all evening. She squeezed his hand. "I'll miss you too, Scotty, and perhaps some-day I can come visit you in America. I would like that."

At his hotel, they made love, holding each other as if they could never be parted. When he awoke, she was gone. All the next day he phoned her more times than he could remember. He left England bitter and resentful. In the following weeks and months he had continued to call and write. She answered neither phone nor pen.

Now, five years later, he was standing beside her and felt nothing but a slight aggravation, no anger, but curiosity was pulling at him like the relentless G forces of a jet fighter's tight turn.

Dessault slid a cardboard box across the table and took out five carry out dinners in Styrofoam carton, coffee and colas.

Austingrove brightened and reached for coffee. He gulped down half of the tepid brew.

"Bridgett is one hell of a fine pilot," said Dessault. "She'll be flying whichever one of these birds you think is the best. Scott, you'll fly the next best and I'll take whatever is left."

A birdlike screech from Hans Ackermann startled them all. "No! No!" he screamed, his tiny slit of a mouth grotesquely twisted and spraying saliva with each word. "I will fly the first Schwalbe! These are my airplanes, this is my Jagdverband!"

Bridgett backed away and the men stood frozen, unable to comprehend this 70 year old, physically handicapped man flying anything, let alone a 550 mile per hour antique jet fighter of questionable airworthiness.

"I will not let you do this," he continued to rant, his eyes burning into Dessault with rage. "I am the one who kept them safe. I have taken care of them. They are mine!" His face was getting red and he trembled all over. His small fists were clenched so tightly his knuckles looked like bare, white bones.

"Whoa, Ackermann," said Dessault. "Don't get all worked up. We can discuss this. Perhaps we just assumed that you wouldn't want to fly the Two-Six-Two again."

"I have to," Ackermann said. "Don't you see? I *have* to."

Gordon touched Ackermann's shoulder. "Easy, Hans. We can work this out." Ackermann looked up at him, anger still in his eyes. His cheeks puffed in and out as if he was about to sob.

"Hans, do you think you can, I mean, are you physically able to handle a fighter plane again? You know, its been a long time since you've flown."

"I have more time in the cockpit of the Schwalbe than any man alive on this earth today." His shoulders straightened. He held his head erect, proudly.

"I can fly. I have sat in the cockpit and have operated the controls for many, many hours, months, years. Yes, I am not a physically handsome man, but I can still move pedal, control stick, throttle, and my eyes can still see the instruments. What else must I do?"

"Well, for one damn thing," said Dessault, "you've got to be able to react with split-second reflexes. What the hell do you think you'd do in an emergency?"

"What do you think *you* would do in an emergency, Major?" Ackermann stepped forward and slapped Dessault across the face.

The big man was stunned and instinctively swung a right cross at the old man's face. Ackermann easily ducked the punch and rapidly hit Dessault four times in the stomach before Dessault recovered his balance. Ackermann's punches were not damaging. Dessault barely felt them. Ackermann ducked another vicious swing that spun Dessault around and in two swift strokes, he yanked Dessault's jacket down over his arms and shoved him head-first into the lockers. Dessault banged against the lockers and stumbled around to face Ackermann, his face red with rage.

"You questioned my reflexes, Major," said Ackermann. "I think that now there is no question of who has the better reflexes, Ja?"

"I'll be damned," said Dessault, a wry smile softening his face. "OK, you crazy old bastard, you've got yourself a ride." Only Dessault knew that this decision came as a great relief.

They broke off into small groups and finished eating. Dessault gulped down the last of a sausage and pulled a stencil and a can of spray paint from his bag. He went to the first plane and carefully positioned the stencil and sprayed his golden scimitar emblem on each side of the plane's nose.

Austingrove stood watching. "Looks pretty good Skipper," he said truthfully.

"Tennison fixed me up with the stencil and this yellow paint. I guess we can imagine it's gold," he said, and headed for the second Me.262. "Scott, how is it looking? Are we anywhere near ready?"

Austingrove took the last of the coffee. "You

know, Major," he said. "We could keep on working on these ships until we're all old and wrinkled. Fact is, they're about as ready to fly as we're ever going to be able to make them."

"Well, hell, then," said Dessault. "Let's get started on getting started."

He took Austingrove out of the hearing range of Schwerin and Ackermann and said softly, "Tennison Barquelay told me that the Munich Air Expo is going on starting tomorrow for a full week. Barquelay suggests that since there will be hundreds of military and private planes flying in and out of this area, it would be a damn good time for us to fly out of here, hopefully unnoticed."

Austingrove nodded, "Just give me a couple more days."

"OK," said Dessault. "Barquelay will send a fuel truck from his flight facility at Munich, but the timing has to be just right. The truck can't hang around that old airdrome waiting for us, and we sure as hell can't sit around on our Messerschmitts out there for very long either."

The next morning, Bridgett Barquelay went into Wolfshütte and called her father with the prearranged, coded message of their planned departure.

"Daddy, the kids are leaving home the day after tomorrow, Thursday," she told him. "Can you take care of them?"

Tennison Barquelay's voice was filled with delight. "Oh, yes, my dear," he said. "I will be so very pleased to provide for their every need. Give them my love, won't you?"

Austingrove had cleaned himself up, shaved and put on a clean shirt. He had been watching for her return from the village.

"Bridgett, what the hell happened?" he said. "Why did you pull that disappearing act on me in Ramsgate?"

Bridgett held her gaze steady, looking directly into his eyes. "After all this time, you still haven't figured out why I left like I did?"

"No," said Austingrove. "For whatever reason you had, I just think it was one hell of a cruel, unfeeling way to treat someone."

"Yes, well believe me, it wasn't a party for me either, you know. I was very happy during the time we spent together, but that last evening I couldn't sleep. I laid there thinking about what you said, you know, about me joining you in the States." She turned away, losing Austingrove's gaze.

"That wasn't a proposal or anything," said Austingrove. "I just wanted you to see, to share with me, some of the wonderful places you'd never been."

She turned back. "Scotty, I was a young RAF Lieutenant. I had the rest of my enlistment before me. I had worked very, very hard for my commission and I wanted nothing more than to be the best. Don't you see, it wasn't you, or going to America. It was simply me and my job. My duty, if you prefer. Duty simply won't allow me to bugger off to some bloody place anytime I wish to. You, of all people, should realize that."

"You're so sure that I understand that now, what made you think that I wouldn't have understood it then?"

Bridgett turned to face Austingrove. Her eyes filling with tears. "I couldn't tell you," she said. "I was falling in love with you and simply didn't have the nerve - or as you might say, the guts - to face you. So, I ran." Her face turned stern. "I won't say I'm sorry, Scotty. I did the right thing for both of us and you know that's true."

Over the years, Austingrove had considered that very fact. Yes, it was true. He had been totally infatuated with her, but there were too many negatives in the relationship.

"OK, Limey," he said, "but when we get back to Roughscuff, I'd like to take you to dinner, OK?"

"Just dinner, Yank." She tenderly touched his face, "I'm over it, Scotty. You must get over it too." She turned away and walked to Dessault's side.

Austingrove went back at the pile of dirt, shoveling with frustrated vengeance.

While the others were engrossed in digging out the tow tractor, Ackermann slipped through the small tunnel into the hidden bunker. "Mein Fuehrer," he saluted smartly. "With your approval, we must prepare to leave now."

The two corpses stared dead ahead.

He slid the rotted suitcases to one side, spreading their split sides open to expose their contents. There were seven metal tubes, each filled with rare gold coins of France, Austria and The Netherlands. There were four hardwood boxes of diamonds and rare gems and several velvet bags filled with jewelry, all contraband from conquered countries. He carefully placed the treasures in a canvas duffle bag.

"God, what a stink!"

Ackermann spun around, the canvas bag falling to the floor. Major Dessault squeezed the rest of the way into the room, Austingrove and Gordon crawling through the hole behind him.

"We've been wondering where you've been sneaking off to, Ackermann," said Dessault.

Austingrove and Gordon slowly took in the scene. "My God, Cody, " said Austingrove. "This ought to make your little old history-loving heart happy."

He went to the radio operator's table, gently picking up and examining a rotted code book. Gordon, all the while holding his nose, carefully eyed the multitude of papers scattered about the larger table, trying to decipher some part of it. Only then did he take notice of the couple on the couch.

"Oh, Sweet Jesus!" He stepped closer, recognizing the two skeletons and realizing the macabre story they told. "Lieutenant Ackermann, is this who I think it is?"

Ackermann looked panicky. "No! It is no one you

would know. Just a German officer and his frau," he said.

"It's Hitler and Eva Braun," said Austingrove solemnly.

Gordon leaned heavily on the table. "This will change every history book in the world. Every history book that told of Hitler and Eva Braun's death is wrong, dead-ass wrong." He looked at Ackermann. "Hans, we have to tell the world about what happened here."

Ackermann stood trembling. "You must leave here at once," he commanded.

"Like hell, Lieutenant." said Dessault. "I saw that loot you stashed in the duffle bag." Dessault walked over to the remains of two people on the couch. "And as far as I'm concerned, both that, and this lovely couple, if they are who we think they are, will have to be turned over to Tennison Barquelay and the British government when we get to England."

Ackermann jumped Dessault, slamming him back against the wall. Fifty years of accumulated dirt and dust cascaded down on the two men and billowed up around them. Dessault was stunned, shaken, and his legs folded up under him.

With amazing quickness and agility, Ackermann dove for the couch. He landed in the woman's lap scattering bones. Her cranium wobbled, then fell to the floor and rolled toward Austingrove. Ackermann thrust his hand down into the rot that was the cushion and came up with a black, evil-looking Luger pistol.

Austingrove snatched up the skull and in one swift movement hurled it at Ackermann. The old man dodged it easily, leveled the Luger at Austingrove and pulled the trigger.

The ancient slide exploded open, sending a shower of hot pieces of brass bullet casing back at Ackermann. Only a puff of dust left the end of the barrel that was pointed at Austingrove.

Gordon grabbed the damaged pistol from Ackermann's hand. The old man just stood looking at his right hand, blood dripping to the floor from a multitude of small cuts from flying brass. He looked from Gordon to Austingrove and began to cry.

"Oh, shit," said Dessault, now revived. "Let's get out of this stink hole. Load up whatever the third plane will hold with this stuff. Get IDs, papers, books, whatever. The Brits will determine if that's Adolf and his babe."

Tired, sore, and covered with dust, the Major looked like an old gray ghost.

CHAPTER EIGHT

The small German tractor was in amazingly good condition. It had been covered with a heavy tarpaulin when the dirt roof fell in on it. Only one tire was flat, but when filled, it held air well enough. The battery was serviced, and the radiator filled. It had no brakes, the brake lines were rotted away. The engine's oil was black and thick, but there was no replacement oil available, so the engine was rotated over manually to loosen everything up and to get the oil circulated. It started in an instant, filling the chamber with noise and thick, black smoke.

Inspector Schwerin complained bitterly about the smell, as he did about most everything. He was so disagreeable that none of the three Americans wanted to deal with him and his complaints. That was to his liking. It gave them less of a chance of discovering that he had been diligently grinding the steel of his handcuffs against the coarse edge of the cement trough that ran alongside his pallet. The steel chain was cut more than three-fourths through.

The next day was Wednesday, and as the sun settled behind the tall trees, four men began to crank down the huge hangar ramp leading to the world above. The electric motors were rusted out, totally un-repairable, but the German engineers had provided for motor or electrical failure by fitting hand cranks to each of the twin gearboxes. Dessault and Austingrove on one, Gordon and a sullen Ackermann cranked the other, the rusty hinges screeching in agony as the door began to lower.

Ackermann's injuries inflicted by the old Luger were minor and the Americans had calmed him down, assuring him that he would surely be a celebrity in the outside world. They convinced him that the treasure should try to be returned to those countries from which it had been stolen. He reluctantly agreed. He was sullen, yet cooperative.

"What about the Kraut?" Dessault asked Austingrove. "Do you think we can trust him with a plane?"

Austingrove threw his weight into the crank and

grunted. "I talked to Cody and he seems to think that Ackermann has resigned himself to the fact that he hasn't a choice. He thinks the Ersters will either kill him or put him in the slammer for the rest of his life. He represents exactly what they want to eliminate."

He shifted his weight and pushed up on the old iron crank handle. "I guess we've got to give him a go. Christ, with his experience in the Two-Six-Two, he may be the only one able to get one to Roughscuff."

"Yeah, well," said Dessault. "He'd better watch his ass. He messes with me one more time and I'll put him back down there in that stinking pit with his Nazi friends."

Beams of moonlight began to teeter over the treetops and into the underground hangar as the ramp was lowered. Two thirds of the way down it stopped. The cables on both sides became slack, and the ramp hung in space, unsupported. The men stopped cranking.

"What the hell now?" said Austingrove.

"She's jammed," said Dessault. "Try cranking it back up a ways, then let it down again. It might just be hung-up someplace."

The men strained at the handcranks. The ramp would go neither up nor down. "How about if we put just a little slack on the cables and then go up there and put our weight on the ramp," suggested Gordon.

The men set the cables and climbed up to the outside. Long shadows spread across the landscape and the sky was showing scattered spots clear of the cloud cover that had persisted since their arrival. They carefully walked out onto the slanted ramp. When it was evident that it was stuck solidly, Dessault attempted to break it loose by jouncing on it.

"It is jammed good forever, I think," said Ackermann.

"Bull crap," said Dessault. "Gordon, go below and see if you can eyeball the hinges on this thing. Maybe its hung-up on gobs of rust or something."

Dessault and Austingrove sat down on the grass-covered ramp. "It would sure be the shits if after all of our work we can't get the planes out of there," said Dessault.

"Major," said Austingrove, "I'm so tired, I don't care if we get them out or not. If I'd known how tough this was going to be, I think I'd have jumped aboard a plane back to the States the minute I got out of that hospital."

Dessault was quiet for almost two minutes. Then he stood up and turned to Austingrove. "Y'know, Scott," he said, "You're really a screwed-up mess."

Austingrove was shocked, "What do you mean by that?"

"I mean that you left college early to join the Air Force to try to live up to your dad's and your brother's expectations. Then you served with distinction in 'Nam but all you do is piss and moan that you were given a raw deal. You have a great position with *Jet*

Fighter! but you just plug along, doing as they say, not exercising any initiative or displaying your talents." Dessault stopped, waiting for a reply. Getting none, he continued. "You have one terrific gal that I think is crazy about you and you treat her as if she had cooties. Damn, Man, you're young, strong and good-looking. You'd better get your life in gear pretty soon or you'll end up a frustrated, lonely, old son of a bitch. You need to get these airplanes to the States more than you realize. Not for the fame or the money, but for your own self-worth. You need to do something extraordinary, Man, and those damned old pisspots sitting down there in that hole may be your last shot at it."

Austingrove knew that everything he said was true. He didn't reply. He knew that Dessault was talking to him like that in an effort to snap him out of the lethargy he had been burdened with lately. The man spoke to him as a father would to his son, and Austingrove appreciated that. He couldn't come right out and say it though, and that bothered him. He'd have to show the Major that he was back on track by his actions. "OK, Major, let's go get those - what did you call them, 'pisspots?' - up and out of here, and into the air."

Austingrove joined Gordon under the ramp. "The Major was right," said Gordon. The hinge runs the entire width of the ramp. Its crammed full of rust and dirt and roots of trees and grass." He poked at it with a screwdriver. "All along the hinge under here it's got itself all rolled up in a gob. Its all jammed up in the hinge."

"Yeah," said Austingrove. "Look, there's a bunch of cases of thirty millimeter shells back behind the last plane. Let's go get them."

"You plan on shooting the ramp down?"

"Well, sort of. Come on."

Gordon drug the case of ammunition over to the steel table. He and Austingrove went to work twisting the shells from the casings. They poured the black and silvery grains of gunpowder into tubes of rolled up pages torn from Me.262 parts books. The end of each roll was twisted tight. When they had twenty rolls prepared, they cut twine into eight inch sections. One of these was inserted into one end of each of the tubes.

The powder charges were set aside while the men dug holes into the dirt and bored holes into the roots holding the ramp.

A tube was placed into each hole, their wicks dangling out like a row of commas. Each fuse was longer than the next, in each set of five fuses. This would allow them to be lit one after another, the longest first. They would burn down, each reaching the powder charge simultaneously.

Austingrove lit the old candle on the table and gathered the men together. "It's going to take a closely coordinated effort," he said. "We'll each have five fuses to light just as quickly as we can. I have one here to test so that we can see how long it takes for it to ignite." He touched the end of the twine to the candle's flame. "One, two, three, four...There." He snuffed out the flaming fuse underfoot. "We'll have about four seconds to light-off each fuse, that means it will take the four of us about twenty seconds to have all twenty lit. I figure we'll have about ten seconds to get under cover."

"Those little packages will blow all that stuff from the hinges?" asked Gordon.

"Well, probably not all of it, but it should blast away most of it." Austingrove looked at Dessault. "What do you think?"

Dessault spoke, "Let's get at it, dammit, these things won't light themselves."

Schwerin was moved into the safety of the generator room. "That old gunpowder will not explode, you fools," said Schwerin. "It will only fizzle like a wet piece of wood."

"Shut up, ass-eyes," yelled Dessault.

Bridgett positioned herself at the doorway. She was to call out "Time!" when the twenty second lighting time was expended. When she called out, everyone was to head for cover, even if they had not lit all of their charges.

Each of the four men struck a match and stood by one of the fuses. At Bridgett's signal, they touched the matches to the first of their five fuses. They quickly worked their way across their rows of powder charges.

"Time!"

Austingrove, Gordon and Ackermann dropped their matches and raced to the shelter of the row of lockers.

Dessault was fussing with the last of his fuses. It had slipped out of the charge and fell to the floor. He was trying to poke it back into the hole when Bridgett called time.

"Major!" screamed Austingrove. He saw the fuses burned almost to the charges. He sprinted from behind the locker and tackled Dessault just as the twenty blasts rippled across the jammed hinge. The explosions blew dirt, grass and pieces of root into the hangar, blowing over the lockers on top of Gordon and Ackermann and sending Bridgett reeling backward into the generator room.

The massive ramp shook, groaned and began to fall. It hit the floor with the force and accompanying noise of its 16,000 kilogram weight.

"Get the hell off me, Mister." Dessault shoved Austingrove. They were covered with dirt and weeds and roots. Austingrove staggered to his feet, stunned by the shock and noise of the blasts.

"Major," said Austingrove, "you're going to get me killed one of these days."

It took three hours to clean the dirt from the planes and from the people. The fresh, clean night air filled the chamber. This, and the success of the ramp blowing, had everyone's spirits high. At 8 P.M., with an overcast sky above the ramp opening, they were finally ready to move the planes out of the hangar.

The towbar was attached, and the tractor, Gordon at the wheel, began to haul the first plane up the ramp. The tractor slipped, fought for traction and gradually jerked its way up the grassy slope of the ramp.

The fighter was positioned facing an opening in the trees that led to the road to Wolfshütte. The second plane was quickly brought up and positioned behind the first. The space behind the pilot's seat headrest was crammed with the duffle bag of treasure and the bones, papers and equipment from the hidden bunker. Bridgett Barquelay would be flying it. Then the third Me.262 was towed out into the moonlight, Austingrove already in its cockpit repairing a bad microphone cord.

Bridgett was in the hangar, gathering up a stack of papers, mostly German aircraft manuals and forms. She slid them into a plastic envelope. Behind her, Lieutenant Schwerin said, "You won't be leaving an old man down here, all tied up like this, will you?"

Bridgett ignored his comment, slipped a tan bomber jacket over her red sweater and picked up her RAF helmet.

"We have time for a little romance, Fraulein."

This time, Schwerin's voice was right behind her. Startled, she spun around. He threw his manacled right hand at her face. Instinctively, she yanked the fiberglass flight helmet up for protection. Schwerin's fist slammed into it, sending it flying off into a corner of the big hangar. She kicked hard up between his legs. He grunted, spat out a profanity she didn't recognize and followed his right with a left. She ducked right into it. The remainder of the handcuff's chain was caught between the man's tough fist and her soft face. Her blood spattered Schwerin as she was spun away, crashing down onto the hard cement floor. He quickly climbed the dirt stairway and exited the way he had entered sixteen days before.

The towing tractor was again attached to the first jet and the four men worked frantically, stretching cables of heavy webbing from the main landing gear of each plane to the nose gear of the next. Gordon had determined that the tractor was strong enough to tow all three down the road at once. Austingrove and Dessault hoped he was right.

Once rigged for towing, Gordon mounted the tractor. Ackermann, it was decided by the others, would fly the first plane, the single seater. Bridgett Barquelay would fly the second fighter with the bags of treasure, bones and papers. Austingrove, with Dessault in the back seat, would take the two-place Model B-2A night fighter. Cody Gordon would ditch the tractor and ride the motorbike to Munich. There, he would board a Barquelay Aviation plane for England.

Gordon started the tractor then turned and yelled to Austingrove, "Where's Bridgett?"

Austingrove twisted in the seat, looking to the

second plane. Its cockpit was empty.

Austingrove sprinted back to the hangar. Sliding down the grass covered ramp, he saw Bridgett Barquelay in the dim light, crumpled up on the floor. Blood, glistening black in the moonlight, was spattered across her face and matted her hair. Austingrove cursed. He looked in the direction of where Schwerin was shackled. He was gone.

He carried her to the cot and gently washed away the blood from the gash on her cheek. It wasn't a serious wound, but she'd be sore for a while. He did a quick bandaging job.

Dessault came sliding awkwardly down the slope. "Oh, Christ," he said. "What happened to her, Scott?"

Austingrove grunted as he lifted Bridgett to his shoulder. That bastard Schwerin clubbed her and split."

"We'd better get our butts out of here," said Dessault. "Schwerin will be back here damn fast with an army of his police buddies." They gathered up the papers and her helmet and stumbled up the ramp into the night.

Gordon jumped down from the tractor, running toward the men.

"Schwerin knocked her out and took off," said Austingrove before Gordon had a chance to ask what happened. "She probably tried to stop him." Then he turned to Dessault. "Looks like you'll have to take the number two plane after all, Major."

They lifted Bridgett Barquelay into the rear seat

of the two-place plane.

The little tractor's engine roared and the old clutch slipped and jerked at the tow straps. Slowly the first plane began to move. The stretch of the webbing was taken up and the second and third planes began their strange caravan slowly across the field, zigzagging around craters and onto the road.

The moon gave Gordon just enough light to see ahead. He gradually pushed the tractor's throttle to the floor and soon it was rolling along at nearly 10 miles per hour, the three German fighter planes trailing behind like ducklings following their mother.

The strange caravan rolled up to the entrance of the deserted airfield. Unable to swing the tractor wide enough, Gordon had to individually tow each plane through the gate. This slow procedure took almost an hour more than they had planned. Barquelay's fuel truck driver made use of that time by topping off all three planes with jet fuel. He wanted to stay and watch them takeoff, but Austingrove told him of the expected arrival of the police, so he quickly left.

The Me.262' s were lined up side by side at the end of the runway. It was felt that the starting procedure would be faster that way, and Austingrove didn't want the jet engine blasts blowing dirt and dust back into the other planes.

The three pilots huddled together and went over details of takeoff. Ackermann ran through the check lists, even though each of them would have to repeat the process once they were strapped into the cockpit.

"The plane's radios are working on Tac Channel One," said Austingrove. "But I don't know about any other working channels. We'll have to give them a try once we're airborne. Ackermann, your call sign will be *Ace.* Major, you'll be *Deuce* in the Number Two plane and I'll be *Trey.*"

Dessault nodded and stepped forward.

"We'll climb straight out above this cloud layer to three thousand meters and turn onto three-hundred-ten degrees. We'll maintain that heading until we cross the Rhine River. To the west there is a village called Monchengladbach. You can identify that town by the four roads laid out in an X pattern going into and out of town.

The city of Dusseldorf is to the east. If you can see it, you're too far east. It should take about fifty minutes to get to that point. We'll be past the mountains by then, and hopefully, we'll be able to keep below the ceiling. At that time, we should be on a heading of two-seven-zero degrees for about ninety minutes. Follow the canal that runs along the border. Hold that heading and it will take you straight across the Channel, right up the River Thames, to Roughscuff Field. If the weather and the cloud cover is as bad as it is here, just dead-reckon it on those headings for those time periods.

The German Air Force will have to intercept us from this field." He pointed to a spot on an old aerochart. "Right here. Hopefully, we'll be to the fork in the Rhine and onto the Belgian-Dutch border before they find us. Once we're on the two-seventy degree course, we'll be flying a straight line along that jagged border, alternately in Belgium, then in The Netherlands, and so on. That should drive them nuts."

"Do we land if they show intent?" asked Austingrove.

"Christ, yes. I don't want anyone getting killed. These are great prizes, but your life is a hell of a lot more important than ten thousand of these old Kraut flying machines."

"One last thing," said Dessault. "Remember to stay just under three thousand meters altitude. Without oxygen, anything higher will be dangerous. By flying at that altitude and using your best cruise R.P.M. throttle setting, we'll have just enough fuel to make it to Roughscuff. Good luck."

Dessault stepped back, folded the old chart and stuffed it into his flight jacket, just as he had done hundreds of times in hundreds of preflight briefings in three wars.

Gordon called that he was ready with the power cart for starting the engines. The flyers shook hands and pulled on their helmets as they headed for their planes. Both engines on the Number One plane, Ackermann's, started smoothly without the all-too-often tailpipe fire that the temperamental Junkers Jumo engines were known for.

The starting procedure was agonizingly slow.

Gordon positioned the cart at each engine, inserting the extension shaft and while holding pressure against the power cart. He started the small gas engine, then motion the pilot to start the jet engine. He strained to hold it in place as the jet engine began to turn. He had to hold it until he saw fire erupt from the tailpipe of the jet engine. Often, the extension shaft would spin furiously out of its socket and hurl skyward, sending Gordon diving face down in the dirt.

Dessault was uneasy and took some time before he signalled Gordon that he was ready. The second plane's engines spun to life without a hitch.

In the Number Three plane, Austingrove set the throttles, nodded to Gordon. First the left engine, then the right spun to life.

The trio of twin engines sent clouds of dust blowing across the airfield, over the road and up into the early morning sky.

Austingrove closed the canopy and was about to snug down his shoulder harness when he heard a low moan from the rear seat. Bridgett Barquelay had awakened.

"Did you stop that bastard Schwerin?" she asked.

"No, he got away clean," said Austingrove, "and we've got to get out of here before he comes back. How are you feeling?" Bridgett was struggling up out of the seat, reaching forward to release the canopy latch. It popped up, letting cool air and the noise of the jets rush in. "I've got to get to my plane."

"Whoa, Girl. You're going to ride this one out in

the back seat."

Realizing that she was still disoriented and shaky, she paused, then sat back. "Damn, I'm letting you down."

"It's OK, Bridgett." Austingrove had to shout over the noise of the six jet engines idling, "The Major is a really fine pilot and feels OK with flying the second plane."

"Damn, damn, damn," she said.

"Besides," he continued, leaving the canopy up, "We don't have time to be switching planes. We've got to get airborne before the German Police are all over us."

As if cued, bright lights suddenly sprayed across the field, illuminating the planes, blinding the pilots. Austingrove could make out a police car and what looked to be a mechanic's van racing through the dust. Behind them, four semi trucks raced across the field, each with dual exhaust stacks blowing trails of black Diesel smoke into the air. He saw one flatbed, and the three others were pulling huge covered trailers. A warbling siren pierced the air. They spread out in front of the planes, blocking the runway.

Austingrove leaned forward to see out of the windshield, released the brakes and eased the left engine's throttle ahead. The Me.262 obediently moved forward, rocking gently and turning slowly to the right. He'd drive around them, somehow, even if he had to take off down the road. Then he suddenly braked hard, rocking the plane violently to a stop.

"What is it?" said Bridgett Barquelay.

"Look up ahead. We've got more company."

From over the top of the trees that edged the west side of the field, another four sets of bright lights suddenly appeared. They surged forward. Now illuminated by the truck's lights, Austingrove saw four black helicopter gunships drop down between the trucks and the German fighter planes.

The helicopter's cannons were aimed directly at the nose of each of the fighters, as if waiting for just one wrong move.

"I guess Schwerin called in the German Air Force for help," Austingrove said. He pushed the twin throttles ahead, simultaneously locking the left brake, spinning the plane around. Twin jet engine exhausts were now pointed at the approaching choppers. "I'll blind them with dust and try for the road."

"Wait Scotty, that looks like Daddy's security force!" said Bridgett. The four big, black, fierce-looking choppers slowly turned as if choreographed, and faced Schwerin's assembled trucks.

Austingrove could hear loudspeakers giving what sounded like orders in German. There were exchanges on both sides, then the vehicles began to back away. Their lights went off. They turned toward the edge of the runway, the helicopters herding them along. The strip in front of the planes was now clear.

Knowing that the others wouldn't be paying any attention to him while this drama was taking place, Hans Ackermann threw open his plane's canopy and lifted himself over the edge of the cockpit. He knew that this would be his last chance to get to the Fuehrer's plane. He must be the one to fly them to the rendezvous. The Americans would take them to England where they would be imprisoned. He could not let that happen. He dropped to the wing, then to the ground. He ran in his awkward lope to the second plane and clamored up to the cockpit.

"Fire! Fire!" he yelled at Dessault. "Your engine is on fire - get out quickly!" Dessault popped his shoulder harness free and quickly climbed from the cockpit. He stopped alongside Ackermann.

"I don't see any damned fire," said Dessault. He yanked the little man up to his level by the front of his flightsuit. "What are you trying to pull, Ass eyes?"

With every bit of his strength, Ackermann brought his knee up into Dessault's groin. Dessault let out a growl and his knees buckled. His grip on the German's collar loosened and Ackermann shoved him toward the sloping rear of the wing. Dessault lost his balance, slipped, and fell from the rear of the wing right into the blast of the left engine's exhaust. Even at idle, the jet engine's force blew him rolling in the dirt fifteen feet behind the plane.

Ackermann slid into the seat, slammed the canopy closed, released the brakes and wriggled into the shoulder harness as he advanced the throttles, deftly steering the plane to the center of the runway. A quick final instrument check. He pushed the throttles to their stops and began his takeoff roll. *It is now just as it was before*, he thought. *I have lost nothing!*

The Me.262 quickly gathered speed, its wings wobbling slightly as it bounced along the uneven grass strip. Then the wings steadied as the plane lifted free of the ground. Its three landing gear rotated into their wheelwells and the Me.262 disappeared into the overcast leaving two columns of black jet exhaust smoke as the only testament to its flight.

Austingrove couldn't understand why Dessault had suddenly decided to takeoff first, but he must have had a reason. He looked toward Ackermann's plane, expecting it to be the next to go. It stood, canopy open, the cockpit empty.

Austingrove was startled as Dessault, covered with dust and smelling of jet fuel, was suddenly at his side, yelling over the noise, "Your Kraut buddy shoved me off my damn plane and took off. He's got the damn plane - and the loot."

Bridgett Barquelay was suddenly out on the wing. "Get in, Major," she commanded. "I'll take the other plane."

"No! Bridgett!" yelled Austingrove. But she was already out of the plane, running to the single-seat Me.262. From the way she was moving, she looked as if she had completely recovered from the blow to her head. A figure carrying an assault rifle leaped down from one of the helicopters and ran toward her. She stopped, they met and hugged. A short talk, and they parted.

"That looked like Tennison Barquelay," said Austingrove. "Damn crazy family," he said. He was unstrapping, about to climb out and go after her.

"Hold it Scott," said Dessault. "Let her take it. She's one hell of a lot better pilot than I'll ever be, and she's current in all kinds of jets." He needn't say more as the Number One plane taxied past them and began its run down the strip. They watched silently as the plane got smaller and smaller, rapidly eating up the length of the runway.

"C'mon, Babe," urged Austingrove. "Get it off. Get it up!"

"She's off," said Dessault. "Now, for Christ's sake, let's get going!"

Austingrove closed the canopy, "You strapped in, Major?"

"Roger, Scott. Get your ass in gear!"

Austingrove carefully advanced the twin throttles. The jet engines each belched out a stream of fire onto the ground from quantities of unburned fuel that had puddled in their exhaust cones during the long period of idling. Then they blew themselves clear and began to develop the thrust needed to move the fighter forward. The plane rocked gently from side to side. Austingrove slid the throttles forward and felt the pressure of acceleration press him back into the skimpy seat cushion. The rocking quickened as did the pace of the plane as it ate up runway. The airspeed indicator's needle crept up to 220 Km/Hr, the first of Ackermann's markings. Austingrove pulled back on the control horn. The Me.262 leaped off the ground, stabbing its pointed nose into the cloud cover. The pressure of acceleration was joined by a heavy downward push on the pilot's seat as the ship shot skyward. He pressed the rudder pedals to brake the rotating main wheels, pushed up the safety cover and pressed the Landing Gear Up button. He raised the flaps as soon as the gear rattled up into their wheel wells.

Austingrove broke out of the overcast layer at 8,000 feet at 450 Km/Hr. The sky was bright, clear and a deck of low clouds lay below them like a huge, rumpled bedspread.

He had endured weeks of a mole-like existence in the underground assembly plant, coming out only at night to ensure their secrecy. Now, the sun was painfully bright. He squinted ahead through his sunglasses, the reflection from the white cloud layer below adding to his discomfort.

He gently pressed the right rudder pedal and the Me.262 responded immediately. He eased off and they were on the first compass heading. He eased the throttles back while watching the engines exhaust cones and keeping the exhaust gas temperature under 700 degrees centigrade. When the cone started to retract, he advanced the throttles just enough to extend it again. This was the best cruise r.p.m. for the engines.

He scanned the sky for the other Messerschmitts. A speck slightly to his left appeared. It grew. It rapidly approached, blurred in Austingrove's eyesight. Then he saw that it was a beautiful Me.262, gracefully arcing toward him. The plane dropped below, circled around, and took a position just off their right wing tip. Bridgett Barquelay smiled at them through the canopy.

Austingrove slipped on the old headset and cranked-in a radio frequency for plane-to-plane communications. Bridgett did likewise. She answered his short radio call immediately.

"Negative, *Trey,* I haven't seen *Ace,* over," she said.

"Well, we'll probably never see Ackermann again" said Austingrove. "With all those goodies aboard, no telling where he'll head, and I'm sure he planned to do just what he did."

"We shall keep good thoughts, *Trey,*" said Bridgett. "He may find us - or we him."

"Roger, *Deuce.* Did *The Dealer* (Tennison Barquelay) give you anything?"

"Rog, *Trey.* He said that he filed an international flight plan for three helicopters direct to Roughscuff. He said fly low and slow, and try to look like choppers," she laughed. "'Might fool the radar', he said."

"OK, *Deuce.*" Austingrove wasn't convinced they'd fool anyone's defence radar, especially if Schwerin had alerted the German Air Force. They needed an hour flying time to reach the English Channel. If they weren't discovered and forced down or shot down by then, they should be clear to make it all the way across the English Channel to Roughscuff Field.

Austingrove had the throttle set for maximum cruising range. They needed to conserve fuel in case Roughscuff was fogged-in and they had to go elsewhere.

The plane handled amazingly well. The whistling sound of the twin jet engines was barely audible. The Me.262 was as smooth and as quiet as any fighter he had ever flown and Austingrove already felt comfortable with it. He noticed that Bridgett had moved away about one quarter mile off his starboard wingtip and was maneuvering the plane in a series of slight turns and shallow dives and climbs. She too was getting the feel of the agile jet fighter.

Austingrove called back to Dessault, "Would you try to keep an eye on her, Skipper? I can't keep a check on her, and we should watch out for any trouble."

Dessault had not let the plane out of his sight since the rendezvous. "Hell, yes, I ain't got a damn thing else to do back here," he said.

CHAPTER NINE

U we DePoel sprawled across the dilapidated sofa. It was the only soft piece of furniture in the Ready Room of the 311 Squadron. He glanced at his watch, noting that he had two more hours of standby until he was relieved.

Normally, a flight of four F-16 fighter pilots were on standby at all times. Each watch stood four hours. On this day, however, DePoel was the sole standby pilot. His base at Volkel in southeast Netherlands was nearly empty of planes and personnel. The two Dutch Fighter Squadrons stationed there, the 311th and 312th, were flying demonstrations and hosting a large static display at the Air Expo in Germany.

Defense of their country was left up to DePoel at the Volkel base and one squadron of F-16s at the Gilze-Rijen air base to the west.

This is such a pitiful waste of time. DePoel thought, *I would like to go home*

He certainly didn't expect to be scrambled. Surely there wouldn't be any war games scheduled by the *Commando Taktische Luchtmacht*, (Tactical Air Command) during the Expo, and no sane country would dare attack Holland, a heavily-defended, well-equipped NATO member, before, during or after that air show.

The Alert Klaxon suddenly clattered noisily. DePoel's trained reflexes catapulted him to his feet. He snatched up his helmet from the rack at the door and bolted outside. His F-16 was just 50 meters from the flight shack.

Running to it, he yelled out loud, "Damn! This is craziness! Why must they do these insane things to us?"

The ground crew appeared from behind the plane and by the time he reached it, the cockpit cover was off and the power unit was started. All that was needed was a pilot.

He clambered up the ladder and tugged his helmet on while a ground crewman clicked the harnesses about his body.

"Do you have any idea what is going on?" he asked a crewman, "is it a practice alert?"

"I don't know, Sir, we are surprised just as much

as you, Sir."

In just under eleven minutes, DePoel's F-16 was wheels-up, climbing to intercept whatever initiated the scramble alert.

The two Me.262's turned northwest at the exact time they were directly over Monchengladbach, Germany. The cloud cover persisted. "I can't see much down there," said Austingrove.

"Yeah," said Dessault, "I thought the weather might clear as we got away from the mountains. No sweat though, just turn to two-seventy magnetic and hold that course for ninety minutes. We'll surely see the channel when we get over it."

They were paralleling the Dutch/Belgium border, on a course to the Straits of Dover and then on into England. Bridgett held formation, just off Austingrove's right wing tip.

Static suddenly crackled in Austingrove's headset. "*Trey*," said Bridgett, her voice sounding weak and distant over the ancient radio.

"Go ahead, *Deuce*."

"Scotty, there's a hole in the ceiling just off to the right, ahead of me, I'm going down to see if I can get a visual on where we are."

Austingrove was apprehensive, but also felt that if anyone could handle it, Bridgett could. "OK, *Deuce*." He almost added, "be careful," but then he realized that she is a professional jet pilot, not a child. She didn't need to be told to be careful.

"See if you can find that damn canal," said Austingrove. A blast of static distorted her reply.

He watched the Me.262 peel-off and swoop downward. He was again touched by the grace and beauty of the German plane. He watched until it disappeared through a mist-ringed pore in the clouds below.

Four French Mirage SBA fighter-bombers of the 23rd Squadron of the *Force Aerienne Belge/Belgische Luchtmach* (Belgian Air Force) at Kleine Brogel air base scrambled. It was routine. They did it each time a Dutch aircraft approached their border without previous clearance. Although there had been no incidences of actual aggression, a constant and fierce animosity existed between the Dutch and the Belgians. This time, however, there was a difference. Two targets were traveling northwestward and a single, fast moving blip just departed the Volkel Dutch air base.

The Operations Officer was sure that the fast moving target was a Dutch F-16, but the other two were unknown. He scanned through the computer readouts of clearances issued to NATO and saw that three helicopters were scheduled to be enroute to England from the Air Expo.

"Two-three Squadron Leader," radioed the Operations Officer, "be advised that three British helicopters have been cleared to transit direct Munich to London. Intercept, identify and report, over."

"Affirmative, base. Leader Two-Three, out."

Flight Leader Philippe Vessom couldn't count how many times squadron Mirage jet fighters had been scrambled. It seemed that the Dutch were constantly trying to annoy them. Since that country's military had become unionized, discipline, uniformity and efficiency had been lost. Enlisted personnel no longer obeyed orders. They wore long hair, beards and nose rings and had become shabby derelicts without pride or substance. Officers could no longer demand that orders be followed. The troops would merely sit-down, complain to their union leaders or go on strike. Initiative, respect and efficiency was unknown. Vulgarity, sloppiness and laziness, all union labels, ran rampant. Vessom knew that the pilots were as well poorly trained, self-absorbed and with few moral attributes.

He glanced over his left shoulder. The fighters were stacked below and behind him in a left oblique formation, precisely spaced, flying as one.

Vessom had the two targets just in range, showing on the upper edge of his scope. They were over Netherlands' airspace, flying parallel with the border. At this point, they were a problem for the Dutch. But he must watch and patrol the Belgian border in case it was a ruse.

From the north, Uwe DePoel's F-16 broke out of the clouds at 3,300 meters. He should have had target confirmation from Tactical Data Operations by now, but the radios were silent. He knew that Tac Ops was understaffed, and he wondered if indeed there was anyone on duty there. He had his orders. They were of primary importance and dictated that he intercept any aircraft violating Dutch airspace and initiate a challenge. If the it were ignored, he must warn them once again and then, unless advised otherwise by Tac Ops, he was authorized - no he was duty-bound - to lock-on one of his AM-9M Sidewinder air-to-air rockets and shoot the offending aircraft out of the sky.

When within 100 miles, the F-16's APG-66 Radar could pinpoint the target and lock-on to it. DePoel setup the programmable radar, adjusted his airspeed to Mach 9.6 and for the first time since takeoff, looked away from the wide-angle Heads-Up Display (HUD) and outside of the cockpit.

The top of a bright white layer of clouds stretched out below him. It reminded him of the white and rumpled cotton pad his mother used to spread out under the Christmas tree. To the west the coastal overcast abruptly stopped as if lopped off by the sweep of a huge blade. He imagined the resort beaches along the coastline. They must be enjoying sunny skies, and he wished he were there.

Bridgett Barquelay leveled out as soon as the Me.262 punched its streamlined nose through the bottom of the clouds. She was shocked to see that she was streaking along a mere two miles south of a large city. They were suppose to be flying over open countryside. She rolled the fighter up on its left wing and scanned the ground for a recognizable landmark.

"There," she said, "those two rivers look familiar."

She leveled up the wings and opened her map. A pair of rivers, bowed like an American cowboy's legs, spread south from the city of Eindhoven. She took another look to confirm her position. They were ten miles north of their planned flight path. She turned, following a southbound road, and scanned the landscape. Ahead, the road crossed a canal. According to her map, they should be directly above that intersection, on a heading of 270 degrees. From there the Belgium/ Dutch border snaked back and forth all the way to the coast. They would be alternately in each of the neighboring country's airspace.

"C'mon Baby," she pulled the control horn back and the Messerschmitt's nose obediently swept upward, stabbing back into the white ceiling. She held the controls steady while in the near-zero visibility of the clouds. Without modern flight instruments, and not knowing the accuracy of those she had, Bridgett played it cautiously. As long as she held all of the flight controls in the position they were as she entered the clouds, the plane would continue to climb straight for the couple of minutes it took to break out above them.

Scott Austingrove didn't see the Me.262 break out of the clouds. He didn't see it sweep gracefully around behind him. But then suddenly there it was, upside-down, whistling overhead. Dessault jumped so violently, Austingrove felt the plane shake.

"Jesus!" said Austingrove, "What the hell is she doing!"

"She's a nut." said Dessault. He smiled, remembering her aerobatics at Roughscuff Field.

Bridgett rolled the fighter back pilot-side-up, waggled the wings and made a sharp, definite turn to the south.

"We must be too far north," said Dessault, "better follow that crazy damn woman, Scott."

Uwe DePoel had acquisition and tracking on his target. Still too far away for identification, he slowed to Mach 8.8 and held his course, approaching slightly from above and behind. The radio crackled. He was advised by Tac Ops that the target aircraft was on a direct course for the secret Dutch Nuclear Research Facility at Tilburg. Now it was only 25-miles from that sensitive research area.

Some of The Netherlands' NATO partners were openly hostile and opposed to that facility and the work being done there. All squadron pilots had orders not to allow any aircraft within a ten mile radius of the plant.

DePoel's radar was tracking the encroaching aircraft and his Sidewinder missiles were armed. He would be acting in direct defiance of his orders if he waited to visually identify the target. He must bring it down as it reached the 10-mile zone. He would be doing this before he was close enough to know who's aircraft and pilot he was destroying. He was not sure if he could do that. But he feared that he would soon find out if he could ambush and kill in cold blood.

He accelerated back to Mach 9.6, hoping that he might get a glimpse of the target before he fired on it.

But time and distance were working in concert, spreading the chances of getting out without a kill.

He selected Number One Sidewinder and flipped up the launch switch safety cover. The HUD showed normal target acquisition and tracking. He went through the procedures just like he did in the training exercises at the Tactical Air Combat Center at Nellis Air Force Base in America. But then the sweat came from the desert's heat, now his flightsuit was soaked from icy fear.

Time and distance dictated the release of the rocket. It left the F-16 in a white corkscrew of hot exhaust and cold contrail. Uwe DePoel selected Sidewinder Number Two and readied it for firing. He stared at the HUD as the number one missile streaked away toward its target.

His eyes widened as he saw another target enter the display. It swept up, over and ahead of the first. Both targets suddenly turned southward as if they knew of the launch from DePoel's F-16. Immediately, four additional targets came into range. DePoel couldn't know that they were the flight of Belgian Mirage SBA's. They were moving much faster and were about ten miles beyond the first target. DePoel couldn't understand what was happening, but he realized that firing the Sidewinder had been a huge mistake.

The first two aircraft obviously had superior, advanced Threat Detection radar to be able to turn away from a missile launch so soon, so far away. The four new, fast moving targets must surely be escort fighters. They would now be launching retaliatory rockets at him.

Uwe DePoel jammed the throttle forward, kicking in the afterburner. At the same time he frantically called for additional support fighter aircraft. His missile hurled onward in its radar-directed, heat seeking path of death.

Scott Austingrove banked the Me.262 smoothly, losing just enough altitude to become level with Bridgett in the Number One fighter. As the plane dropped, a blurred streak tore past the canopy at an incredible speed. It shot between the two German planes, trailing a white contrail.

Austingrove had been shot-at enough in Viet Nam to recognize that streak as a deadly air-to-air missile.

"My God," said Dessault, "somebody's shooting at us!"

"Oh, man!" said Austingrove, "we must have strayed into a sensitive area," He increased their airspeed. "It must be the Dutch Air Force. I hope to hell they see that we're leaving."

"Get down into the clouds, Scott." said Dessault.

"That won't do any good, Skipper," said Austingrove, "without IFR flight instruments, I'd probably have us upside-down into the ground. Besides, the Dutch are flying F-Sixteens and clouds don't hide anything from their radar and missile systems."

"Yeah, you're right" said Dessault, "but let's get our butts out of here anyway, and damn fast, Captain!"

Austingrove had the Jumo engines turning up to the red line that Ackermann had scribed on the tachometers. He began to jink back and forth, dodging left and right, up and down. He was hoping that if there were any more rockets heading their way they would lose their electronic fix. The aircraft would be presenting a constantly moving target. With luck, the rockets would miss just like the first one did when they suddenly turned.

Bridgett saw the near-miss as well. She saw Austingrove's Me.262 begin its gyrations. At first she thought it had been hit and was going out of control. Now she realized that the apparent haphazard flying was actually evasive maneuvers. She began the same erratic flying, careful to increase the distance between the two planes as she did. They didn't need a midair collision to spoil their day.

Dessault had quieted since the near miss, but that ended as he blurted out a loud "Holy crap!" Austingrove was startled by the sudden outburst. As he snapped his head around, he saw what stunned Dessault.

To port, at least three or four miles away, a fiery ball with shooting trails of smoke and fire was spinning crazily across the sky. The Sidewinder had finally found a target. Austingrove had no idea who or what had caught the deadly missile, but he gave thanks that it wasn't one of the Messerschmitt Me.262s.

Flight Leader Philippe Vessom was surprised to see the two targets, now much closer, suddenly turn left. Now they were heading directly on an intercept course for his flight of four Belgian Air Force 5BA Mirages. They were approaching the border, slowly and openly, without any stealth or attempt at deception.

"Two-three flight," he called over the tactical channel, "Acquire and track two targets three-hundred-sixty degrees relative. Ready arms." He tracked and locked onto the single fast moving target approaching from the north.

He had no sooner armed his two AIM-9P Sidewinder missiles and the Threat Alert began sounding its warning horn. A missile had been fired and it was coming their way. Vessom stabbed the throttle and rolled the Mirage hard to the right, diving and rolling in an evasive maneuver. The other three Mirage's broke formation, each in a different direction, releasing chaff to confuse the missile's radar.

The last plane pulled up, ejecting flares to attract the heat-seeking Sidewinder. But it was mere seconds too slow to react. The missile locked onto his blazing afterburner, ignoring the flares and chaff, and flew right up the plane's exhaust cone. The explosion blew the 5BA in half. The nose section from just behind the cockpit was hurling end-over-end, spewing flames from what was left of the Number One fuselage fuel tank.

Philippe Vessom watched the flaming pieces scatter across the sky. He was amazed to see the canopy suddenly fly from the spinning nose section and its ejection seat blast away in a white stream of rocket exhaust. He rolled the fighter to the left and pulled up, just in time to see his pilot's parachute pop open. Cold sweat was flooding Vessom's flightsuit, helmet and face. He was shaking. That was something he never considered would happen, him shaking with fear in a combat situation. But there it was, and it made him angry.

He rolled the Mirage back to face the two threat aircraft. He put the nearest one right in the middle of the target acquisition square of the heads up display. It indicated that the Sidewinder missile was locked-onto the target. He flipped up the trigger guard and placed his finger on the firing switch.

Bridgett was shaken by the explosion. Some unsuspecting pilot had died instantly, in a plume of flame. He died for no reason, just some rocket-happy jet jock with a hair-trigger finger. She felt a sudden, deep sadness and for a moment wished she had never gotten involved in this crazy fiasco.

After five minutes on the southerly course, she tried to put her thoughts of the exploding plane and its pilot out of her mind. She was a trained combat fighter pilot. She must not let emotions affect her performance, and she would not. She checked her watch, calculating that they were now directly over the Belgian/Dutch border. She swung the fighter across the other plane's nose, waggled her wings, and turned to the 270 degree heading.

Austingrove banked the Me.262, holding its nose in a smooth, steady sweep across the horizon. As the compass neared the 270 degree mark, he eased off the right rudder pedal and relaxed his slight backward pressure on the control horn. The Me.262 obediently steadied up on the new heading. He decided not to continue with the evasive flying. He reduced the power slightly. He must conserve fuel.

He figured that whoever threw that first hard ball at them would have hurled more by now, if they were going to. The two planes had obviously presented a threat to Dutch security or to their air space sovereignty. But he thought it was unconscionable that they would fire on an unidentified aircraft without first intercepting and identifying to whom it belonged. And he had a sour knot in his gut for the poor damn pilot that been in the way of that errant rocket.

Austingrove figured that they were only seventy

miles from the coast. He looked at the airspeed indicator. It showed 448 kilometers per hour. He tried to do the mental mathematics that would determine how long it would take them to reach the coast at that speed.

He wished he'd paid more attention to metric conversion figures. "Major," he said over his left shoulder, "what's the time required to go seventy miles at four-hundred-forty-eight kilometers per hour?"

"How the hell should I know? said Dessault, "I haven't messed with the metric system since I left the Air Corps."

"Well, see if you can figure it out, OK?"

"Christ, Scott," said Dessault, "I know I said I had nothing to do back here, but doing your navigation figures doesn't make it a party, you know." He pulled a pencil from the arm pocket of his flight jacket and began to figure.

"Fifteen minutes, Scott," said Dessault a moment later, "then another twenty two minutes or so to Roughscuff Field."

"OK," said Austingrove, "We've got enough fuel for about an hour. Looks like we'll just make it."

Not one of the three people in the duo of Messerschmitts was aware of the four Belgian 5BA Mirage jet fighters approaching them from behind at more than 925 kilometers per hour.

Squadron Operations advised Flight Leader

Vessom that the pilot of the Mirage that took the missile had been recovered. He was shaken and confused, but unhurt.

In his anger, Philippe Vessom was ready to release a pair of deadly Sidewinder air-to-air missiles. Then his two targets suddenly veered right. They were now so close to the snakelike border that he wasn't sure if they were in Belgian or Netherlands airspace. Their slow speed and seemingly innocent demeanor had him confused. But more-so, he was extremely curious as to why they would fire an air-to-air rocket at his flight without provocation.

He had calmed now and he decided that he must follow his orders. He must find out what type of aircraft they are before attacking.

Traveling at twice their speed, he would be upon them in a moment. If they were the helicopters that had left the Air Expo, he would visually check to see if they were equipped with missile hardpoints. If they were, he would force them to land. There would be an investigation as to why they shot down a Belgian fighter plane.

At the horizon, two specks appeared. That would be them, Vessom thought. He ordered the flight of three Mirage jets to reduce their airspeed. Eight Sidewinder missiles were still armed and at the ready. He silently prayed they wouldn't be given a reason to use them.

The two targets framed by Vessom's windshield rapidly grew. He determined that they were airplanes, not helicopters. Then, an instant later, he recognized them as a pair of World War Two German fighter planes.

The swift Mirage jets were overtaking the Messerschmitts by more than 400 kilometers per hour. Vessom ordered his flight to orbit above the jets and to stay within Belgian airspace. He eased the throttle back and lowered his flaps to the landing position. As his airspeed dropped below 460 kilometers per hour he lowered his landing gear. He advanced his power slightly. The Mirage steadied up and eased alongside the Me.262s.

Vessom was astonished to see the Nazi fighters. He knew that several examples still existed in a scattering of museums, but was unaware that any were still flyable. He was also unaware that there had been two-place models built, but one of these was, and both looked to be perfectly restored, even to subtle weathering of the paint and insignia. He flew for long moments staring at the planes before looking back into the cockpit of his fighter.

He scanned his inventory of radio frequencies. He tried all of the tactical channels. But he received no indication that the German plane's radios were operable.

Vessom smiled in his oxygen mask as he saw the first pilot discover him so close alongside and jump, startled. Vessom held up his right hand with the fingers curled, as if holding a microphone. He worked his thumb up and down as if actuating a push to-talk microphone switch.

The Me.262 pilot shook his head. There would be no radio communications.

Vessom pointed ahead and then held up both hands, palms up, as if in a shrug. The other pilot understood and scribed the letters U and K in the air. United Kingdom. Vessom understood that they were headed for England. These were certainly not helicopters, but there were two of them, traveling in accordance with the flight plan. Vessom decided that it must have simply been a miscommunication about the aircraft being choppers.

The antique planes had no hard points for missiles. It was obvious that they could not be responsible for the wild rocket shot. He decided it must have been a crazy Dutch hot-shot fighter pilot that had become excited and let one fly. And if that were the case, he would be the unidentified fast-moving target was coming right at them.

Vessom knew that it would be a Dutch F-16. He also knew in his heart that it had been the plane that fired the missile. He pulled up, raised his landing gear and flaps and climbed at full throttle to meet the approaching fighter.

The three other fighters of his flight were still orbiting above. Vessom radioed them with orders to return to the airbase. He would handle the crazy man in the approaching jet.

The plane would undoubtedly wait to fire another missile until it identified the slow moving pair, as well as Vessom's Mirage.

Now Vessom was ignoring the border. The plane's action of firing at such a long range at an unidentified target was unconscionable, and he would pay, regardless of political delineations of airspace.

Vessom locked onto the jet as it was framed in the HUD. He could see it clearly now, approaching at Mach one or better. Vessom fired one Sidewinder missile. There will be a price to pay, thought Vessom, but right now it's a bargain. The missile hit the F-16's left wing. The plane exploded in a white and red maelstrom of flame. He felt a grim satisfaction as he watched the momentum of its supersonic speed carrying the flaming wreckage over the border and into Belgian territory.

CHAPTER TEN

The Me.262 burst through the top of the cloud cover like a breaching whale. Hans Ackermann pulled the throttle back slowly, leveled out and scanned the heavens about him. This was the first time in half of his lifetime that he felt truly alive. All the glory and excitement of being one of the Luftwaffe's elite jet fighter pilots came rushing back into his life. He was like a young man again. His movements were quick and positive. His airplane was smooth and fast. He felt as he had long ago. He was invincible.

"While the stupid Americans are flying north-ward, Mein Fuehrer," Ackermann said to the bones in the rear compartment, "we will fly west, passing south of the Ardennes Plateau. We will drop down below the clouds near a town that I know of called Mezieres. We will be only one-hundred-forty kilometers from the coast."

Ackermann knew this route well. He had flown it many times as a young man. He would fly along the southern border of Belgium and France, just as the Americans were doing along the northern border between Belgium and The Netherlands. Their courses would bring them both to the coastline a mere 70 kilometers apart.

"I must first deal with the Americans, then we will rendezvous with the Dornier flying boat." He thought better of making such a bold decision alone and hastily added, "of course, if that is to your liking, Mein Fuehrer." He once again took the silence behind him for Hitler's approval.

"It is an unexpected opportunity, Mein Fuehrer. In the last weeks of our beloved Third Reich, an American plane of the Golden Scimitar Squadron, in a cowardly maneuver, damaged my aircraft. I was nearly out of petrol, almost gliding back to Sangerhausen. I was unable to engage the swine. The American attacked me from behind, then ran." Ackermann shifted his position in the seat, checked the compass and engine instruments and wiped the sweat from his face and back of his neck. "I know it is this Major Dessault who is responsible, and I must avenge that cowardly act." Remembering his last flight in the Me.262 caused icy perspiration to erupt from his every pore. His hands shook on the controls. He envisioned the American's bullets tearing through the fragile skin of his airplane. Then the fire, the horrible fire. He trembled violently. His tremors shook the entire airplane through his tightly clenched fists on the control horn. He wanted to scream out in his agony, but he choked down his misery. There was another way to vent his terror.

He had ensured that the 20mm cannons on the plane that Major Dessault would fly were armed and ready. He was proud of the clever way he had switched planes with the American. He had to be the one to fly this plane, the one with The Fuehrer and Eva Braun. But he feared that the old ammunition would be bad, or so volatile that it would all explode at once. He must find out.

Ackermann flipped up the safety cover on the cannon trigger under his right forefinger. With the cover out of the way, he was able to squeeze off a burst of fire. One, then another longer, and another, even longer. He roared like a pathetic tiger, guttural sounds and spittle bursting from his deformed mouth. It excited him to feel the airplane jerk spasmodically and see gray cannon smoke billow up over the plane's nose. Tracer shells streaked away from the fighter, insuring that indeed, the deadly 20 MM cannon were operable. The firing of the guns thrilled him just as would a sexual release. And now it was over. Now he was spent. He let up on the trigger and slowly dabbed the sweat from his face. He knew now that he and the Messerschmitt were ready.

Calmed, Ackermann wiped the spittle from the windshield and peered through the smeared glass, getting the plane back on a straight and steady course. His eyes scanned the billowing cloud formation ahead and below. He was looking for a particular and peculiar mountain top that jutted above the overcast, a landmark formation that indicated that he had reached the tiny village of Mezieres. It was a mountain crest that reminded him of a Tyrollian hat, complete with the decorative boor's tail. Unmistakable. But he could see ahead for miles, and it was not there. *Am I mistaken? Have I forgotten?* he asked himself.

He checked his compass heading. Although he couldn't be wholly reliant on the accuracy of the ancient instrument, it was about all he had. That, and his memory. He was sure he had been airborne long enough to be very near Mezieres, but his old reliable landmark, the hat-like peak, was missing.

Ackermann noted that the sun was directly behind him. He was most certainly on a westerly heading, as he should be. But where, how far along this route? His watch told him he should be near his only landmark, so he must drop below the clouds and visually determine where he is. If the cloud layer was thick enough to hide the Tyrollian hat mountain, he had a chance of diving down through the mist and blindly flying right into the side of it. He would see it only an instant before the crash, much too short of a time to make any sort of evasive maneuver. But he had no choice, he must determine where he was.

Ackermann shifted his weight, scooting forward in the seat so as to see better through the small forward windshield glass. He took one last wipe at the sweat that formed on his forehead and ran cruelly down into his eyes. He leveled up the plane's wings, pulled back the twin throttles slowly, carefully, and allowed the nose to drop below the far-off horizon.

The Me.262 plummeted into the gray haze of the clouds. Ackermann held the stick and rudder pedals steady, watching the altimeter's black needles spin down. He was a "seat-of-the-pants" pilot who rarely flew entirely on instruments. He had always had a natural feel for the airplane and for its relationship to the horizon. But time had stripped him of that talent.   Ackermann   was   unaware   that   the Messerschmitt had continued its dive beyond a mere descent. It was now approaching the vertical, the tail of the plane sweeping a broad arc over the top, giving Ackermann the sensation of his own weight pressing into the seat with one force of gravity. One G. It was the same feeling as normal, straight and level flight, but it was unsettling his stomach, and he began to feel the first effects of vertigo and airsickness.

The plane continued in its falling loop. Now totally upside down, it was in an inverted flat spin. It broke through the ceiling and into a gray, misty sky, directly over the village of Mezieres.

Ackermann was horrified to find himself upside down, virtually out of control, falling leaflike toward the ground. It took a full 10-seconds for him to realize his situation. In that short burst of time, the plane was 600 meters closer to smashing into the hard, cold earth.

The plane was upside down, rotating to the right. If Ackermann had even been taught how to recover the airplane from such an awkward attitude, he couldn't remember the lesson. But he had to do something now, by the book or not. He smashed down hard on the left rudder pedal, shoved the control horn forward with all his strength and carefully advanced the right engine to full power. The Me.262 stopped its rotation and the nose obediently rose. Ackermann gave it full left stick. Suddenly, the plane swiveled around. Ackermann saw the sky flash by, then the windshield was filled with the little town of Mezieres. He quickly pulled the throttle back and neutralized the controls. The plane went into a controllable dive, right side up, but with less than 800 meters of altitude.

Ackermann carefully eased the control horn back into his stomach and the responsive fighter began to pull out of the dive. It roared over the village, less than 30 meters above the town's church steeple.

He was too weak to do anything more than to hang onto the control horn, guiding the jet into a slow ascent. He slumped in the seat, drenched with chilling sweat. His heart beat so hard it rocked his entire body. His head ached and his vision was blurred. He vomited into his lap and coughed violently, spattering the instrument panel and windshield with bloody bile. From the way he felt, he suddenly faced the grim proposition that he was dying.

Bridgett's Me.262 was performing perfectly. She was thoroughly enjoying the flight in the old plane. It was smooth and powerful, without all of the modern, complicated equipment. She was reminded of her Father's 1933 MG sports car. She loved driving that old roadster and she was beginning to love this old airplane. If there was one thing in need of improvement, it would be the seat. It was not as form-fitting and as well padded as the modern jets. She had to shift her position occasionally to remain comfortable. And the sounds in the cockpit were vastly different than those she was used to. In the modern jet fighters there was a constant buzzing, humming, and clicking, the sounds of electronics and automatic controls. In time, and with the help of the thickly padded flight helmets, one soon became unaware of those sounds. But in the Messerschmitt, the sounds were louder; a whistling of wind over the canopy and the throbbing of the twin jet engines; a pulsing, low moan that, she supposed, could very quickly lull you to sleep.   Perhaps, thought Bridgett, the German engineers designed the seat to be uncomfortable in an effort to keep their pilots awake.

She looked over to the other Me.262, just slightly behind her. Austingrove saw her looking and gave a thumbs up. She noticed too that the Belgian Air Force Mirage was about 400 meters off, escorting them out of their territory. It had been gone for some time, then had returned. The other three were nowhere to be seen.

Sensing that something had suddenly changed, Bridgett checked ahead.

The billowing white clouds were gone, replaced by an expanse of emerald blue sea. Lighter and darker tones made bold sweeps of color over the surface. The sunlight was reflected up at them in shimmering sparks of brightness. They had reached the Straits of Dover.

Bridgett looked back to Austingrove, waving and pointing ahead to attract his attention. He acknowledged her excitement with a nod and a condescending smile. She watched as the Belgian Mirage pulled ahead, waggled its wings, then pealed off in a graceful turn. She noticed that one of the Sidewinder missiles was not in its place under the right wing.

But it was time to start thinking about the landing at Roughscuff Field. They would have to fly by the control tower and watch for the controller's green spotlight signal. That would be their permission to land. Tennison Barquelay will have briefed the controllers and everything should be ready for their arrival. Each would lower their flaps and gear on the downwind leg and the other would give the landing gear a visual check to be sure they were down and securely locked.

Bridgett was feeling an excitement she had not experienced since she and the Me.262 lifted off the grass in Germany. She had established a rapport with this old airplane. She felt a familiarity, a compatibility that she had previously experienced only in the little de Havilland Tiger Moth trainer and the American T-33 jet trainer. Every other plane she had flown had been without that mystique. She attributed that feeling to the airplane having the personality. She knew that without that rare and mysterious bond between a frail human and the inanimate flying machine, flying was merely a mechanical function, with little enjoyment and limited satisfaction.

Flying was always fun for Bridgett and she yearned to feel the agile and responsive German fighter perform. Now, with the end of the flight approaching, she wanted to get the most out of the last few minutes she had with this plane.

She scanned the engine instruments, tugged her seat belt and shoulder harness tighter, pulled back the throttles and shoved the control horn forward. The Messerschmitt fell forward, gathering speed as it dove. She felt light in the seat, as if she was merely falling through space along with the plane. It gave her a delightful light-headedness. The view forward was a solid expanse of blue sea dappled with flashing whitecaps. Bridgett pressed the control to the right and the plane rotated one hundred eighty degrees. She pulled back on the control, eased the throttles forward until the tachometers registered seventy percent power and pulled up in a graceful sweeping loop. The lightness became a steady downward pressure more than three times her weight as gravity forces tried to compress her into the thin seat cushion. At the top of the loop, she rolled the plane to the left. No longer inverted, she completed the Immelmann maneuver every bit as smoothly as would Herr Immelmann himself. She heard a whoop of delight an instant before realizing that the joyful yell had come from her.

She saw Austingrove and Dessault in the other Me.262 holding a steady altitude and course, now about two kilometers away. She dropped into a shallow dive, picking up speed and thinking, *Don't you ever have any fun, Scotty?*

Hans Ackermann passed over the seaside village of De Panne and turned northward. He would intercept the others shortly. They would be on a westerly course, heading for the mouth of the River Thames, just a few miles from Roughscuff Field. He was feeling better now that he'd had time to calm down.

Coughing up blood had worried him, then he reasoned, *I'm an old man. It is likely that I have many things wrong with me. Perhaps the blood is of no im-*

portance. But he was not truly comforted by that thought. It would be ironic that the years he spent living in the dampness and dust of the underground lair, the haven that had protected him, would be the eventual cause of his death.

Ackermann was unaware that the others had been flying above a heavy overcast and when they reached the straights of Dover, they would be at a greater altitude than they, or he, had planned.

He was straining to see the sky ahead of him. Even with the spittle and blood wiped from the windshield his old eyes could barely make out the horizon.

He would not have seen the two Me.262's if Bridgett had not given into her urge for some aerobatics. He saw the plane swoop down, roll and curl upward.

Ackermann watched the Me.262 climb back up to altitude. Then he saw the other fighter, some distance off, headed for England. He thought that the looping plane looked like the single-seater, the one that he still believed to be flown by Major Dessault. It was he who was his prey. It was the Major who bragged about flying over Germany in - what did he call them - *Jugs?* He was now only moments away from avenging what that man did to him.

He eased the twin throttles slowly up to 95 percent power. Unlike modern jet engines, Ackermann had to adjust the mixture controls to reach and maintain the proper exhaust temperature. Too cool and he'd risk a flameout when maneuvering. Too high of a temperature would damage the engine, even to the point of causing an explosion.

He pulled the nose up and the plane responded with instant agility. The G forces pressed Ackermann back into the seat. He saw his vision blur, felt his heart begin to pound like a thousand marching troops. He tried to raise his head forward to keep the other plane in sight, but he didn't have the strength. He relaxed and watched the altimeter spin. He would simply estimate the amount of time it would take to be above and behind the Major.

Ackermann leveled out at 3,000 meters. He could see the lowlands, canals, bays, and harbors of The Netherlands below his right wing, and in the distance, the fog shrouded British Isles lay low on the horizon off his left wingtip. He had not seen Great Britain since he escorted a flight of Junkers bombers in 1942. He had shot down three Hawker Hurricane fighters in just a few frantic minutes of aerial combat.

He rolled the Me.262 up on its left wing and saw the Major's plane below and ahead of him. He pulled his goggles down to shield his eyes and shoved the control forward.

Bridgett was content to follow along a bit more than a kilometer behind and some 500 meters above Austingrove and Dessault. It pleased her that they would now have to strain around and look back over their shoulders to see her. She felt that she had been herded along on this flight, watched constantly, except for her recon trip below the clouds. She was independent enough for that to bother her. *But then, it is after all, their airplane,* she reasoned. She smiled as she recalled how she had faked radio failure. Being watched was one thing, but having to constantly report-in was entirely too much for her to bear.

This was when she really loved flying. Alone, high above the earth, the sun warming her through the shiny plexiglas canopy, with the drone of fine engines audibly caressing her, was her element. This is what she lived for.

A rattling, clattering sound snapped her head around. She saw pieces of aluminum bursting from the right wing. The plane shook as a succession of explosions sent torn aircraft skin peeling off and blown aft in the slipstream.

Bridgett thought that the starboard engine had exploded. She quickly scanned the instruments, finding all indications within acceptable limits. Just then Ackermann's Me.262 streaked by her right wing, so close that she could see the smoke still streaming from the cannons. He rolled right, pulling up to position himself for another attack.

Bridgett knew it was Ackermann. Austingrove and the third Messerschmitt was still in her view ahead.

She snatched up the microphone, "Scott, I'm under attack by Ackermann," she said, "he's shot up my right wing and I'm sure he's going to be heading back for another run at me."

There was no answer. Austingrove had turned off all of the communications equipment thinking that it was inoperative.

"Scott, you bastard," she screamed, "answer me!"

She glanced behind her and saw the German fighter rolling down out of the cloudless sky, the sun right behind it, blinding her.

"Well, blast you, dammit," she said, "You'd do bloody well not to mess about with this RAF-trained little girl!"

She snapped the Messerschmitt into a tight roll to the left. The moment the plane was inverted, she pulled back on the control horn and saw the sky replaced by the dark blue sea, she reversed the controls and the plane rolled back to the right. She sucked it up into a climb, ending up with Ackermann's plane above and squarely in her gun sight.

She watched the right wing the entire time, fully expecting it to fold up from the damage and send her spinning into the channel below.

Bridgett had no idea if the guns in her plane were armed. *Ackermann's obviously are*, she thought. She flipped up the trigger guard and gave the red lever a quick squeeze. The Me.262 vibrated with the release of two cannon shells. She saw one tracer in the pair scribe an ineffective arc behind Ackermann's plane.

"The next won't be just for effect, Mate," she said aloud.

Ackermann was not satisfied with his first pass.

He waited too long to fire, underestimating the speed of his fighter. He should have begun his firing as soon as the other plane was well in his sights. No waiting next time, Major.

He pulled the Me.262 around in a tight turn to the left, the G forces smashing him into the seat, again blurring his vision. He straightened-out sooner than he wished to. The pressure was simply too much for his aged frame to endure.

Bridgett had expected him to continue around, take advantage of her lower airspeed, and again be in an attack position behind her. His sudden change of direction put him directly in front of her. She slammed the control to the right, her snap roll avoiding an air-to-air collision by mere few meters.

Ackermann watched the fighter streak by. He saw the pink RAF helmet and the pilot's hair pinched out around the back of it. He realized it was not Major Dessault. It was the girl, Bridgett Barquelay, that had taken off in his plane. He was stunned. He had no desire to kill that young girl, he wanted the arrogant swine that was suppose to be flying that plane.

Ackermann pounded his fist on the side console. "This is not right!" he shouted aloud. "It is not him! It is not fair!"

Tears blurred his vision and his vengeance became defeat. Now he only wanted to show her that it was all a mistake. He would level out, slow, and lower his landing gear, the international sign of surrender. He pulled the throttles back and watched the airspeed indicator drop to 400 kilometers per hour. He pressed the landing gear down button and felt the main gear start to rumble down out of their wells. The nose gear popped out next, making the Me.262 nose upward. Ackermann held it down with forward stick and leveled it up.

Bridgett pushed her plane to its limit in an effort to catch Austingrove in the number two plane. He was now almost four kilometers away.

Ackermann expected the other plane to setup for another pass. But he was astonished to find the sky empty. Had he sent it into the sea with his first feeble burst? He doubted that, but where was it? He twisted around in the seat, seeking the answers. Then he saw the single-seat Messerschmitt diving away, heading back toward the other.

Ackermann raised the landing gear. He brought the plane up to 450 Km/Hr and climbed up 4,000 meters. He must have time to think, a moment to reassess his situation.

Dessault alerted Austingrove to Bridgett's dog fight with the other Me.262. "It's that crazy kraut bastard," he said.

Austingrove turned the fighter back and pushed the engines up to their maximum 8700 r.p.m. He saw Bridgett's plane diving down toward him, but with no one in pursuit.

"My God," he said, "Ackermann must have armed his guns. I wonder if he did the other plane's."

"Christ," said Dessault, "I'll bet he did. He thinks I'm the one who shot him down back in forty-four and probably thinks I'm flying that other plane. Try our guns, Scott."

Austingrove flipped up the trigger guard, checked ahead, and gave the trigger switch a quick jab. Nothing happened. He squeezed it again, then again and held it. "Nothing, Major," he said, "they're inoperative."

Bridgett's fighter leveled out and she expertly worked it over to Austingrove. She was frantically pointing to the throat microphone each wore. Austingrove went to the radio panel, switched to the tactical channel they were using when her radio quit. Immediately Bridgett's voice scratched out of his headset. "Scotty, Ackermann's up there. The bloody bastard tried to flame me!"

"Bridgett," said Austingrove. "has your radio been turned off?"

"Booger the bloody radio, Scotty, we've got to do something about Ackermann. He's mad."

"Bridgett, drop down to a few hundred feet above the water and run for Roughscuff." said Austingrove. "I'll hold just above you. He won't be able to get a clean pass at you that way. Get going."

"Crap off on that, Yank!" Bridgett sounded angry. "I damn well won't sit there and let him blow you away to get at me!"

"Bridgett," said Austingrove, "We think that he's after Dessault. He believes that somehow by shooting the Major down, he will avenge his defeat in World War Two. He's planned this from the very start, that's why he had to get into the Major's plane. He thinks Dessault is flying your plane."

Austingrove swung the Me.262 up and over Bridgett's. "Get on down there and let me cover you."

From the back seat, "How the hell do you think you're going to cover her when our guns are dead?" said Dessault.

"I don't think Ackermann is sharp enough to concentrate on Bridgett and get in a good shot if we keep him distracted. He'll get flustered." said Austingrove. "We'll just keep in his way, outmaneuvering him and dodging his shots."

"You're as damn crazy as Ackermann, Scott," said Dessault. "If he's trying to get me, he'll give up on Bridgett as soon as he realizes it's not me in that crate, then it'll be our ass."

Austingrove watched Bridgett as she nervously looked around, up and behind, searching for Ackermann. He knew Dessault and she were right. Ackermann would simply blast them out of the way to get to Bridgett, never realizing that Dessault is in this plane. He could only hope that Ackermann's guns would fail, he'd have plane trouble or perhaps finally realize that he doesn't really want to destroy these beautiful aircraft. *No, the man's crazy,* thought Austingrove, *he's not going to give up on trying to shoot the Major down.*

As if his thoughts were a cue, he saw Bridgett

stiffen, staring out over her right wing. Austingrove followed her gaze and spotted the speck coming at them fast and low. There was no question that it was Ackermann.

Ackermann made up his mind that he didn't want to shoot down the girl, but if he had to do that in order to get to the Major, he certainly would. Listening to the plane-to-plane communications angered him. *Mad? She thinks I am mad?*

He dove behind the other two Messerschmitts then turned to intercept them. He would make one pass from the side, where they had no defense, then circle upward and behind them for his second pass. The sun would then be behind him. He was confident. The same tactics had worked before, and surely, they would work for him again.

He saw the two ME.262s flying stacked, low over the sea. He could see that the two-place plane was attempting to cover the other. *How noble,* he thought. *How noble, Herr Austingrove, but how useless and stupid an attempt.*

Ackermann centered the top Me.262 in his gunsight. He wouldn't make the same mistake he'd made before, waiting too long to fire. When he had it squared in his gunsight, he swung the plane's nose just a degree to the right to lead the target. Ackermann pulled the trigger and felt the Me.262 shudder, smoke curled past the cockpit and he smelled the acrid aroma of the burned gun powder that seeped into the cockpit. Ackermann held his course, watching the tracer of every third cannon round burn a straight white path toward his target.

Austingrove calculated about when Ackermann would fire. A moment before, he radioed Bridgett, "Cut right, hard! And stick down on the water!" He saw the flashes at the nose of Ackermann's plane and the smoke blow back along both sides of the fuselage.

Bridgett banked right, dropping closer to the surface of the Channel. Austingrove pulled up and rolled right, hoping to come up between Ackermann and Bridgett. He was stunned to see the tracers flash by just below his right wing tip, and realized that Ackermann had him targeted, not Bridgett. He must know that Dessault is not the one flying the other Me.262. He rolled back to the left as Ackermann shot by, pulling up for another pass.

Austingrove slammed the stick to the right as Bridgett's Me.262 accelerated upward directly in front of him, in pursuit of Ackermann.

"Bridgett, Dammit. Break off! Break off!" Radioed Austingrove.

"Break off yourself, Scotty." Bridgett sounded excited, almost breathless. "This bastard is after you, not me, you know, and you've got no guns, have you? So bugger off, Yank."

"She's going to do as she damn well pleases," said Dessault. "That's one crazy woman."

The   Me.262   fighters   that   Bridgett   and

Ackermann flew were lighter and faster than the two-place model which Austingrove and Dessault were flying. They pulled away from the two-seater, climbing into the sun. Ackermann would not know that Bridgett was behind him and Austingrove prayed that she could get a good shot in before he discovered her there.

Bridgett had been at the top of her class at the Aerial Warfare Training Center at R.A.F. Station Leeming in North Yorkshire. She used that training now, hoping that she had learned well and forgotten nothing. She held the fighter slightly below the climbing Me.262, so that when Ackermann rolled over the top, she'd cut at the same instant, making her deficit in distance an immediate asset. She would end up close enough, but still out of his sight, for a clean, effective shot.

But Ackermann didn't simply level-out, instead he pulled the Me.262 up and over in a loop. Now he was looking straight out of the top of his canopy at the nose of Bridgett's fighter. He finished his loop at the top with a half roll, then smoothly pushed the Messerschmitt over into a dive.

Bridgett was not expecting these maneuvers and Ackermann's plane shot past her, accelerating to establish an offensive position. She rolled hard and fast to the left and saw Ackermann, his speed already greatly increased, pull up and cut to the right to be setup for a shot at her undersides. Bridgett cut the Jumo engines back to idle, quickly levered in 20 degrees of flaps and pulled the nose up. The Messerschmitt's speed dropped to 180 Km/Hr and the plane stalled.

Ackermann rolled out of his right turn and saw his target roll away from him, exposing its bare undersides to his cannon, a perfectly spaced 450 meters away. He mentally calculated how much he need to lead the fighter, and with a slight pressure on the right rudder pedal, the nose of his plane swung into position. Ackermann squeezed off six rounds from each of the four 30 millimeter cannon, confident that a clean kill was assured. But his target suddenly stopped as if tethered to a mountain. Ackermann was stunned. He spat out a string of curses and leveled up the planes attitude. That was the worst possible maneuver he could have made, but he was confused, suddenly tired, and for the first time in his life he felt defeat was at hand.

Then he was looking down the flaming cannon barrels of a Me.262. It was Bridgett. She was coming at him from the left, well out of the cone of his gunsight.

He saw flames erupt out of the 30 MM's snouts. He felt the impact of the rounds smash into the fuselage just behind his seat. He felt the explosion as the side of the plane was blown open and he screamed his birdlike shriek as his seat was torn from beneath him. He was hurled upward and forward, smashing through the canopy. Ackermann's right leg, permanently bent, was jammed between the windshield frame and the jagged edge of the broken canopy. He was catapulted out of the cockpit, his torso slamming again and again against the side of the plane. An agonizing death came as his body flailed in the slipstream of the falling Messerschmitt.

CHAPTER ELEVEN

Bridgett didn't see the cannon shells streak from the nose of her plane. Their course was momentarily obscured by plumes of gray smoke that curled over the nose, engulfed the canopy, to finally be swept behind. But she saw them tear into Ackermann's plane. She saw the aft fuel tank explode and the sky ahead of her fill with flames and shredded remains of the Messerschmitt fighter. She jerked the control hard to the left, but was too late to avoid the debris she was hurling into. An incredible rattling and banging shook the plane and the starboard engine began a deep rumbling roar. It was about to flame out and Bridgett could only hope that it didn't explode from all the metal it was ingesting.

The staccato throbbing of the twin engines in synchronization abruptly ended as the starboard engine's roar was silenced. The plane rolled to the right and shuddered. Bridgett pulled the right-hand engine's throttle back, shut off the fuel pump and generator and turned the fuel selector handle to the port engine. With the right engine dead, she had to push the left engine's output up to 100% just to keep the Me.262 in flight. She cranked-in some rudder trim. This allowed her to relax the pressure she held on the left rudder pedal since the moment the engine flamed-out.

But she knew that at full power, the Junkers Jumo jet engine would last but a few minutes. She remembered how the German flight manual flatly stated that one should "...land as soon as possible as operating engine will not hold up long at full throttle operation" and she was on one engine, somewhere over the dark, cold waters of the Straits of Dover.

Scott Austingrove pounded on the instrument panel in frustration as he attempted to force the plane climb faster to assist Bridgett. He wasn't exactly sure what he could do, but he knew that he had to try. Then he saw Bridgett stall, roll and fire into Ackermann's plane. He and Dessault watched in grim horror as Ackermann was savagely thrown from the cockpit and beat to death in the Messerschmitt's death plunge into the sea. He prayed that Bridgett had not seen Ackermann's gristly end.

"Bridgett's lost an engine, Scott," said Dessault. A thin trail of white smoke coursed aft from the right side of the Me.262.

"Damn," said Austingrove. He smashed down on the mic button, "Bridgett! Bridgett! Close the throttle, cut-off the fuel and the fuel selector!"

A static-filled reply came immediately, "Got it, Scotty. I'm OK. I've got FOD (Foreign Object Damage) on number two."

"Don't worry about that girl," said Dessault. "She knows what she's doing."

The two Messerschmitts turned back toward the English coastline at 400 Km/Hr. The aerial combat maneuvering had cost them some precious fuel and Austingrove quickly calculated that they would be some three to five minutes short if the German fighter's fuel gauges possessed any degree of accuracy.

Austingrove reduced power and fell in alongside the crippled plane. Bridgett gave him a long look through the canopy as if silently asking for help, yet knowing there was nothing he or anyone else could do. Getting to Roughscuff Field would simply be a matter of luck. He gave her a "thumbs up" and looked back through the windshield toward the British coastline.

"Scott," said Dessault. "You might try pulling back your RPM to seven-thousand and easing out four or five degrees of flaps. You'll increase the lift of the wing and the nose should drop just a tad. That should extend your range a bit."

"Been reading up on the flight manual, Major?"

"Damn right," said Dessault.

Austingrove looked out to the left outboard flap where the degree indicators were painted. He pressed the Flap Down button next to the landing gear controls on the left side of the panel.

"Five degrees, Major," he reported. Then he eased the throttles back to 7000 revolutions per minute. It seemed that the plane was going to nose over into a dive, but it stopped short, and the airspeed stayed at 400 Km/Hr.

"What about Bridgett, being on one engine?" Austingrove asked.

"She can lever in about four or five degrees flaps, but she'll have to keep her RPM up." said Dessault. "Have her try it."

Austingrove radioed the suggestion to Bridgett. She carefully nudged the flaps out five degrees. She left the throttle alone and felt the plane pick up speed. "That worked, Scotty, I think I can pull a little power off the port engine to try to save it, OK?"

Austingrove saw her plane pull slightly ahead as the speed increased. "Give it a shot, but be ready to ease on more power if the plane acts like it's going to stall."

"Rog." She said. *That's exactly why I turned off the bloody radio, Scotty, I don't need constant direction, you know!*

The planes fell in line just as Austingrove saw the low rolling hills emerging from a cover of low clouds and fog. Soon the cliffs of Dover and entrance to the River Thames was visible. Once over Ramsgate near the north point, it would be a mere ten minutes to Roughscuff Field.

Bridgett's one remaining engine began to lose power as the strain of maintaining flight overheated the powerplant. She was unable to add power as the Exhaust Gas Temperature gauge crept up to the 700 degree centigrade mark - the absolute maximum. She was slowly losing altitude.

"Scotty, I think my engine is about to make pudding of itself."

Austingrove shut his eyes, straining to come up with some sort of answer for her. "Major, got any good ideas?"

Dessault shook his head. "Sorry, Scott. Just tell her to try to hold on to as much altitude as she can. And she'd better not drop her gear or flaps, that will put her into the ground straightaway."

Austingrove keyed the mic. "Look, try to keep it hung up here as best you can. We're going to come right up the mouth of the Thames, turn right and take them straight into Roughscuff. You should almost be able to glide to whole way."

He didn't believe that, and knew that she wouldn't believe it either.

"Scotty, I'm going to set her down with the gear-up and just five degrees flaps." She sounded calm, professional.

"Roger, *Deuce.*"

There would be no more talk, their every thought and movement must be dedicated to bringing the two planes to a safe landing. Austingrove pulled the nose up slightly, dropping off some airspeed. Bridgett pulled ahead. He leveled out behind and slightly above her right wing and dead starboard engine. In this position he could keep his eye on her progress without being in view to distract her.

The planes entered the mouth of the great river. Bridgett gradually dropped down to 650 meters. The valley beyond Ramsgate would give her a slight bit more height above the ground. She made her right turn, losing more precious altitude and swept over the town at a mere 400 meters.

A distant tree line suddenly disappeared as the fighter swept down into the valley. A low-lying fog that wasn't visible from above as the sun shone through it, suddenly became a gray curtain in front of her. As the plane entered the mist, the view ahead was blanked out. Bridgett calculated that she would clear the first stand of trees, but beyond that it would be a gamble, the odds based on her luck and her reaction time as obstacles came into view.

She saw the vague shadowed form of tree tops ahead. She realized that she would not clear them after all. She pushed the left engine's throttle forward to its maximum. The overworked engine came up to 8,900 RPM, far above the dangerous limit. The plane responded, accelerating up and over, a mere meter above the treetops. Then the engine made one last anguished roar, flamed out, and began to shake as its insides came apart.

Bridgett cut off the fuel switch, closed the selector valve and then flipped up the stop so that the throttle was able to be pulled back to the stop position alongside the other one. She leaned forward, straining to see ahead. The plane glided over another row of trees and the light gray cement of a runway with its black stipes of tire marks filled her windshield. She was crossing its width without the power or altitude to turn onto it.

She eased back on the stick. The nose came up and the Me.262 settled into the soft grass, its tail just missing the concrete. The jolt was amazingly soft. The plane was sliding on the damp grass, its smooth underside working like a child's sled. She saw the trees bordering the north side of Roughscuff Field ahead and pushed hard on the left rudder pedal. The fighter slued sideways. She jammed the right pedal down and the disabled Messerschmitt rocketed through the tree line between the only two trees that would accommodate its wingspan.

A stone wall, green with moss from more than a hundred years of damp English weather lie ahead. Bridgett knew that to hit the wall at the speed it was skidding on the slick grass would destroy the ship.

The hydraulic pump supplying pressure for operating the landing gear was located on the left engine. With that engine not running, there was no hydraulic pressure to operate the landing gear. But the German designers had provided for such an emergency by equipping the Me.262 with an air supply tank for just such an eventuality.

Remembering that, Bridgett actuated the emergency landing gear switch. She heard the rumble as the landing gear doors began to open. The leading edges of the frail doors dug into the ground and pealed upward, scooping great quantities of English soil into the wheelwells. The plow-like effect rapidly slowed the Messerschmitt. It finally came to a stop, punching its pointed nose into the mossy wall at barely walking speed.

Bridgett quickly unlatched her shoulder harness, released the canopy latch and stumbled out onto the wing. The time in the seat made her legs almost unworkable. She stumbled and fell to the ground, thankful to be home in one piece.

Austingrove watched in horror as wisps of fog gradually enveloped Bridgett's plane. The valley was a basin of mist, the plague of all pilots; the English fog. The Messerschmitt disappeared. Austingrove pulled up, advancing the throttles. He must find Roughscuff and lead Bridgett to it if possible. Knowing that he was clear of the other plane, he dropped down, straining to see some sort of landmark through the grayness. "Major, keep a lookout for a landmark, OK?"

"Yeah, Scott, I am. But it's damn soupy down there," said Dessault, Then, "Wait! There's a break. I can see some trees and a road!"

Austingrove recognized the road to Ipswitch as the fog seemed to dissipate along its route. Roughscuff was just north of the road. They should be very near to it.

A red and white checkerboard pattern suddenly formed from nowhere and filled the windshield. Austingrove jammed the stick to the left and smashed down on the left rudder pedal just in time to send the Me.262 screaming past the Roughscuff control tower.'The panic maneuver put the fighter right in line with the runway. Austingrove slammed his finger onto the landing gear down button and heard the rumbling of its mechanism. The plane nosed up as the nose gear slid out of its wheelwell. Austingrove cut the power and the Messerschmitt slammed down on the Asphalt runway, its ancient tires howling in protest. It bounced twice and then stuck. Austingrove pressed down hard on the tips of the rudder pedals to actuate the brakes. The plane came to a lurching stop at the extreme end of the strip.

As the engines stabilized, Austingrove switched off the left fuel pump, and closed its selector valve. He lifted the safety latch from its detent and retarded the throttle. The left engine whined downed to silence. As the same procedure stopped the right engine, only the ringing in the ears of the airmen was left.

"Damn nice bunch of landings, Scott," said Dessault. He was busy unlatching seat and shoulder harnesses.

Austingrove released the canopy latch and swung it up. He stood in the cockpit and scanned the field. There was no sign of Bridgett's plane.

Half a dozen emergency and service vehicles came screaming up the runway with warbling sirens and flashing colored lights. The first truck pulled up. Four men in chemical suits leaped out and ran to the plane. "Out! Out!" the first one commanded. Austingrove and Dessault climbed down from the plane.

"Have you seen another Messerschmitt?" called Austingrove. As usual, after flying, he was practically deaf, the loud whine of the jet engines still ringing in his ears.

"No, Sir," said the first man, "but we heard another jet just after you buzzed the tower."

"Wait, I didn't *buzz the tower...*"

Dessault stepped in front of Austingrove. "I think this man needs to be reprimanded for his reckless flying, and I hope you'll see to it." He turned to Austingrove, grinning. "You should be ashamed..."

"Up yours...Sir!" whispered Austingrove.

A Range Rover pulled up and a man in mechanic's coveralls leapt out and ran to the men. "Got a report that one of your Mates went in just beyond the tree line, over there." The man pointed to the north. "Where's the third ship, Sir? We were told there would be three coming in."

"Lost one on the way," said Dessault. "Let's go!"

The driver drove the Rover like a mad man, bouncing across the strip, sliding wildly on the damp grass, toward the trees at the edge of the field. "Look!" he yelled, startling the fliers.

At the edge of the line of trees, a small figure walked dejectedly, dragging a pink helmet alongside. Bridgett was heading for the main field's buildings.

"Yahoo!" yelled Austingrove. "She's OK!"

The Range Rover pulled alongside Bridgett. Austingrove and Dessault jumped out and ran to her. She stopped, dropping her helmet, and raised her arms in a questioning gesture. "Where have you Yanks been?" She grunted as Dessault grabbed her in a full body hug, lifted her from the ground and swung her in a wide circle.

"Where's your damn old airplane, Bloke?" Austingrove smiled.

"Oh," she said as Dessault let her down. "I made my own little landing field just on the other side of those trees. I have to share it with a bloody cow!"

They walked to a space between two trees that framed a trio of ruts. The furrows started just at the edge of the runway. Through the trees they saw the Me.262 sitting with its nose crumpled against the stone wall.

"Hell of a job, Bridgett," said Austingrove.

*   *   *

The English dawn was cooled by a thick layer of coastal fog that dimmed vision, but amplified sounds. Occasional laughter or a yelled request echoed across the air field from the opened doors of the Barquelay Aviation hangar.

Hazy morning sunlight reflected off the polished floor of the facility, radiating soft beams of light upon the highly arched ceiling. Men in blue coveralls with "Barquelay Aviation" imprinted across the back and a stylized "BA" on the left breast were already at work disassembling the two German fighter planes.

The B-2a model was in the rear of the hangar, with Bridgett's damaged fighter still hanging from a mobile crane's straps at the front. The nose and cab of the crane protruded out of the hangar so that they would have to remain open, putting a chill inside the building.

Scott Austingrove walked to the hangar from the crew facility barracks. He slept at the airfield, falling into bed at 7 P.M., and not getting up until after 8 A.M. A light breakfast that included a great urn of coffee was ready for him.

Cody Gordon had flown in on Barquelay's plane from Germany, the starting engine still with him. They ate breakfast and now they were ready for the job of carefully taking their treasures apart for shipping.

Three huge shipping containers, each over 12 meters long and with a volume of more than 67 cubic meters each, were placed in a row, side by side under the hangar's overhead crane. Two of the big steel shipping boxes would hold the two fuselage assemblies and all four of the engines, while the third would accommodate the four wings, nose cones and horizontal stabilizer assemblies. When filled with the carefully padded and protected aircraft parts, they would be tightly sealed and locked. The three containers would be lifted back onto truck beds to be transported to the London docks.

Each of the BA crew were experts, fully trained in aircraft maintenance and service. Some had even built small aircraft in a hangar provided by Barquelay for employee projects and hobbies. But even with that, the Americans wanted to be involved in the process. After all, they would have to reassemble, and later, fly the ships once they were back at the Dessault Flying Museum in California.

Gordon began work on a journal of notes and drawings of each section of airframe as it was separated from the whole. The crew started on the two-place night fighter while others were stripping the damaged wheelwell doors from the fighter. They would have to get the landing gear into the down position in order to remove the slings and move the crane from the doorway.

The bleat of a car's horn echoed through the structure. Major Dessault sat with a smiling Tennison Barquelay in a black Bentley at the hangar door.

"Mister Barquelay. Major," said Austingrove.

Dessault looked haggard. He was unshaven and still wearing the sweaty clothes from the flight. "After I left you last night, I flew to Munich and met Tennison," he said. "We picked up Gordon and flew back this morning. On the way back we took a good look at about where the Kraut went into the channel. The plane is someplace on the Foreland shoals, probably in pretty shallow water."

"Don't you think it's probably in a million pieces?" said Austingrove.

"I don't think so, Scott. I saw it hit the water. It was pretty much in a flat spin as it went in. It seemed to float a moment, and then sink. It may not be too horribly torn-up. And remember, Scott, its got a satchel full of loot in it."

Austingrove had written-off the plane, but if recovered, it would be of great value, even if not complete. They could use its parts and engines for the other aircraft, not to mention the booty.

"Tennison has arranged for us to take a workboat out to look for it," said Dessault, and turned to Gordon, "Scott and I are going to take a look for the crazy kraut's plane, I want you to stay here and see that this end of the project goes smoothly."

CHAPTER TWELVE

The harbor at Caldoon was protected from the North Sea by a block jetty that curved out from a northern point of land. It was primarily a fishing port, but some specialized workboats moored there because of its proximity to the larger commercial ports to the south.

Fog rolled off the cliffs surrounding the harbor like a wispy waterfall, then dispersed as if by magic. At sea, visibility was almost a mile, good for the time of year.

They boarded the 18 meter long *Expedient* in Caldoon Harbor at noon. *Expedient* was a well worn workboat, low in the water, the sides of her black steel hull were rippled with dents as evidence of her history of hard work. The wheelhouse stood a full 16 meters above the steel decks and shone brightly with a fresh coat of white paint. The superstructure stood out in stark contrast to the rest of the ship. Her name was painted in red block letters on both sides of the cabin. She sat with just one spring line to the dock, her diesel engines noisily pumping black smoke from two rusty dry stacks.

Captain Billingston Black, called "Black Bill" by his cronies along the Caldoon docks, was a native of the West Indies. He was an honest six foot four with bulging muscles straining at his clothes. His black, curly hair was cropped short, and he sported massive Muttonchops sideburns that waved like semaphore flags with every movement of his jaw. Black pulled the starboard engine out of gear and the boat eased its steady pull at the spring line. He slipped it from the dock's cleat and with hands the size of frying pans, he advanced the throttles and steered the ship away from the dock.

Dessault was intrigued by Captain Black. He had never met a black man who spoke very proper English with a very pronounced British accent. And Captain Black - Dessault couldn't bring himself to call him "Black Bill" - carried a typically British reserved demeanor, but could flash a huge, sincerely warm smile when amused. His two deckhands - one a skinny Scot with very bad teeth he called Andy, and the other a Vietnamese, Shin, who was constantly nodding and bowing to everyone - were given commands with respect, dignity and calm authority. Dessault instantly liked the man.

The workboat cleared the jetty, its bow nodding up and down in an easy swell. The twin engine's stacks belched out cloud of black smoke and a made a chugging, clanking noise that gave both Americans an uneasy feeling about the Diesel's dependability.

Captain Black ran the engines up to cruise speed and they quieted, smoothing out as if this was the speed they were meant to run. The boat lurched ahead as it picked up speed. The Captain dialed a heading into the ancient autopilot and engaged its clutch. The Wood-Freeman autopilot was of 1950s vintage, a corroded and dirty relic. But a lifetime at sea as deckhand, fisherman, tug operator, salvage skipper, and workboat owner had given the big black man the ability to keep even the oldest equipment operating smoothly.

Austingrove and Dessault were with him in the cramped wheelhouse. They bent over nautical charts of the Straits of Dover and the southeastern coast of England.

"We were flying at two-seven-zero degrees from about here; Knokke, Belgium, and passed just north of Margate, here," said Dessault, scribing lines on the chart. "I remember that this point of land," he poked the pencil at a prominent headland on the north side of the river's entrance, "was at about forty-five degrees off our right wing." He drew a line at 45° from the first line to the landmark. The two lines crossed at a point about 18 kilometers from land, just off the entrance of the River Thames.

Using a brass compass and a pencil, Dessault measured the distances from where the lines crossed to the lines of latitude and longitude. He transferred those measurements to the scales at the side and bottom of the chart. "Captain Black," he called, "I plot one degree, thirty-four point two minutes east, by fifty-one degrees, two minutes north."

Captain Black punched the numbers into the Satellite Navigation receiver. The SATNAV, a modern electronic navigation unit, was in stark contrast to most of the other equipment aboard the *Expedient*. The SATNAV almost immediately gave him the compass heading to the position, his boat's speed and the estimated time of arrival. He adjusted the boat's heading with the old autopilot and she obediently swung four degrees to port. "Very well, Major, we shall be there in two hours, twenty two minutes."

Austingrove rolled the chart and slid it into its slot in the chart rack above the plotting table. He joined Captain Black at the helm. Dessault found a stool alongside the table and sat looking out at the sea.

At the exact moment that Austingrove was wondering how the Captain planned to raise the airplane off of the bottom of the ocean, Captain Black began to tell them. His crew was below, attaching weights on the bottom of two large cargo nets. The nets would be dropped to the sea floor when the plane was located and dragged in a circular pattern, spread by the outboard-powered skiff carried aboard *Expedient*. Captain Black would hold the boat in position over the plane until each of the nets snagged the Messerschmitt. Then the crane would slowly raise the plane to the surface where cables would be added to the lift. Then it could be brought aboard.

It was hoped that the plane could be located using the huge recording fathometer mounted alongside the helm station. Intended for finding schools of fish, it burns an electronic picture of the bottom on a paper scroll as the boat moves along the surface. Anything as large as the Me.262 will show up as a mound on the flat seabed.

Their quiet thoughts were shattered some time later as a clattering noise arose from the aft deck. The two deckhands were taking the nets to the crane, the weights banging on the steel deck. They dropped the rope eyes of the nets over the crane's hook and spread them out.

Captain Black pulled the twin diesel engines back to an idle. Their ragged sound returned as the big boat's forward speed bled off to dead slow. "We are very near the coordinates you gave to me," said Black.

The two men watched the black and gray lines progress across the paper of the recorder. In the corner of the wheelhouse, Dessault slept.

The three hours of crossing a 10 kilometer grid time after time, produced no indication of anything as large as an airplane on the bottom. The steady drone of the engines and the motion of the boat lulled the men back into a drowsy watch, struggling to stay awake.

When a large target began its sweep across the chart, it was like an alarm clock going off. Captain Black punched a button on the SATNAV that would record the exact position and allow them to return to the same spot on the ocean floor repeatedly.

Shin went forward and released the safety chain and allowed the anchor to lower into the sea, pulling a large, rusted chain from a hawse pipe on the deck. Shin watched Captain Black and when Black nodded, Shin released the brake and forty fathoms of chain reeled overboard. At the Captain's nod, Shin braked the windlass. The boat was backed-down to set the anchor. With the boat stopped, the deck crew quickly launched the skiff. The motor started on the first pull and the Scotsman, Andy, idled around behind *Expedient,* waiting for the net to be lowered into the water. Shin went to the crane and began to raise the nets. The two men worked as if it was something they did routinely, without direction or comment from their captain.

The rattling gears of the huge cargo crane startled Dessault to wakefulness. "We find it?" he said.

"It is possible, Sir," said Black, moving quickly to a control station on the back deck. "There is something quite large just below us." He turned the bow directly into the swells and with the help of the boat hanging on the anchor, he manipulated the two shift levers, skillfully holding the big boat directly over the object.

Lines, one dangling from the rear of each net, were fitted with orange floats. They were allowed to drift on the surface as the nets disappeared beneath the water. Andy retrieved the first one and secured the line to the sampson post in the center of the skiff. He began to circle, dragging the net along behind the boat. The boat was suddenly jerked to a stop as the net snagged on the object below. Andy untied the line, letting it fall back into the water. He sped to the second orange buoy, secured it aboard and began the same procedure, but in the opposite direction. Half way through a full circle, the second net caught.

Shin began to ease pressure on the crane's cables. The lines tightened and began to vibrate as the load below started to be taken up. A great jerk vibrated the entire boat as the lines shook and the second orange buoy was yanked below the surface. "Bloody damn!" yelled Captain Black. "We lost one net, the load slipped out and took the tow line with it."

"What do we do now?" asked Dessault.

"We manipulate the one net we have control over and hope that we can release the snagged buoy," said Black.

The boat crew worked the crane, the skiff, and the position of *Expedient* in an effort to regain control of the second net. Two hours passed without progress.

"We can not free our net," said Black, "and we can not lift the plane with the one alone. I am afraid that we must dump our nets and return at a later time with more nets and try it again."

"How deep is it here?" asked Austingrove.

"It is shallow, only 32 fathoms."

"That's about a hundred and ninety feet," said Austingrove, "Do you have diving gear aboard?"

"Oh, yes," said Black. "We have complete SCUBA equipment. But none of us are divers."

"I am. A hundred-ninety feet is about twice as deep as I've ever gone, but I think I might be able to retrieve the line, or at least be sure of what we're snagged onto."

"Shin," said Black, "Prepare one set of diving gear. Bring a suit for Mister Austingrove, if you would, please." The man bowed and ran off. "You are sure of this?" he said to Austingrove.

Austingrove wasn't sure that he could free or reattach the net, but he was sure that he wanted to give it a try. His diving experience was strictly sport diving at the various Channel Islands of Southern California, and the thought of diving nearly 200 feet down intrigued him. He had never had a desire to go below 60 feet while sport diving. It seemed that there was little to see beyond about 10 fathoms. There would be plenty to see here at 32 fathoms. But he estimated that at that depth he would have less than 10 minutes time on the bottom to get the nets arranged. Longer than that would be dangerous.

The diving suit was an old-style dry suit.

Austingrove stepped into the opening at the front of the waist, crammed his arms into the sleeves and tugged the suit up over his shoulders. The old equipment smelled musty and he wondered how well it would keep the icy water out. The suit's wrists were tightly rolled and the opening in the front had to be closed, rolled and sealed with a rubber ring. A sheath was sewn into the outside of the right calf. A rusting, jagged-edged knife was held in the scabbard by an elastic loop. He took it out, felt the edge, and returned it to its place.

While Black kept the boat on station, Dessault helped Austingrove into the fins, a pair of old U.S. Divers Duck Feet, the weightbelt, and a single 72 cubic foot air tank. Shin brought up a bucket of seawater. Austingrove dipped the face mask into the water, shook it out and spit onto the inside of the glass. He rubbed it around on the glass and gave it a quick flush in the bucket. The saliva keeps the lens from fogging.

Austingrove fitted the mouthpiece and took a couple of deep breaths, He gave a thumbs up, pressed his mask to his face and fell over backward into the dark channel water.

Even with the dry suit, Austingrove felt the sudden chill of the water. The exposed parts of his face and his hands instantly became as cold as he had ever felt. He rolled face downward and waited for the bubbles to clear. He checked his breathing and began his descent into the blackness below.

The column of ropes disappeared into the depths. Austingrove put his hand on the nearest and used it to guide him down. It would also prevent the current from moving him away. He descended slowly, completely focused on the ropes, expecting to see the nets and the plane at any minute. At 5 fathoms the darkness was almost total, a gray glow from above providing just a few feet of vision.

He found it impossible to judge how fast he was pulling himself down the lines. He would be able to judge his ascent using the bubbles from his SCUBA tank's regulator, but there was no reference when going down with the bubbles streaming up behind. It seemed like a terribly long time until he suddenly came upon the top of the cargo nets. One net was stretched out to the right and the other hung slack, swinging in the current. He eased himself down that one.

Then he saw the Messerschmitt. It was right side up, hanging crookedly in only one of the nets, its left wing dug into the sandy bottom. The other net was prevented from enveloping the plane by the wing jabbed into the seafloor. The orange buoy had been jerked underwater as the plane slipped out of the net. Austingrove found the line, pulled it free from beneath the wing, sending a great cloud of silt billowing up around him and the plane. He released the buoy and rested, floating gently with his right arm and leg around the net.

As the silt settled and visibility returned, Austingrove gathered up an armful of the slack net and worked his way to the wingtip stuck into the sand. He had to move slowly to keep the silt settled, but it still rose like gray smoke as he stepped onto the bottom at the wingtip. Working in nearly total darkness, Austingrove grasped the wing at the aileron cutout and lifted. The wing slowly pulled up out of the sand. He felt it lose suction as the bottom released it. He quickly pulled the net around the end of the wing and worked it along the leading edge. He blindly pulled the net toward the fuselage until he collided with the engine nacelle. He stopped and rested. The plane had rolled back, the left wing again resting on the bottom, but this time it was in the netting.

The visibility improved with the settling of the silt, and Austingrove pulled the net as tightly as he could under and around the front of the number one engine nacelle.

He swam around the right side of the plane, inspecting the plane's position. The tail stuck out of both of the nets. He saw that the rear of the wings were snagged, and with the mass of weight forward, it looked to Austingrove as if it would balance when lifted off of the bottom. He had done as much as he could to secure the plane. He figured that he had just enough time to check for the bag of Nazi booty that was in the plane's cockpit.

He ducked under the tail assembly and started up the left side of the fuselage.

An impact from behind sent him hard against the side of the plane. He was pinned against the fuselage and began to roll along its side as something huge and strong moved toward the front. His tank banged against the aluminum, then he was rolled completely around. His mask was torn off and his head was banged hard. He was turned once again and he pushed out hard against the huge mass that was crushing him.

The unmistakable rasp-like hide of a very big shark tore his hands with razor-like slashes. There was no pain. The iciness of the water, the sharpness of the cuts and Austingrove's fear numbed any other sensations he may have had.

He opened his eyes and saw a black cloud of blood forming in the water in front of his face. The sinister side of a giant shark cruising alongside the downed airplane filled his vision. He was shoved and rolled the length of the fuselage like a wad of modeling clay being formed between a child's palms. Its tail slammed him into him one last time, sending him falling backward into an opening in the fuselage. The shark dodged the nets and disappeared into the dark expanse. The monster had not seen Austingrove or it surely would have taken him to be a seal and attacked.

Austingrove pulled himself up, bumping into something blocking the opening. He ducked under it and blindly felt along the wing for the face mask. Without the mask, his vision would be even more limited than it was. He frantically pawed along the wing on his hands and knees. He might not even see the shark coming back again without the diving mask.

He bumped something with his hand and it drifted toward the edge of the wing, *That might be the mask!* He dove for it, grasping blindly at the object. He felt the soft rubber and the hard glass and immediately calmed, he had found the mask. He pushed himself up from the edge of the wing, pulled the strap over his head and blew the mask clear of water. It took a minute for his eyes to recover from the stinging saltwater. He sat back against the side of the plane, waiting for the silt to settle and watching for the shark's return.

Then, as his eyes cleared and the silt was once again taken by the current, it became apparent that the object blocking the hole was the decapitated trunk of Hans Ackermann.

Austingrove eased closer. He saw that the side of the plane had been blown open by Bridgett's cannon fire. She had hit the rear fuselage fuel tank that sat directly behind the pilot. The side of the plane, the canopy and the pilot's seat were gone. It was this hole he had fallen backwards into. The canvas bag of loot was also gone.

Ackermann's ripped and torn bloody torso was suspended from the forward front corner of the cockpit, hung there by his unbending right leg. The sharks had ripped at his body until all that was left was an almost indistinguishable mass without head or arms. Austingrove realized that most of the blood he saw was Ackermann's, not his.

Austingrove pulled at Ackermann's boot, twisting the leg outward, then pushing down. He wanted Ackermann's body out of the plane. The man was dead, ripped to totally unrecognizable shreds. There was no reason, thought Austingrove, to take him back to the surface. There was no family, no one up there for this poor old man, and the horror of his condition would serve no other purpose but to repulse those still living. The body bobbed and swayed, sending bits of flesh and organs drifting free. More blood, as black as ink at that depth, darkened the water. The remains of Hans Ackermann finally came loose and slowly floated away between the nets, as if following the giant shark. Austingrove sat for a moment, silently honoring the old German fighter pilot.

He felt that he might vomit, but shook the scene from his mind and began his ascent from the ugliness of this place. At that moment his tank began to ring, alerting him to the fact that his main supply of air was running out. He reached to the side of the tank and pulled the reserve handle down. The ringing sound stopped. His time on the bottom was spent.

He knew that he would have to rise slowly, but had no decompression table to know exactly how long he should take to traverse the 32 fathoms. He had studied the Navy Standard Air Decompression Tables and remembered that being at 32 fathoms, or 190 feet for about fifteen minutes, should require him to take about fifteen minutes to surface. He had heard that in the early days of SCUBA diving, the old-timers would rise slower than the smallest bubbles from their breathing apparatus. He had no better gauge, so he watched his bubbles surge upward and kept a slower pace, staying below them. The threat of air embolism, "the bends," was a companion on every dive.

He wanted to look up to see if he could see the hull of the boat, but kept his eyes sweeping the sea around him just in case that huge shark, or another of its species, decided to return for another look.

As he inched up the ropes, the light from above gradually increased and his visibility improved. After 10 minutes, he felt it was finally safe to look up to see how far he had to go. He rolled onto his back and looked up at the bottom of the *Expedient*. He felt his stomach knot and a cotton-like bloating of his tongue as the first symptoms of nausea began. He'd felt on the verge of being ill since discovering Ackermann's shredded torso, and now the sight of the boat above him, a moving, twisting, undulating and deformed dark shape brought bile to his throat. He slued himself back to the vertical and grabbed onto the ropes and cables with both arms and legs.

Austingrove closed his eyes. He knew that deep dives could cause a medical condition called Nitrogen Narcosis - Some called it Rapture of the Deep. He had heard horror stories about divers hallucinating and in severe cases experiencing an intoxicated state of well-being. It is such a strong feeling of ecstasy that some so afflicted removed their diving gear while deep below the surface, imagining that they could breathe underwater without it. In most cases, they died.

His momentary panic subsided and he realized that only his vision of the boat was distorted. Everything else was normal. He opened his eyes and looked around him. He wasn't hallucinating, there was something happening to the boat.

Austingrove ventured another look. There it was, that dark waving form, above him. He squinted through the half-light, trying to grasp what he was seeing. Then, as it came into focus, it became apparent that the black form was not the *Expedient,* but the underbelly of a monstrous shark. A full 10 meters long, hovering above him, slowly circling the ropes. The huge beast seemed to be waiting for him, blocking his progress to the safety of the waiting boat.

Alerting him to take action, the SCUBA tank again began to ring with a metallic sound each time he took a breath. His tank was nearly empty. He figured he had only a few minutes more before it would get increasingly harder to breathe. Then, when the tank had insufficient air pressure to activate the diaphragm in the regulator, it would shut down, and when that happened, he'd better be above water.

He had no choice now but to continue upward. Upward to the mouth of the shark, or to the deck of the boat. He slipped the old knife from the sheath at his right calf and began to kick the fins gently, rising to his fate.

Expedient was rocked by sea swells that had increased steadily the past hour. Wind chop created waves that slapped the steel sides of the vessel, sending spray cascading onto the crew and deck. Each wave sent a resounding bang throughout the boat. Dessault was becoming tired of the wet and of the noise. He wanted to get Austingrove back aboard, the plane secured and the hell out of there. He wasn't all that fond of boats and water anyway. He paced the lee side, occasionally looking into the boiling spume for some sign of Austingrove.

"Major," Captain Black's voice boomed over the noises of ship and sea. "I believe we have a bit of a problem here, Sir." He stood, wet and shivering at the helm station aft of the wheelhouse. At that position he could keep the boat on station and watch the fathometer through the rear cabin window, and he saw something that bothered him.

"What is it, Black?"

"There is a large fish circling our haul lines, Major. It appears to be a quite large shark of some variety. It looks to be half as long as *Expedient* here."

"Oh, Christ," said Dessault, staring at the long, dark blip on the fathometer. "How the hell is Austingrove going to get past that thing? Is there something we can do from up here to scare it off?"

"We have some small explosive devices that we use in shallow water to scare them off. This chap is about four fathoms down. I suppose it might work."

"Oh, shit yes," said Dessault. "and you could blow Austingrove all to hell too." He went to the side of the boat and looked down.

"We could throw the first two or three off to the side, well away from your friend and his visitor. Then Mister Austingrove would know what we are doing, and be prepared. He might even descend a bit, just to get out of the way, you know."

"OK, Captain. I'd bet he'd rather be blown up than eaten, anyway."

Captain Black called to Shin to bring the small bombs. He was there in a moment with a dirty plastic bag swinging in his hand. He bowed. He handed Black the bag and produced a Bic lighter from his pants pocket.

Black carefully lit the wrinkled, black fuse. Dessault recognized the explosive as an M-80, a plaything of his teens. Black waited a moment to ensure that it would stay burning, and tossed it far beyond the end of the crane.

There was a muffled thump and a white dome of foam belched up on the surface of the water, then quickly died.

Both men turned to the flickering screen of the fathometer. The black form still hung close to the lifting lines. "I'd say that it went off a bit too shallow, wouldn't you?"

Black's calm analytical tone annoyed Dessault. "Yeah, yeah," he said. "Throw a couple more of those bastards. This time right on top of that son of a bitch."

Black tossed another, this time not waiting to check the fuse. He threw it low and fast so that it would sink farther before detonating.

They heard two thumps in rapid succession and saw a repeat of the welling-up of water. The menacing shape on the fathometer was gone. Two minutes later, Austingrove broke the surface and was roughly dragged aboard by the crew. He fell to the deck, stripped out the mouthpiece and spit the foul taste toward a scupper. He jerked off the face mask, rolled over and kissed the dirty steel of *Expedient's* deck. "Thanks for the bombardment, guys," he smiled, "I was in a bit of bind down there."

Dessault caught Austingrove as his eyes glazed and he fell backward. A stream of bright red blood drained from his nose and joined the bloody handprints mixed with seawater on the deck. What should have been the whites of his eyes were blood red and his skin was as ashen as that of a dead man's. "Black!" shouted Dessault, "what the hell's wrong with him?"

"I am not sure, Major, but I think it may be the bends, and we'd better get him medical attention as fast as possible."

Captain Black's words were lost in the clanking of the windlass bringing the Me.262 to the surface.

CHAPTER THIRTEEN

The clatter of a gurney rattling down the hospital corridor awakened Austingrove. He felt the comfort of the bed and the warmth of the covers. He heard the unmistakable hospital sounds; the paging of doctors, the mumble of hallway conversations and the hissing of oxygen being pumped into him. He did not open his eyes, rather, he preferred to carefully gather his thoughts, assess his condition and try to remember how he came to be where he is. *Ah, alive. In a hospital. Warm and comfortable. The plane! Did we get the plane?* Sleep again pulled its black shroud over him.

"If he's going to be OK, why the hell is he sleeping so long?"

Austingrove barely heard another voice answer Dessault's question, but it was far off and soft. He remembered waking before, but now he seemed more alert, more able to handle wakefulness. He slowly opened his eyes. The room was softly lighted. He was glad of that. Even the soft lights burned into his pupils. Images formed. Dessault, Gordon, Bridgett. *They're all smiling like they're glad to see me.*

"If I'm going to be OK, why the hell am I sleeping so long?" He smiled.

Bridgett warmly hugged him, holding on tightly and for so long that Dessault said, "Christ, Bridgett, let the man breathe."

Austingrove noticed his bandaged hands as he reached up to hug Bridgett. The memories of the dive, finding Ackermann, the shark and his encounter with the second shark came back to him. "Did we get the plane aboard?"

Dessault told him that the Messerschmitt was retrieved and was now setting outside the hangar at Roughscuff, being totally flushed with fresh water and sprayed with preservative oil. He explained that Captain Black called Tennison Barquelay from *Expedient.* Barquelay dispatched his company helicopter to pick up Austingrove and take him to the Hospital in Ipswitch. Austingrove had spent four hours in a Royal Navy recompression chamber, and was unconscious for two days.

"The medics want to keep you here for a day or so to be sure you're fully recovered," said Gordon.

A large nurse carrying a small paper cup and a stern look parted the visitors. "Here, now, Here, now."

She handed the pill and cup to Austingrove. "Take this, and I'm afraid your friends must leave now, visiting time is past, you know." Austingrove noticed her name tag identified her as W.W. McFarland. "Ah, a Scottish lass, I see," said Austingrove. "And what might the W.W. stand for?"

"Well, it isn't 'Wonder Woman'. Now take your sleeping pill. I've got more than just you to attend to, you know. I can't be standing around here all night jabbering." She gave the men a scowling look, took the empty cup and hurried away.

The men said short good-byes and filed dutifully out of the room. Bridgett held back. She hugged Austingrove again, whispering, "You owe me a dinner, Yank. And I'll not let you out of it." Her smile was as warm and as tender as Austingrove remembered it could be. She kissed him and hurried out. He was left alone with the sweet warmth of her lips and the lingering scent of her perfume to comfort him.

"What the bloody hell?" said Bridgett Barquelay.

The big hangar doors at Barquelay Aviation banged open and the roar of four diesel truck engines echoed throughout the building. Twelve black suited men rushed in. Some brandished guns, most had sections of pipe. One man grabbed her arms and twisted them behind her back. The man smelled of sweat and whiskey.

"What the *bloody* hell?" she repeated. "Let go of me you stinking bastard!" A strip of rough, foul-smelling tape was pressed across her mouth. She was forced outside and pushed face down into the rear of a small black van. The man expertly tied her hands and feet with a length of coarse twine.

The seven B.A. mechanics were herded to the side of the hangar, pushed and kicked if they moved too slowly. They were tied with sections of cord each of the raiders carried. One of Barquelay's men was clubbed when he resisted and lay unconscious on the floor.

Their attackers wore no masks and made no attempt to hide their identity. They didn't speak, they simply made grunting noises and swung their clubs if their prisoners didn't move quickly enough.

Only a few small parts of the Messerschmitt fighters were left to be packed into the containers and the men went to it. As each was filled, they secured the two steel doors with large locks and towed the loaded shipping containers to the hangar's door. The crane quickly lifted each onto a truck.

A man with a vicious-looking machine pistol stood frowning at Barquelay's men until a shrill whistle sent him fleeing to the last truck.

Bridgett's attacker climbed into the passenger's seat of the van. Then the driver jumped in. She recognized the large frame of Inspector Karl Schwerin. Three more men clamored into the van. The convoy roared off across the ramp and up the road toward London.

It took a full twenty minutes for the mechanics to work themselves free. The flight line ambulance was summoned for the injured man and the rest ran to tell Tennison Barquelay what happened.

Cody Gordon pulled up to the hangar. The three shipping containers packed with the two disassembled German fighters were gone. Only spots of oil and small clods of dirt and grass were left to indicate that they had been there. He ran to the administration building. Two police cars stood outside, their engines running and lights flashing. He crashed through the swinging doors at full pace. Tennison Barquelay stood talking to a uniformed policeman. Gordon could see two plainclothes constables at a conference table in the next room. They were interviewing the six B.A. mechanics that were assigned to disassemble the planes.

"Mister Barquelay," he said, "what is going on? Where are the planes?"

Barquelay held up his hand to momentarily hush him, spoke a few more words to the policeman. They shook hands, and then he turned to Gordon. "They are gone."

"They're gone?" said Austingrove. "What the hell do you mean, 'they're gone'?" W.W. McFarland, the nurse who had brought him his nightly pill, was pushing Austingrove's wheelchair down the hospital corridor. Gordon, almost trotting alongside, explained what had happened at Barquelay Aviation.

"And Schwerin told one of the mechanics to tell you something," said Gordon.

"What's that?"

"That you and the Major are wanted for two murders in Germany," said Gordon. "Bridgett and I are wanted as accessories."

"Oh great. Hilda Göettz and Ackermann. Right?" asked Austingrove.

"You got it, Pal."

As they reached the admitting area, Austingrove grabbed the wheelchair's wheels, bringing it to an abrupt halt. He sprang up out of the seat and the two men headed for the door. "Wait! Stop!" called the nurse. "You can't do that! I have to take you in the chair!" The men didn't hear her as they sprinted across the parking lot to Gordon's car.

Austingrove and Gordon arrived at Roughscuff Field. Twenty minutes before, Tennison Barquelay sent his helicopter with Dessault aboard to search for the loaded trucks.

"I've called the Transportation Authority to detain them if they try to use the Chunnel," said Barquelay. "They have only two ways out of the country," he said, "by Chunnel or by ship. One or the other, and they surely can't hide for long."

The "Chunnel," a recently opened rail tunnel under the English Channel, is a 50 kilometer route to France. Barquelay had connections at both ends.

If they used it, he would know about it immediately. Both British and French authorities were alerted to the kidnapping of his daughter.

"I'd like to search the harbor area," said Austingrove, "could I borrow a car?"

"My dear boy, of course. Take the Bentley, it has a radio. Both the helicopter and my office can talk to you, and you them. If something turns up, you must alert us so that we can assist."

"Of course," said Austingrove. "I think we should be armed too, Schwerin and his gang certainly are."

"My boy," said Barquelay, "you are not in America or Germany now. Guns are only for some police and the military in the U.K. You can get in your knickers in quite a twist if you are caught with a firearm. And it would indeed be a high crime should you happen to shoot someone."

"Mister Barquelay," said Austingrove, "your daughter's life is in jeopardy here. We need some sort of defense if we're going to be able to get her back."

"My security chaps are legally armed. It would be advisable for you to take four or five of them with you."

"OK, good," said Austingrove, "but I only want two." He knew that too many approaching hunters often spook the prey.

"Very well," said Barquelay, "I'll send Colin and Jeremy with you. They are experienced in this sort of thing. Both of these lads came to us from Scotland

Yard."

Colin Fishe crammed his six-five frame into the Bentley's back seat. His shoulders nearly spread the width of the car. Jeremy Dunn, smaller but as tough looking as an English bulldog, slid in beside him. The two uniformed guards introduced themselves as if they were guests at a formal dinner. "I am so very glad to make your acquaintance, Mister Austingrove," said Fishe. "As am I," said Dunn, "we are quite privileged to have the opportunity to be working with you gentlemen."

Austingrove and Gordon drove to the commercial dock area of London. Jeremy Dunn directed their search. They began a systematic tour of each of the streets, alleys and docks. Forty containers were found, none of them the ones they had to find.

"Scott, Dessault here," the radio scratched, "you on?"

Gordon took the microphone. "Go ahead, Major, we're on."

"What color were those containers?"

Gordon turned to Austingrove, "You remember what color they are?"

"Yeah, sort of a light green."

"Scott says light green, Major."

"OK, there is a container ship at the end of Harrington Dock and there are three greenish looking containers still on trucks. You guys won't be able to see them, they're parked in behind a bunch of others."

Dunn knew Harrington Dock. It was about two

miles from where they were. "Roger, Major, we're on our way."

They pulled into Harrington Dock Road five minutes later. Austingrove drove slowly until they could see the ship and the containers stacked three high on the dock. Leaving the Bentley, they walked toward the pier, keeping close to the wall of the dock's warehouse and watching for Schwerin's men. An overhead crane was loading containers onto the aft deck of the ship. It was methodically loading its way forward. The light green containers were well forward. It would be some time before they were in turn to be lifted aboard.

The men reached the corner of the warehouse. A large, dark-suited man in street clothes stood at the top of the gangplank leading up to the ship's deck. He was watching the loading procedure aft. He turned away out of the wind to light a cigarette and the four men sprinted to the stacks of containers. They worked their way up to the green boxes.

"That's them," said Gordon. "See the sticker on the side, it says they are consigned to Barquelay Aviation."

"OK, Pal. The hell of it is that we don't know where Bridgett is." Austingrove leaned back on a shipping container, watching the man on the ship.

"Barquelay's man said they took her away in a small black van without any markings on it." said Gordon. "Let's look around here before we do anything heroic, she might not even be here."

"Damn," said Austingrove, "I should have had the Major looking for the van, not the containers. How about you sneak back to the Bentley and describe the van to the Major and have him start looking for it, OK?"

"Right. I'm on my way." Gordon took a quick look at the sentry aboard the ship and slipped around the corner.

Austingrove knew that Gordon's heart wasn't totally into accosting the Germans. He felt that his friend would be of more value looking for the van and Bridgett Barquelay.

He jabbed a thumb toward the ship. "Fishe, you stay here and keep an eye on that guy. If he looks like he's spotted us, or tries to leave, get him."

"Righto. I'd love to pop him a good one, Mister Austingrove," said Fishe.

"It's probable that you'll get your chance," said Austingrove. "And you guys call me Scott, OK? Dunn, let's you and me nose around this place."

"Aye. Call me Jeremy, OK?"

They carefully worked their way through the stacks of loaded containers to the side of the ship. There they could see the entire length of the vessel and not be seen by anyone aboard. He went aft, looking among the cargo containers for the van.

The overhead crane was about to lift the last container of a stack and take it aboard the ship. Two dockworkers hurried away to be ready at the next stack. Just then Austingrove spotted the black van parked at the gangplank. Now he was sure that Bridgett was aboard the ship.

"That's the van, Jeremy," he said. "Let's hop a ride on that container."

The two men sprinted to the container just as it was lifting from the dock. They jumped onto the end of it, out of the operator's line of sight. The door latch handles gave them a foothold and the latch rods at the opening end of the two doors provided hand holds.

The huge box soared upward, slowed and then moved sideways over the ship. Austingrove saw Barquelay's helicopter hovering over the channel. He didn't know if he imagined it, or if he actually saw Major Dessault watching him from the chopper, his mouth hanging open in awe. He looked to see if anyone on the ship had noticed him. There were only two dockworkers aboard, and they were busy securing the other containers. His ride came down softly atop another of the cargo containers. They slid down the latch rods, got a foothold on the bottom container and shinnied down onto the ship's steel deck.

He trusted that the crew, and the Germans, if indeed they were aboard, would be concentrating their attention on the side of the ship laying to the pier. He motioned Dunn to follow him down the seaward side. Reaching the superstructure, he checked each companionway and peered into each port. At the galley, they heard voices speaking in German. Austingrove peered into the companionway that ran the full width of the superstructure. There were doorways along each side, the first one was open. He eased into the dim companionway and carefully looked into the room.

Schwerin sat with two other men around what appeared to be the ship's dining table. Except for the masks, they were still dressed as Barquelay's men described the raiders. They wore black suits that appeared to be the type police Special Weapons And Tactics (SWAT) teams use. Austingrove could not understand what they were saying, and Bridgett was not in the room.

He eased back out to the side deck. He was eager to deal with the sadistic Schwerin, but he had to find Bridgett before anything else.

As he neared the next port, he heard Bridgett's unmistakable voice, "Get away from me, you filthy bastard!"

"Jeremy," Austingrove whispered, "take a look in there, I'm going to check for a way in."

Dunn pulled a huge revolver from the holster at his hip and looked through the partially opened port. A ragged plastic curtain obscured most of the room, but he could see that it was a small stateroom, probably for a ship's officer of lower than Captain's rank. There was a desk attached to the bulkhead directly across from the doorway. The bunk was built into the inboard bulkhead and Bridgett was on it, her hands tied, and her blouse torn down from her shoulders, exposing her breasts. A large man stood in front of her. He had pulled off his black suitcoat and was unstrapping his bulletproof vest. That answered one main question, were the Germans equipped with protective chestpieces?

The man casually tossed the vest into the corner of the room. He reached down, taking Bridgett's breasts in his hairy hands. At that moment, Austingrove burst open the stateroom's door and shouted the only German word he could remember, "*Achtung!*"

The man turned to Austingrove and then saw the dark, round muzzle of Dunn's revolver protruding through the port. He reached for his suitcoat but was not fast enough to beat out the two 9 millimeter slugs that slammed into his chest. Blood, bone and skin splattered Austingrove, Bridgett and the bulkheads. The man was spun around by the impact. His eyes bulged with disbelief and he spat out an epithet at Austingrove. He tried again to reach his gun, but his legs collapsed and he crashed down onto the steel deck. He would not have landed harder if he'd been hit by a truck.

Bridgett struggled up from the bed, pulling her torn blouse over her shoulders. She looked as if in a daze.

"Jeremy, " shouted Austingrove, "get Bridgett out of here." He dashed to the forward corner of the superstructure and ducked in behind a stack of cargo containers. The two men who had been with Schwerin emerged from the companionway, guns in hand. They were met with a blast of automatic rifle fire from

Dessault in the helicopter. They ran back into the ship, across to the other side of the superstructure and headed for the gangplank.

Dunn entered the diningroom. "Miss Barquelay, It's me, Jeremy Dunn. We must get you out of here." Bridgett hurried from the stateroom into the dining area.

Bridgett stopped and stood unblinking at Dunn. She opened her mouth to speak, but it was too late. Schwerin clubbed Dunn from behind with the butt of his pistol. He fell in a heap at Bridgett's feet. Schwerin yanked Bridgett back into the small stateroom.

Austingrove heard Bridgett scream in terror. He abandoned his chase of the two Germans and burst into the dining area. He stumbled over Dunn's crumpled form, and reeled to the table.

"Look out, Scotty!"

Austingrove dove to Dunn's side and pulled the pistol from his holster. Schwerin fired two rounds from what sounded to Austingrove like the same short-barreled .38 caliber handgun he used to kill Hilda Göettz. The bullets ricocheted off the steel walls of the dining room. Austingrove rolled under the table.

"Let her go, Schwerin," he called. "We've got the ship surrounded and a helicopter overhead. You can't get away."

"I know that you will allow nothing to happen to your woman, Mister Austingrove," Schwerin yelled back. "So remove yourself and your people from this ship - Now!"

Austingrove knew that Schwerin would not give a second thought to killing Bridgett. He also knew that there was indeed the possibility that he'd kill her anyway if he was allowed to leave the ship. He imagined her bullet-riddled body being pushed from the speeding van as Schwerin escaped. The thought fired shocks up his backbone and he felt his stomach churn. He had to keep them both aboard. "No deal, Schwerin."

"Deal?" said Schwerin. "You are in no position to accept or deny any sort of *deal*. You move away, I leave the ship, the girl lives. *That* is the *deal*."

"I'm moving to the gangplank, Inspector," said Austingrove. "Release her there and I'll do nothing to stop you. You can leave the ship. I give you my word on that."

"Oh, yes, I am going to leave the ship. And I do not need your word, and there is nothing you can do to stop me. Get out of here or you both die now."

"OK, OK. I'm leaving. Don't hurt the girl." Austingrove moved out of the dining room and sprinted to the starboard side of the ship to where the gangway led down to the pier. He saw two of Schwerin's men, stripped of their weapons and body armor, being loaded into Barquelay's Bentley on the dock below. Austingrove positioned himself at the top of the ramp, squatting down behind the ship's bulwarks. He would be hidden from Schwerin as he stepped onto the top platform of the gangplank. Austingrove would have to grab him then, going for the gun. Hopefully, Bridgett would be able to pull away and run.

A shuffling of feet announced their approach. Austingrove heard a muffled whimper from Bridgett and tensed. Schwerin's legs became visible at the opening in the bulwarks. He had her in a headlock with his right arm, and his left hand held the gun under her chin. Austingrove dove upward, hitting Schwerin hard in the face with his shoulder and grabbing the pistol with both hands. He jerked it as hard as he could away from Bridgett. It fired. The tremendous noise stunned Austingrove. The end of the barrel was a mere two inches from his left ear, pointing into the air. Schwerin lurched backward. He swung Bridgett around with his right arm, lifted her up, and with one arm hurled her over the side of the ship. Austingrove didn't hear her scream. Nor did he hear the scream abruptly stop. His ears rang from the report of the pistol. He slammed Schwerin against the bulkhead and repeatedly banged Schwerin's right hand hard against the side of the ship's superstructure.

Schwerin smashed down viciously on the back of Austingrove's head with his left hand just as the gun was knocked free. It skidded along the deck, through a deck scupper, and overboard.

Austingrove went to his knees, stunned. Schwerin stumbled down the side deck toward the rear of the ship. Austingrove rolled over, pulled Dunn's pistol from his jacket pocket and staggered to his feet. He knew that most, perhaps all, policemen carry a standby gun somewhere on their person. He imagined that Schwerin was so armed and couldn't take the chance that he wasn't. He shuffled along the side of the superstructure to its aft end, his head pounding and his ears ringing. He scanned the stacks of shipping containers. Schwerin was among them somewhere, and wouldn't be easy to find.

Colin Fishe and a dazed-looking Jeremy Dunn ducked in beside Austingrove. "Any idea where he went?" asked Gordon.

"No. Let's split up and go down both sides. Keep a lookout on top of those containers, they're easy to climb," said Austingrove. "You OK, Jeremy?"

"Aye," muttered Dunn, obviously ashamed of being ambushed as he had.

Fishe and Dunn started down the starboard side. Austingrove the port. It was slow work, checking each stack on all four sides, and on top. They came to the end. There were three stacks of two containers remaining. The crane just set the last of the second layer and was swinging the first of the top layer into position. The crane operator maneuvered the loads from a control cab directly above the lifting cables. His cab moved along with the load. He could see all around it, but not directly below the lift.

Austingrove stepped back. He thought he saw movement on top of one of the containers.

The crane swung its huge load over the end stack of two and lowered it smoothly and quickly. Austingrove saw Schwerin suddenly stand up and try to run just as the great steel box was lowered onto him from above.

A muffled scream came from between the two containers. Schwerin's arm, a gun still in his hand, jutted out from between the steel boxes. It convulsed spasmodically before the gun finally fell to the deck.

Fishe, his pistol drawn, and Dunn came around the corner of the stack just as a gushing stream of blood reddened the side of the lower container. They heard a horrible cracking, snapping noise as Schwerin's body was crushed between the loaded containers.

CHAPTER FOURTEEN

ere, now.   Here, now." Nurse W. W. McFarland barged through the four men standing at Bridgett's hospital bedside. She hesitated, looking at Austingrove, then at Gordon. She knew there was a reason she should reprimand these two, but couldn't quite remember for what.

Bridgett Barquelay lay with her right leg elevated with a cast from her ankle to the center of her thigh. She had suffered two fractures of her right leg, but that had saved her life. When Schwerin catapulted her over the side of the ship, she landed on the top of a stack of shipping containers. She had fallen only about twelve feet. Her impact was absorbed by her leg, saving serious injury to her head and body.

"Schwerin's henchmen ratted on their boss," said Austingrove. "The German police have taken them. We'll have to make a deposition as soon as you're able to. But at least they've cleared us on Hilda Göettz' murder. And the German government has said that they want nothing to do with the Messerschmitts. They think that we bought them from Schwerin. Schwerin knew about Ackermann's sack of jewels. He evidently overheard us and saw us stash them in the plane. He thought they were still in the crated planes someplace, that's why he was so eager to get hold of them."

"Unfortunately," said Barquelay, turning to Austingrove, Dessault and Gordon, "the three of you may be facing serious weapons charges. The British government and police do not think much of civilians going about shooting people." He flicked an ash from his topcoat, "I have made calls to some of my associates, however, and we may find that the circumstances of the shooting will be taken into consideration. I shouldn't be too concerned, but be ready to answer questions regarding the matter."

Having taken Bridgett's blood pressure and temperature, Nurse McFarland wedged her way back through the men, again eyeing Austingrove and Gordon. Unable to remember, she shook her head and went on.

"I think Wonder Woman likes you, Pard," said

Austingrove. With a grimace, Gordon delivered an elbow to Austingrove's rib cage.

"Do you have a sincere interest in her, Scott?" Barquelay's question took Austingrove totally by surprise.

Austingrove could only nod. He was surprised when Tennison Barquelay asked him to join him at the Felixstowe estate for luncheon as they left the hospital, and this question surprised him as well. He now realized that the invitation was because of Bridgett. He felt like a tin can on a pistol range; all setup and ready to be shot down.

"You know, Bridgett is an exceptional woman. She is, however, approaching a time in her life when she should be thinking of establishing a family," said Barquelay.

He went on. "Bridgett is a warm and loving person, as I'm sure you realize. But she has devoted almost her entire life to aviation. And, I might add, she is exceptional in her ability," he paused, relighting his pipe. "I feel that it is time for her to experience more of what life is all about. She must come to realize that if aviation is the only thing she ever aspires to, she'll surely end up missing the more meaningful things our very short lives have to offer." He stopped. A gray haze of smoke curled about him. Austingrove enjoyed the aroma of the tobacco. He idly wondered if he should take up smoking a pipe.

"Well, do you have any thoughts on this, Scott?"

"Oh, yes, Sir. Everything you said about Bridgett is certainly true. That is, about her abilities as a pilot, and her devotion and, well, I don't know about what she would like to do with the rest of her life. Have you asked her?"

"God, yes, man." Barquelay stood and took the three steps to the fireplace, and leaned on the mantle. He frowned at Austingrove. "You are a young man, Scott. You will someday be an old man. And that time arrives much too soon. I have only Bridgett now. Her mother passed-on more than five years ago and I am very alone, except for Bridgett."

"But Sir, if I may say so, you have so very, very much," said Austingrove. "A wonderful business, political position, friends, and I'm sure Bridgett appreciates her place in your life." He was hoping to remove himself from the line of fire by switching the focus onto Mister Barquelay.

"Psssh!" The sound of a ruptured tire spewed from his lips. "Oh, Yes, I have my work and a place in the Air Ministry, but as for friends, I fear not." Barquelay returned to his chair.

"You see, all of my acquaintances of my age are thoroughly involved in their families. And that is as it should be. I have tried to establish personal relationships with some of those at Barquelay Aviation, but I'll tell you, Young Man, there is a wall that, regrettably, must be maintained between myself and my people at B.A." His pipe died and he placed it in the silver tray at his elbow. "There is something a man in my position learns very early in life; position and money simply buys loneliness. In the past I have had parties, inviting all of the personnel at Barquelay Aviation, and I have found that an air of uneasiness always exists. But my most shocking discovery is that the rich are not the snobs, Scott. It is the poor, or those with less, that are truly the snobs. The poor have never been rich, but the rich, in most cases, have at one time or other, been poor. I have tried to make friends with workmen and shopkeepers and they always express regret that they cannot visit me here at my estate because they 'don't feel they belong' here." He poured two glasses of cognac and handed one to Austingrove.

"What if I said to them upon visiting their home that I 'don't feel that I belong' there? I should say they would be most offended, right? If any one strata of the populous are snobbish, it is indeed, those with less wealth."

"Yes, Sir. I can see that you are somewhat socially isolated," said Austingrove.

Barquelay brightened, straightening in his chair. "But a *Family* is the answer. I want Bridgett to have a family. A husband and children, you know, grandchildren that I can enjoy during my last years.

Austingrove silently wished that this same conversation had taken place five years ago. At that time, he would have jumped right in front of the speeding bullet. But now he was uncertain. "Surely she has her choice of many men," he offered. After all, she is a beautiful, talented and charming woman."

Barquelay opened a small pipe tool, and began to dig at the buildup of black scale in the bowl. "She has had a number of men friends. Mostly Royal Air Force chaps. She seemed happy enough with each one of them, but for only a short time." Barquelay blew through the stem of his pipe and placed it back in the tray, squinting at Austingrove.

"In not one of them was I able to detect husband or family potential. Nor did I see anyone of them as a future head of Barquelay Aviation."

Austingrove realized that Barquelay had just upped the stakes. *He wants a son-in-law, he wants a husband for his daughter, he wants grandchildren, and on top of all of that, he wants someone who could take over Barquelay Aviation. It was,* he thought, *an extraordinary opportunity for the right man, but I am not that man.*

"I have never seen her quite so happy as she was when she was with you a few years back. Scott, how do you feel about Bridgett? At one time she suggested that you were getting quite serious."

"Well, Sir, that was a long time ago, and I was..."

"My God, man!" blurted Barquelay, "You're not married, are you?"

"No, Sir," said Austingrove. He was getting very uneasy and began to wish that this evening would end. He glanced at his watch. And he didn't like the feeling he was getting; being pressured into something as serious as marriage and family.

"Bridgett is a wonderful woman, but I'm not so sure that we share the chemistry that it takes for being anything more than just friends," said Austingrove. "Mostly, that's up to Bridgett, and I think that she is the kind of person that will work hard to get whatever she wants. So far, she hasn't indicated that she has a great interest in me, other than as a colleague and as a friend."

"Well, blast it all." said Barquelay, and became sullen and untalkative.

They finished their cognac and Barquelay silently drove Austingrove back to Roughscuff Field. As they parted Barquelay finally said, "Scott, I know that you are a good chap and that you care for Bridgett much too much to ever do anything to harm her. I would simply ask you to keep your mind and your heart open to her. Good night, Son."

Austingrove flailed his way through the night, unable to sleep, unable to lay still. His mind crammed with thoughts of Bridgett, what his life would be like with her, leaving Dessault and the flying museum and *Jet Fighter!* Magazine, and finally, living in England and running Barquelay Aviation. It would take many more sleepless nights, he was sure, before he reached a decision.

A damp, gray and gloomy morning greeted Austingrove and Gordon. They went to work cleaning and repairing Ackermann's plane. It was their intention, as recommended by Dessault, to fix it up and give it to Barquelay Aviation. The seawater had not time to do much damage, but it was important to remove every trace of it from the aluminum airframe and the engines. The men worked steadily for three days, reducing the Me.262 to lines of parts and pieces on the hangar floor. The other two planes were still packed in the ship containers. They had been reopened so that flight manuals and parts books could be removed for what would be Barquelay's jet.

Gordon poured Austingrove a cup of tea from a Thermos. "You know, Scott, with your one kill in 'Nam and these three German planes, you are now almost an Air Force Ace, man!"

Austingrove threw a punch at Gordon's shoulder, intentionally pulling it.

"Up yours," he smiled. "Look, I'm going to run over to the hospital and see how Bridgett is doing. Do you have any message for that nurse over there that has the hots for you?"

"Yeah, tell her I died and she's all yours now!"

"Hello, Scotty, I'm glad you came." Bridgett was propped up in bed, her leg protruding from the blankets. She wore a blue nightgown with a delicate lace pattern, her favorite lipstick and her hair put up in two pony tails.

"You look great, Kid," said Austingrove. He kissed her forehead and lightly stroked her cheek. He remembered that she liked that caress. "How's the leg feeling?"

"Oh, the bleeding leg is fine, it's my backside that's getting sore from lying in this miserable bed."

Austingrove dragged a chair across to the bed and sat, holding her hand. "I'll take you and your backside dancing when you get all healed up, how's that?"

"Feels better already," she said. "What have you been up to?"

"Your father invited me to Felixstowe for lunch and a few drinks yesterday. Do you know that he's concerned about you, Bloke?"

"Concerned?" she sat up in the bed. "Concerned about me? What in the world for?"

"He thinks it's getting about time for you to raise him a mess of grandkids. He's worried that you're; 'not experiencing the truly meaningful things available to us in this short lifetime of ours', or something like that."

"Oh, my," she flopped back against the pillows. "He thinks I'm an Old Maid, does he?"

"That's about it, I guess." Austingrove said. "On top of that, he has as much as offered me a position with Barquelay Aviation if I stay in England."

"Why, that old codge!" said Bridgett. "He just thinks he can order me to get married and you to come live here?" She stopped, closed her eyes and shook her head as if trying to dislodge an ugly hat. Then she opened her eyes wide and sat erect. "Oh, my God! He means for you and I to get married?" She said the word 'married' as if it held some sort of evil connotation.

"I guess something like that is what he has in mind." Austingrove was enjoying seeing her squirm.

"Oh, yes; 'or something like that' it is. He just wants someone like you to head-up B.A. He doesn't think that I am capable of handling it. I'm merely a woman, you know!" She said 'woman' with the same inflection as 'married'.

As her anger grew, Austingrove decided he'd better quit baiting her. "No, seriously," he said, "I truly believe that he is really concerned that you are missing out on the kind of life he and your mother had together. He just wants to see you to have a family in place before he, you know, *goes.*"

"Oh, fine." she calmed. "But *you?*" Again, she stressed the word as if it was dirty.

"Well, hey," smiled Austingrove, "I'm not so bad. At least I don't drive airplanes into stone walls and fall off of ships." He shifted his weight in the chair and leaned toward her. "I truly think he is somewhat lonely, and he thinks that a grandchild or two would fill that void in his life."

Bridgett thought a moment then took his hand in both of hers. "Oh, I know, Scotty, he means well, to be sure. It's just that I'm not so sure that I'm ready, you know, to become a wife and mother. And I do resent his constant meddling about in my life."

"Well, he loves his little girl and wants the best for her. And believe me, I'm not all that hot for his attempt at being matchmaker for you and me, either."

"Oh no?" Bridgett again looked surprised. "And why not? Oh, yes, you probably have a girl in the States waiting for you, don't you? I suppose she's prettier and sexier than I as well, isn't she?"

Austingrove laughed. "Yep! She's gorgeous. And she's not British, she's an American! A North American F-86 that is, and a lot easier to handle than you would ever be, I'll bet!"

They sat a moment looking at each other, trying to sort out their feelings.

"Ah, I've got to go, Bloke. You get a lot of rest and I'll keep that dinner and dance date open for you. Unless, of course, I meet a prettier and sexier *American* girl." Austingrove hugged her and she kissed him, warmly and tenderly.

"Thanks, Yank."

As he turned to leave, he thought he saw the start of a tear begin to form in the corner of her eye.

The next morning, Dessault joined Austingrove and Gordon at the small tea shop across the street from Roughscuff Field. "We have clearance to leave England," he said. "The Germans may want us to return later, but for now we're free to go back to the States." He took a sip of the tea, grimaced and slid the cup across the table. "We've got the Reno Air Races in just three weeks, and we have a lot to do to get ready. Everything's probably gone to hell back home while we've been screwing around over here."

"When will the Messerschmitts be released?"

asked Austingrove.

"It looks like it'll be a few weeks, Scott." said Dessault. "Barquelay has been handling that through his connections, but as he says; 'It looks rather nasty'. But it's in the works."

Austingrove visited Bridgett at the hospital the morning the Americans left England. He was still uneasy about the position her father had put him into with the not-so-subtle suggestion that he and Bridgett wed. He also felt he was being pressured into the proposition of taking over Barquelay Aviation at some time in the future. What, he wondered, would happen if, after he married Bridgett, Barquelay decided that his daughter's new husband was not capable of, or suitable for, that position. He said nothing about that to Bridgett, and their parting was warm. They joked about her coming to America and hopping around Dessault Aviation in a huge leg cast. But Austingrove was uneasy, eager to get away from there and he knew Bridgett recognized it. He left her hospital room with, "I'm going to call you every day."

Her smile said she didn't really believe him.

CHAPTER FIFTEEN

Austingrove flew the Museum's Russian MiG 15 jet to the Reno Air Races and competed in a demonstration race against a P-51 Mustang Racing plane, "Tang II". The Mustang took the pylons low, tight and fast, its supercharged V-12 Rolls Royce Griffon engine screaming at the top end of its 2,300 horsepower. The Mustang's ability to make turns in less than one-third the distance required by the Russian jet fighter negated the MiG's superior speed, and the World War Two, prop-driven fighter completed the eight-lap race well ahead of the MiG. The crowd was delighted.

At the race's end, Austingrove completed a four-point roll in front of the grandstands and pulled the

MiG up into a climbing turn. He dropped it smoothly down onto the runway on its two main landing gear. He held the nose high and proud until gravity overcame the lift afforded by the plane's speed. The nose wheel settled onto the tarmac with a muted screech. He taxied the MiG past the crowd, waving from the open canopy. The announcer plugged *Jet Fighter!* magazine and Dessault's Flying Museum. That chore finished, Austingrove swung the plane into its assigned spot on the flightline, chocked the wheels and quickly made entries into the pilot's and aircraft's flight logs. He gave the plane a quick postflight inspection while the MiG's engine, a Russian copy of a Rolls Royce turbojet, was still coasting to a stop. He tossed the log books into the pilot's seat and headed for the terminal building.

He was aware that it had been a less than inspired performance. Since returning from England, he was tired, discouraged and had little enthusiasm for anything, and that included flying. The prospect of losing the German planes to the British or German government was another huge disappointment in his life. On top of that, he had become aware of an emptiness that he felt could only be filled by Bridgett Barquelay. He was unhappy and lonely.

He called Bridgett at her father's Felixstowe estate. "Hi, Bloke, how's the leg?" This was his first call in the three weeks since he left England. Each time he thought of it, it was either too early or too late in the day to call overseas. He expected her to be less than thrilled to hear from him after so long.

"Scotty, I'm so glad you called," she sounded nervous, anxious. "I left a message at the Dessault Museum earlier. I've got to talk to you."

"Talk away, Kid. What's got you so fired-up?" Austingrove pulled the door of the small pilot's lounge closed.

"Something's going on here that I can't really understand," she lowered her voice to almost a whisper. "At Roughscuff, there are crews leaving each morning in two lorries. They are gone all day and return in the evening. After dark, actually. I've heard them speak of 'The Messies'." She paused, "Scotty, I think they are talking about 'Messerschmitts' and I'm scared."

"Whoa, Sugar," said Austingrove. "There's nothing to be afraid of, I'm sure."

"There's more, Scotty."

Austingrove reached a chair and pulled it to the telephone counter. "Go ahead."

Bridgett told him of several strangers who came and went, visiting Tennison Barquelay. "They drive up in a big black car, go into Daddy's office, then leave after about a half hour. They are all dressed in black suits and never speak to anyone or even talk among themselves. Isn't *that* a bit odd?"

"Sounds weird," said Austingrove.

Her voice trembled as she began to describe her father's recent actions as bizarre. He was remote, staying to himself, coming to and leaving Roughscuff without being seen. She felt that he was avoiding her.

"It's not like Daddy," she said. "He's acting as if something is dreadfully wrong, Scotty, and he hardly speaks to me."

"That sure doesn't sound like Mister Barquelay," said Austingrove. "Let me talk to the Major about this, Bridgett, and I'll call you tonight. OK?"

"Yes, please do. Oh, Scotty, I must tell you as well, Ackermann's Two-Six-Two has been cleaned, preserved and is all painted up, as if it is going to be displayed someplace."

Austingrove hung up and jogged out to the taxiway where the aviation displays were setup. The Dessault Flying Museum air show display was the cockpit of a DC-3 on rollers, its back open. It was positioned so that the airplane enthusiasts could sit at the controls, looking out over the nose, and operate the throttles, flap and gear handles. For a moment they are flying an actual airplane, albeit with their imagination. Dessault stood at the display's table, handing out Dessault Aviation brochures and answering questions about the MiG-15 and the decapitated DC-3 nose section.

Dessault listened intently as Austingrove told him of Bridgett's concerns. "Damn sure doesn't sound like Tennison," he said. "I'll give him a call and try to find out what's going on."

The blazing Nevada sun dropped behind the western hills and in the coolness of the evening

Austingrove helped Gordon tie-down, refuel and put the MiG-15's canopy, intake and exhaust covers in place. A preflight inspection in the morning, and it would be ready to fly in that day's performance. They were wiping the tires clean when Dessault's voice boomed across the airfield, "Scott! Cody! On the double!"

Austingrove and Gordon jammed the rags into their pockets and sprinted to the Pilot's lounge. Dessault was waiting.

"Scott, at the end of tomorrow's flight, take the MiG directly back to Fullerton. There will be a ticket waiting for you at the BOAC counter for Heathrow out of Los Angeles. I'm leaving tomorrow for San Francisco and will be on a flight to London the day after. We should meet up in London close to the same time." Dessault shook his head. "I don't know what the hell's going on with Barquelay, Scott, but something's not right." Dark rings had formed under Dessault's eyes and his cheeks looked sunken. For the first time, it seemed to Austingrove that his mentor was showing his age.

"Cody, you get some help, load up the gear at the end of Scott's show and drive the truck back to Fullerton," said Dessault. "I'll call you day after tomorrow and let you know what's going on." He was heading for the door. "Take care of things, OK?" Gordon nodded, but they all knew that it wasn't a question. It was a command. The door slammed. Austingrove and Gordon stood in the still room looking at the door and wondering what was happening at Roughscuff Field.

Bridgett Barquelay fidgeted with the yellow rain cap, alternately crushing and straightening it. The hem of her slicker was still dripping rainwater onto the brightly polished terminal floor, leaving her standing as if surrounded by her own personal moat. She had not moved from the window at gate 26 since her arrival half an hour before. Now the huge blue and white nose of the Boeing 747 that carried Austingrove was sweeping around, moving forward, its windshield wipers frantically beating back and forth. It approached the window until she could practically see the aircrew's name tags. The airliner and the windshield wipers stopped in unison, and she saw the cockpit lights come up.

For the first time in her life, Bridgett was lonely. Whenever she needed attention in the past, her father was always near, ready and eager to comfort her. Now she was confused and afraid. Her father's sudden retreat into himself made her realize that this is how it will be when he passes on. She would be without anyone to turn to. This revelation brought with it thoughts of Scott Austingrove. She knew that she certainly did not want to be alone. Austingrove was the only other person on earth that she would want to be near. He could dispel her loneliness with a simple joke and a warm smile.

For the third time in her adult life, she cried for

someone. She wept for her mother when she died so many years ago, and then she wept again, believing that she would never see Austingrove again. She didn't want to cry any more, and she didn't want to be without him anymore either.

A smartly dressed BOAC attendant pulled the skyway door open as speakers echoed throughout the building, "British Overseas Airways Flight number 444 from Los Angeles, now de-planing at gate 26." Bridgett limped to the rope barrier, the lightweight cast on her leg still awkward and uncomfortable.

"Scotty!"

Austingrove was the sixth passenger to come through the door. They embraced, a lingering kiss, and they hurried arm-in-arm for the exit.

"The Major here yet?" asked Austingrove as they buckled into the Jaguar.

Bridgett squinted into the headlights of an approaching lorry, "No, he's due in this evening, eight or so, I believe."

Bridgett pulled the Jaguar into a tight turn, negotiating the roundabout that joined the road to Felixstowe to the highway out of London's Heathrow Airport. Austingrove couldn't dissuade her from driving, she said that the cast was not a hindrance, and since he disliked driving in England, he belted-in good and tight and held on.

As they sped past Roughscuff Field, Austingrove asked, "Going to the Barquelay Aviation guest house?"

"No, I've made-up rooms at the estate for you and

Major Dessault," she reached over and pressed her hand on his. "I want you with me, Scotty. To tell the truth, I'm quite frightened."

The car splashed through a puddle at the entrance to Barquelay's estate, smearing the windshield with mud and blurring the view of the old house. Only one light was visible, and it appeared to be in the grand entrance hall. Bridgett pulled the Jaguar into a garage stall that had been reclaimed from the stables that backed the house. They hurried across the gravel drive and entered by a side door.

"Go up to the first room on the right and get your shower," called Bridgett. "I'll bring a brandy up to you."

She knocked softly on the door of her father's study. Hearing no response, she looked in. The room was dark and empty. As were all of the other rooms.

The shower was Austingrove's first in two days and it revitalized him after the boredom of the long flight from Los Angeles. He pulled on a pair of khaki pants, toweled his hair dry and strolled into the suite's bedroom. Bridgett sat at the vanity. She held out a snifter to him.

"This is your room, isn't it?" he said, taking the goblet.

"Yes, Scotty. Remember what I said in the car?" She stood and put her arms around him. She snuggled her face into his neck, "I said that I wanted to be with you. I'm so very frightened. Hold me."

*   *   *

"Tenny, what the hell is going on?" Dessault tossed his flight bag into a chair and leaned on Tennison Barquelay's desk, looking him straight in the eyes. He knew that Barquelay absolutely could not lie, especially when face to face with someone.

"Harvey," said Barquelay, pressing back into his chair as if trying to escape Dessault's glare. "There is nothing wrong."

Dessault saw the rapid eye blinking that signaled a lie as surely as a semaphore.

"Bull dust!" he raised his voice for emphasis. "You've got Bridgett half scared to death and you've avoided my phone calls. There's trucks running in and out of here with men talking about 'Messies' and besides," his voice softened, "you look like hell. Now, what's going on around here? I'm not going to get off your ass until you tell me, so get with it."

"Harvey, you must leave and let me get this settled," he fumbled for his pipe. "I assure you, it is simply temporary business pressures that are keeping me remote, but it will be finished soon, I swear to you."

"OK, sure, 'business pressures'," said Dessault. "What are the men in the trucks doing and what is a 'messie'?"

"Oh, my dear friend," sighed Barquelay. "I am involved in a cinema project and my company is building a huge model of the Loch Ness Monster. The men are saying 'Nessy', not 'messie', don't you see." He struck a match to his pipe.

"We must do it at the harbor. It is too large to transport on the roads, so we are building it on a barge in the harbor. They travel there daily, and that's all there is to it."

Barquelay's eyes semaphored Dessault again.

"He's lying," said Dessault. He squirted a great gob of catsup on his eggs and reached for another biscuit.

"Why that old snot!" said Bridgett. "Those men were saying 'messies' just as sure as can be. I've heard people say 'Nessy' my whole life. A 'cinema project' indeed. I'll have none of it!" She started to get up.

"Easy, Kid," said Austingrove, taking her hand. "We have to handle this carefully. I think it would be best if you didn't confront your father right now."

Bridgett pulled her hand away, left the breakfast table and walked to the window. "What will we do?" she asked the window.

"I guess the way to check this out is to follow the trucks, right Major?"

"I suppose so, Scott. But we'll have to do it carefully," he looked as if he hadn't slept, and his voice lacked its usual commanding tone. "If Tennison is in trouble, I want to help, but we sure don't want to alienate him or cause him more grief.

They quickly finished breakfast and drove to Roughscuff Field. They parked the Jaguar behind the main hangar while Dessault requisitioned a pair of walkie talkie radios from Barquelay's own storeroom. Austingrove found the truck parked by the airstrip's diner, the driver reading a paperback novel.

Seven minutes later the truck wobbled across the uneven driveway and pulled out onto the road to London. The rear canvas flap was down, keeping out the cold drafts and preventing the men inside from noticing Dessault and Bridgett following in the Jaguar. Nor did they see the Cadet Pilot Program's white and red Cessna 172 lift off and begin circling above.

The Cessna was to Austingrove as a pedal car might be to a race driver. But he enjoyed flying the little ship. Its bouncing and shaking with every air current was unlike the swift, powerful and steady jet fighter planes he was used to.

"Scott, did you get that puddle-jumper off the ground? Over." Dessault wanted to ensure that the radios were working.

"Roger, Major," replied Austingrove. "I'm doing figure eights behind you and the truck. I'm trying to keep them in sight without being obvious. Over."

"OK, I'm going to drop back some," said Dessault. "If we lose them, it"ll be up to you to steer us to them again."

A double click of Austingrove's mic button told Dessault that he had heard and understood.

The truck pulled off the main road and rattled along an unpaved country lane, finally parking alongside an old wooden hangar. With the exception of a bright orange windsock hanging limply from a rusting steel pole, it was the only structure on a well-kept, grass air field. About 1500 meters had been cleared, leveled and kept mowed. The rest of the length appeared to be usable runway of about an additional 3,000 meters, but it was overgrown with high grass and some small shrubs. To Dessault, the field looked to be an old fighter base, a flying field of World War Two.

Dessault positioned the Jaguar so they could see without being seen. The men, he counted twelve, dropped down from the truck and strolled around to the front of the hangar, out of sight.

Dessault and Bridgett left the car and slowly approached the hangar, keeping close to the stand of trees bordering the rutted lane. The hangar's west side was covered with green moss, the boards warped and twisted with age. Bits of gray and green camouflage paint still clung to that portion of the walls sheltered by the overhanging eaves. Lines of rust from long ago driven nails, left rows of spikelike trails pointing downward, toward the damp ground.

Dessault motioned Bridgett to stay put. He eased around the north side of the hangar and peered around the corner. Inside stood the two Me.262s. The model A-1 fighter, the plane Bridgett had flown, was reassembled and looked complete except for the damaged right engine. Its cowling was removed and wiring hung down, apparently ready for the engine's installation. A pair of Jumo jet engines were being worked on in the back of the building. It appeared to Dessault that they were being carefully prepared for installation on the fighter.

The two-place plane that Austingrove and Dessault had flown to England was only partly assembled, one wing and engine and the control surfaces were still in cradles alongside the fuselage. Dessault inched back to Bridgett. She immediately saw that he was furious. His face was red and his jaw was clinched as tight as a Scotsman's purse. "Our damn two-six-twos are in that hangar," his whisper hissed like an overheated steam engine. "They're putting them back together in there. The government didn't confiscate them, your father did."

"No!" said Bridgett. "He couldn't do such a thing." She put her hand over her mouth and turned away.

Dessault softened, "Look, Bridgett, it's obvious that he is involved in some sort of shaky deal here. Maybe he's being coerced by someone. Remember those men who keep coming and going at Barquelay Aviation."

"Yes!" said Bridgett. "They are forcing him to hide the planes from you. That must be it."

"Yeah," said Dessault. "That must be it." But he didn't really believe that. Tennison Barquelay would fight like a berserk bearcat if someone threatened him. Dessault would find out his reasons, by God, and find out right now.

"Scott," he radioed, "Set that piss pot down and taxi it right up to the door of the hangar. And do it fast!" He crammed the radio into his hip pocket, "Bridgett, get back to the Jag. Keep and eye on this place. If Scott or I don't come out in a few minutes and give you a thumbs up, go get the local constables."

Dessault jogged back to the corner of the hangar. He saw the Cessna drop down between two trees at the edge of the field and land crosswise on the airstrip. *Damn, that kid can fly,* he thought.

As the Cessna bounced toward the open end of the hangar, Dessault stepped around the corner, whipping the radio out of his pocket as if it were a weapon, "All of you! Stay where you are!" he shouted. "We are federal officers and this is an official investigation! You will be shot if you try to leave the premises!" The roaring engine and spinning propeller of the Cessna suddenly protruding into the hangar door added emphasis to his claims, if not validity.

The men stood still, stunned, and obviously not about to challenge this mad man. A balding man with thick glasses and a clean white smock sat at a gray steel desk, three stacks of papers and manuals in front of him. Dessault guessed that he was the person in charge. "You!" The man jumped to his feet. "Get over here. Now!" barked Dessault.

"Sir?" The man was nervous, unable to decide what to do with his hands, he fumbled with the pens and pencils in the pocket protector of his smock, his glasses, and finally began to wring his fingers. He made Dessault nervous.

"Be still, Man!" said Dessault. "What are you

doing with these aircraft, and who authorized you to do it?" He put a menacing inflection of anger and impatience to his voice. His years of command made it very effective.

"*Assembly,* is what it is, Sir," he said. His thick Scots accent made it difficult for Dessault to understand him. "We're to have them flight ready in only four more days, Sir, but I don't know how he expects it to be so."

"Who?" bellowed Dessault.

"Mister Barquelay, Sir."

"Damn!" said Dessault. He knew in his heart what the answer would be, but actually hearing it shook him.

"Call Mister Barquelay and tell him to get down here, now! Tell him it's an emergency." He walked past the Cessna, turned the corner of the hangar and motioned to Bridgett. She climbed from the Jaguar.

"It's your father's deal, Bridgett. I'm truly sorry." She sat back in the car, dejected.

Austingrove shut down the Cessna's engine and slipped out of the cockpit.

Dessault told Barquelay's men to carry on. Then he and Austingrove shoved the Cessna out onto the field.

They sat under the wing, silent for a time, then, "Mister Barquelay must have a reason for what he's doing, Major," said Austingrove.

"God, I hope it's a one hell of a good reason, Scott. I can't imagine what it would be though. He stole the planes, lied, and now he is trying to cover up the whole damn deal." Dessault punched the tire of the Cessna in frustration.

Twenty minutes later, Barquelay's Bentley slowly rolled down the lane and emerged from behind the hangar. The man stepped out, looked at Dessault and Austingrove walking toward him, turned and walked slowly into the hangar. He stopped at the first Me.262 and rested his arm on the wing. He looked old, beaten and extremely unhappy.

"Tenny," said Dessault, "what the hell do you have to say about this?"

"I've always admired the way you come straight to the point, Harvey," said Barquelay. "But I think it's obvious. I have taken your aircraft, even after you provided me with one. I have lied, I have alienated my daughter, as well as you, my very best friend." Barquelay put his hands out in a gesture of hopelessness. "I did all of this out of desperation. Barquelay Aviation is foundering. The Labour Party that assumed power just two short years ago has stripped the country's military budget to nearly zero. And most all of my contracts are military; the Royal Navy and the Royal Air Force. They have, as you say, 'dried up' and the future looks bleak as well."

"Well for Christ's sake, man, why didn't you tell me? I'd have given you the damn airplanes if it would do any good."

"I thought that I could manage," said Barquelay. "And not all I told you was a lie, Harvey. At the time the government told me they wanted no part of the Messerschmitts, I was contacted by a friend of mine in the cinema production business. He approached me wanting to purchase some jet fighters for use in a World War Two cinema. I recommended you, Harvey." Barquelay went to the desk and sat heavily on a gray, steel folding chair.

"But then I found out the amount of money he was offering for the planes. I was astonished. So, when it turned out that the German government wanted nothing to do with the Two-Sixty-Twos and I would have them and could provide him with three, and you would never know about it, I began to consider it."

"Would it have been enough money to bail out Barquelay Aviation?" asked Dessault.

"It would have allowed me to pay most of my debts and provide me with a bit of time to restructure and get back in business."

"Well, wait a minute," said Austingrove. "Why didn't you just tell us about it? We could have leased the planes to the film maker and let you have the profits."

Barquelay pressed his fingertips to his forehead and stared down at the floor. Barely audibly, he said, "The airplanes were to be destroyed in the film, and you would never agree to that."

"You're sure as hell right about that," said Dessault. "Tenny, It's damn hard for me to believe what you've done. I had already given you the plane we recovered from the North Sea, and I won't renege on that. But I want you to have your men take those ships back apart and stow them in the shipping containers, just like they were. I'm going to arrange for shipping them back to the States. I'll pay your crew for their time, but other than that, I won't have another damn thing to do with Barquelay Aviation."

Tennison Barquelay did not look at Dessault, Austingrove or Bridgett. He turned and walked slowly to the balding Scot foreman.

"Do what?" echoed throughout the hangar as the surprised Scot was told to begin disassembly of the planes.

Barquelay spoke softly with the man for a moment, then walked toward the Bentley. At that moment a cry echoed through the hangar, "I say! Look at this, will you!" One of Barquelay's men working on the engine from Bridgett's plane, getting it ready for disassembly, had pulled a pile of mangled aluminum debris from the intake. Now he stood back pointing to a ragged duffle bag still jammed into the powerplant. Bright diamonds and gold jewelry sparkled among the bleached fragments of rat-gnawed bones of the cadavers.

"My God," said Dessault, "it's the bag of loot that was in Ackermann's plane!" He turned to Bridgett, "Nice catch, girl!" He swung Bridgett around, laughing.

Austingrove dragged the bag from the engine, spilling jewels and jewelry on the hangar floor.

"Wahoo!" he yelled. "This is incredible!"

Barquelay returned to the group. "What is this?" he said.

Bridgett picked up a diamond bracelet and showed it to him, "It's the bag of World War II pillage that we recovered in the underground aircraft plant. It was in the Messerschmitt when I shot it down. We all thought that it was surely lost when Ackermann's plane went down, but it was blown out of his plane, right into the intake of this engine. That's what blew it up!"

"Oh. Quite nice for you. Most fortuitous," he said and turned to go to his car.

Dessault watched his old friend walk away. He felt that Barquelay's deception was inexcusable, yet he knew how desperation can drive a man to do unthinkable things. And he remembered the numerous times Barquelay had come through for him when no one else would. He realized too that the Englishman's friendship was worth more to him than an entire squadron of Me.262s. "Tenny," he called. "Wait up a minute!"

Barquelay, already in his car, rolled down the window, "What is it, Harvey?"

Dessault leaned on the roof, "You're not getting those damn fighters, Tenny," he said. "But I'll tell you what I'll do, I'll talk to the others and I think they'll agree that we should get Barquelay Aviation back on its feet with the money from those German goodies. A part of it is Bridgett's anyway, and I'd be glad to toss in my share. What do you say?"

"I would say that under the circumstances that is a generous offer." He began to crank the window up.

"I have not accepted charitable donations in the past and I shan't do so now." The window closed and the Bentley pulled away leaving Dessault angry and frustrated.

"What the hell is the matter with that man, Scott?" said Dessault.

Austingrove handed Bridgett the small, gold box he had been admiring and took Dessault's arm. "I've got to talk to you, Skipper." The two men walked out to the Cessna.

"Do you remember me telling you about Mister Barquelay having me out to his estate before we left?"

"Yeah," said Dessault

"Well," continued Austingrove. "He said some really strange things to me. Things about how he is rejected by everyone because of his social position. He feels that he is unable to make friends. He has a low opinion of anyone below his social level, saying that poor people are snobs."

"OK, Scott," interrupted Dessault, "so the man is not perfect, what's your point?"

"My point is, Major, that I think he has some emotional or personality problems, perhaps some kind of persecution complex, that he has kept hidden from you and perhaps even Bridgett. I've seen it before. I've seen troubled people shift from hot to cold and back again in an erratic manner, and that's what he does. Besides that, I think that generally, he's a damn unhappy man."

Dessault nodded and slowly walked to the edge of the runway. He smelled the sweet dampness of the English countryside and watched a black bird settle atop a moss-covered stone wall that delineated the west edge of the field. He too was a damn unhappy man.

Dark clouds moved across Roughscuff Field bringing a steady drizzle with them. The airfield was dark except for the single rectangle of Tennison Barquelay's illuminated window shade. It would be totally quiet as well if not for the light patter of the sprinkle and the light tapping of the keys of Tennison Barquelay's ancient Royal typewriter. A cold wind off the North Sea curled white smoke around the chimney of Barquelay's office, then dissipated it as if it had never existed.

At eight o'clock Tennison Barquelay's driver pulled up to the Operations building and stopped behind an old, black Mercedes that had arrived only moments before. Dessault and Austingrove ducked out of the Bentley, quickly swinging four suitcases through the building's entrance and hastily thanking Barquelay's driver.

They stood for a moment in the foyer, shaking droplets of rain from their clothing.

Dessault had his foot on the first step of the

stairway leading up to Barquelay's office when a single gunshot rattled the windows and echoed its deafening blast throughout the old building.

Startled, he jumped back as a man bolted to the top of the darkened staircase and started down. Seeing Dessault and Austingrove, he tried to stop his forward flight and stumbled, hurling himself awkwardly down the stairs, entangled in his bulky overcoat.

Dessault grabbed the man's left arm as he tumbled to the bottom step and twisted it up behind his back while pinning him to the floor with his knee.

Dessault pulled the overcoat down from around the man's face. "Captain Black!"

Dessault lifted his knee from Captain Billingston Black's back and looked in amazement at the black man's glazed eyes and sweat-covered face. His muttonchops whiskers trembled and his hand shook as if palsied. He let out a low moan.

"Scott, check on Tennison." Said Dessault.

Austingrove took the stairs two at a time. A rectangle of light shone from a partly open door, standing as a beacon directing Austingrove to Barquelay's office. He cautiously peered into the still room. It was furnished simply. A huge dark maple desk and striped fabrics and a minimum of knickknacks or artifacts or even the photos and pictures one would expect in a man's office. It was as austere as a hotel room, and nothing seemed out of the ordinary to Austingrove until he saw light glisten off the surface of a slowly spreading pool of blood from behind the immense desk. Austingrove used the desk phone to call the Felixstowe constable.

Returning to the foyer, Austingrove gripped Dessault's shoulder. "Mister Barquelay is dead, Major. I'm sorry."

Dessault turned back to the cowering Captain Black and jerked the big man to his feet with the overcoat's lapels and held him up against the wall.

"OK, Captain, want to tell us why the hell you killed Barquelay?"

The man's eyes were wide with fear and tears ran down his cheeks, dampening his whiskers.

"I did not kill Mister Barquelay, believe me," he said trembling.

"He called me tonight asking me to come here immediately, that he had a job for my boat. I came as fast as I could, naturally. He was at his typewriter, a gun on the desk. He insisted that I pick up the gun and look at it." He swallowed hard, shook the tears and sweat from his eyes.

"He took the gun from me and stood looking out of the window. I heard the door close downstairs and he said for me to see who it was." Captain Black as crying uncontrollably now.

"I turned to go," he sobbed, "and Mister Barquelay simply shot himself, right then, with me in the room. It was ghastly."

The warbling of police vehicle sirens rose to drown out Billingston Black's sobs.

* * *

It was the kind of persistent drizzle that has a person's clothes soaked all the way through before they realize it. And the rain was iced almost to freezing by a wintery wind that blew steadily off the North Sea. Clouds, as gray and as heavy as the mood of the people huddled beneath them, blotted out the horizons, leaving only the immediate cemetery grounds visible through their mists.

"So he tried to set-up Captain Black as his murderer?" asked Austingrove.

"That's right," said Dessault. "His life insurance doesn't pay-off for suicide, so he thought that he would make it look as if Black murdered him." Dessault shook his head and ran his fingers through his hair.

"It was a clumsy attempt, and thank God it didn't work," he said. "Barquelay Aviation will go to Bridgett anyway, but there'll be no insurance pay-off."

The organ began and Scott Austingrove noticed that only a few of B.A.'s managers and foremen came to Tennison Barquelay's funeral, and they stood to one side, or in the back. It was obvious that they truly felt out of place, just as Barquelay said. There were no tears among his men and their wives, only contrived looks of sadness and honest looks of boredom. Austingrove imagined that Tennison Barquelay would not have been surprised at the light turnout and the heavy disinterest.

The service in the ancient stone chapel was short, then Austingrove, Dessault and Gordon, along with three B.A. staff people, served as pallbearers, sliding the casket into the rear of a highly polished hearse. It pulled away and the men and women walked along behind as it slowly drove to the gravesite.

Austingrove held a black umbrella over Bridgett as the eulogy was read. They placed flowers on the casket and without speaking, walked back to the chapel in the soft rain.

Austingrove worried that he had been partly responsible for Barquelay's death. Perhaps if he had shown some enthusiasm for the man's plans for his daughter and him, it would have given him at least a couple of reasons for living. He didn't want to think that was so, but he did decide that when things settled down, he would ask Bridgett to come to America with him. He wanted her, even if he would not inherit Barquelay Aviation.

Bridgett held up well. She cried softly, few noticing. As her father was being lowered into the earth, she realized that his critical assessment of her future had indeed been very insightful. As she walked from the gravesite, she began to view the world and her life in broader terms; she had accomplished everything she had ever desired in the field of aviation, and all the while she had been self-possessed, not realizing that a full and happy life needed more in it than just airplanes. It needed to include people, family and children. She decided that she would sell B.A., pay what debts she could, and if Austingrove asked, she would go to America with him.

Major Harvey Dessault's grim, downcast face reflected the guilt he felt as he lingered at the gravesite. He regretted his hard-nosed treatment of his old friend. This guilt, either real or imagined, drove him to pay for the entire funeral and interment. While making the arrangements, the realization of his own mortality struck him like a hard landing. In a frenzy of self-pity and remorse he threw himself into trying to save Barquelay Aviation from sure bankruptcy, working night and day at Roughscuff Field, doing his best to save his old friend's legacy. His efforts put him in a London Hospital for five days. Exhaustion, they said. For the first time in several months, the bed rest gave him the luxury of uninterrupted time to think and to plan. He decided that he had done all that he could do at B.A., and it was time for him to get back to Dessault Aviation before it went under as well.

Cody Gordon had flown to England for the funeral and brought news that they had been summoned to Munich, Germany. It would be the final depositions in the Hilda Göettz murder and Karl Schwerin accidental death probe.

They took the Chunnel train into France and transferred on to Munich. Dessault used the hours of relaxation to tell the others of Bridgett's intention to put Barquelay Aviation into the hands of the company's attorneys for sale.

Bright sunshine reflected through the glass domed ceiling of the Munich station as the train eased in. Outside, a warm afternoon greeted them. The weather's effect was immediate as spirits rose and for the first time in weeks, the quartet made jokes and laughed.

In the Munich courthouse Gordon was stunned to see a young image of Hilda Göettz standing quietly to one side. She was tall and slim, with the same bun in her hair and those sparkling, hypnotic blue eyes that lingered in his memory like a beautiful melody. Gordon slipped away from the others.

"You're Hilda Göettz' daughter."

She looked confused, "Yes. Do I know you?"

"I met your mother, and I'm sorry for your loss. I knew her in Philadelphia when your grandfather, Albert Flueger, passed away."

"Oh, yes." She looked down at the floor. "I didn't know my grandfather. Actually, I didn't know my mother all that well, either."

"Well," said Gordon, "she seemed to be a fine woman. I didn't know her well either, but I knew that you had to be her daughter the moment I saw you."

She extended her hand, smiling, "I'm Hannah Göettz."

They sat together during the proceedings, then went to lunch and talked the rest of the afternoon. They spent the next three days together while Dessault, Austingrove and Bridgett returned to England.

On the fourth day Gordon returned to Roughscuff

Field, and the next day the three men left for California. The long flight was quiet and sober, each man thinking of what he'd left behind.

EPILOGUE

Las Vegas, Nevada, the present.

The airplane shuddered, hanging on the ragged edge of a stall. The pilot kicked the left rudder pedal and sent the olive drab P-59A Aerocomet cascading over the top of the climb, falling like a drunken buzzard toward the earth. He glanced over his left shoulder just as a Messerschmitt 262, almost 100 miles per hour faster, ripped past and rolled upside-down. It too fell inverted, finally spiraling in behind the pitifully slow Aerocomet to a combat position of sudden, positive doom for the American fighter.

From below, and in horizontal flight at 490 miles per hour, a British Gloster Meteor closed on the

Messerschmitt.   The German fighter, suddenly trailing a column of white smoke, twisted off to the left. The victorious Meteor redeemed the American pilot from a sure and violent death. The British jet exuberantly performed the traditional victory roll, then dove out of the sun, skimming across the Nevada desert at a mere 500 feet.

The three planes formed-up in a staggered column, the Messerschmitt, the Meteor, and bringing up the rear, the Bell Aerocomet, struggled to stay up with the faster jets. They flashed past the stands at 200 miles per hour, exciting and delighting the more than 25 thousand cheering air show spectators on their feet in the grandstands.

"There they are, Ladies and Gentlemen," blared the public address system's huge speakers, "the world's first jet fighters! Aerial warriors of Germany, Britain and the United States performing a classic World War Two dog fight for you right here at the Las Vegas International Airavaganza!"   The announcer, and indeed most of the spectators, had no idea that none of the planes had ever met in actual wartime combat.

Bridgett swung the Me.262 onto its final approach and eased the throttles back to the idle detent. The plane settled softly to the runway. She smiled, knowing that Scott would be watching her landing, as he always did. She thought of him and their life together and her smile widened.   She understood now that this was what her father had envisioned for her; a real family. And soon it would be complete. She rested her hand just above her seat belt. She felt the slight swelling that in a few short months would emerge as their child. They agreed that he or she would be named Tennison.

Scott Austingrove slid the Gloster Meteor alongside the twin trails of black exhaust smoke from the Me.262 on its landing approach ahead of him. The Meteor landed slower than the German fighter and was able to hang back, keeping an evenly-space formation with the Me.262 and the P-59A.

He felt satisfied with today's show. They had hit upon a popular and unique concept; the world's first jet fighters in combat. And he enjoyed flying the British Jet in the shows, it was smooth, handled well for its age, and was of an attractive design with good visibility and no dangerous quirks. Up ahead he saw Bridgett's Messerschmitt's main tires puff out twin eddies of white smoke as they contacted the runway in unison. *Bridgett sure makes some sweet landings,* he thought. The pavement sped up at him and he slicked the jet onto the runway equally as well.

He raised the visor of his helmet and prepared to pass in review, taxiing along the air show grandstands. He scanned the crowd, knowing that two special people were somewhere among the thousands of cheering fans. He savored the thought that at the end of this performance, they would be beset by his enthusiastic brother and father. They attended every show, and now that neither of them still flew, they lived vicariously through him. Just as he had for most of his adult life through them. He had finally gained the recognition that, in his mind, had eluded him for so long. It had taken him twenty five years to grow out of his feelings of inferiority to his father and brother, but now it was different, they looked to him as an equal. He has their love and admiration, and the love of Bridgett as well.

Although he down-played it, not needing fan adoration, he actually had gained fame in the flying community as one of the men to find and bring back the three rare German jets. And it embarrassed him that he was admired by young and old as a flawless performer in a variety of rare jet planes in air shows all over the world. But in spite of that, he did feel that he had finally become an "Ace" in every sense of the word.

"C'mon, you rattling pile of rivets," muttered Major Harvey Dessault. "Let's try not to pile us up on the damn runway now, there's a lot of folks watching and I don't want you to embarrass me." He always talked aloud to the planes he flew, mainly so that his attention wouldn't wander. The P-59A dipped and wobbled on the final approach, Dessault cursing it constantly. He had begun to enjoy flying again, but the old Bell Aerocomet was as ill-handling a machine as he'd ever experienced. Beside being slow and noisy, it was quick to stall and hard to land.

He cut the throttles and the fighter hit the runway like a sack of potatoes thrown from a truck. The tires squalled in protest and the ship bottomed out on the short landing gear struts, driving Dessault down into the seat with a painful thump. It bounced, landed again and finally, mercifully, stuck to the runway. Dessault slid back the canopy and inhaled the hot desert air.

"Well, you miserable beast, you tried, but you didn't kill me this time!"

The three planes taxied in front of the temporary grandstands to the cheers of thousands. Bridgett, her helmet removed and her hair flowing in the wind, Austingrove and Dessault waving, brought a feeling of closeness for the aviators to the crowd. The jet fighters turned onto the taxiway and pulled up, side by side, at their service van.

Removed from the noise of the air show, the whine of six jet engines coasting-down brought Cody Gordon running from the nearest hangar. He pulled two handfuls of chocks from the rear of the truck and placed them front and back on the main tires of the three planes.

Gordon shared in the increased popularity of the Me.262s and the business success of the Flying Museum too. He also began to get the prime assignments for *Jet Fighter!* magazine. His work left him most weekends free, with only some of them devoted to the air show performances.

If Gordon had any free time, it was spent working

on a book about finding the Me.262s and the adventures of the people involved. The book was progressing painfully slowly, for now he had a wife, Hannah. Two weeks after leaving Germany, he called and asked if she'd come to America. She quickly said yes. They were married three weeks later.

The eastern horizon began to shimmer with waves of the sun's fever even before its daily scorching of the Nevada desert began. Eager to put the more than one-hundred-ten degree temperature in their wake, the three classic jets took off at daybreak and turned west for Fullerton Airport.

Sweat already beginning to darken his flight suit, Major Harvey Dessault led in the slow-flying Aerocomet. Bridgett and Scott Austingrove held a loose formation, hanging back of each of Dessault's wing tips in the Messerschmitt and the Gloster Meteor. The trio of jets climbed to 14,000 feet, the new morning sun glinting off the nose of each plane, flashes reflecting off their emblems, the Golden Scimitar - battle sword of the ancient Persians.

- T h e   E n d -